Military Writers Society of America

Untold Stories

AN ANTHOLOGY

September, 2021

Library of Congress Control Number: 2021946357

ISBN: 978-1-943267-87-3

Red Engine Press
Pittsburgh, PA

Printed in the United States.

Dedication

This book is dedicated to all the men and women who serve or have served in the U.S. Armed Forces and to their families.

INTRODUCTION

UNTOLD STORIES

A few thoughts from the President, MWSA

WHEN THIS TITLE WAS SUGGESTED FOR our 2021 anthology, it really hit home. My father served as a pilot in the U.S. Army Air Force in World War II. He flew P-51s in mission after mission, supporting our bombers flying over Europe. Being a young pilot, he claimed he would never parachute out of an airplane—that he could land anything as long as it still had wings.

One dark night over Germany, heavy flak from the German anti-aircraft batteries below shredded the night sky and in doing so, ripped through his plane setting it on fire.

Despite my dad's proud claims, when the fire reached his boots and the legs of his flight suit, all he could think of was getting out of that plane. In the pitch black of night, having never before parachuted and not knowing what might be below, he jumped. Luckily, he survived but was captured and served the remainder of the war as a POW.

He never talked much about his experience in the war or as a prisoner, and I've always thought his life story would have been a good one. Undoubtedly there are thousand of stories out there like my father's waiting to be told. In this anthology we have been able to collect dozens of them interspersed with poetry written by our members.

Untold Stories

I hope you enjoy this book. We in the Military Writers Society of America encourage our veterans and their family members to write. Not only to preserve history one story at a time, but we believe writing can be a form of therapy much needed by several who have returned home.

Thank you, and enjoy the book.

— Bob Doerr, President, MWSA

Table of Contents

Salina B Baker

1

AMERICA'S FIRST MARTYR: GENERAL (DR.) JOSEPH WARREN

"The Day: perhaps the decisive day is come on which the fate of America depends. My bursting heart must find vent at my pen. I have just heard that our dear friend Dr. Warren is no more but fell gloriously fighting for his country—saying better to die honourably in the field than ignominiously hang upon the gallows. Great is our loss… and the tears of multitudes pay tribute to his memory…" ~Abigail Adams in a letter to her husband, John Adams: June 1775

Painting of Dr. Joseph Warren (1741–1775) by John Singleton Copley about 1765. Copley Gallery, Museum of Fine Arts Boston. Photograph By: Salina B Baker

D R. JOSEPH WARREN WAS A HANDSOME, young 1755
graduate of Harvard, Boston physician, father, husband, Son of Liberty, Masonic Grand Master, spy-
master, and soldier. He provided medical care for rich and
poor, American and English, free and slave. He was deeply
involved with the rebellion and his fellow patriots: John
Hancock, John Adams, Samuel Adams, and Paul Revere,
to name a few. Joseph's interaction with his much older
political mentor, Samuel Adams matured into one of the
most significant of their lives and of the patriot movement.

In early 1764, a smallpox epidemic swept through Boston and the surrounding areas. Joseph went to work for the
physicians' initiative for community-wide inoculation at
Castle William, a fort and smallpox hospital just south of
Boston where he met John Adams.

On the evening of April 18, 1775, with the rebellion
underway Joseph received word from one of his informants
that, under orders from British General Thomas Gage,
troops were assembling at Back Bay in Boston to march to
Lexington and Concord where a stockpile of rebel arma-
ments was stored. Joseph feared for John Hancock's and
Samuel Adams' lives if the British discovered the fugi-
tives. They had hidden in Lexington after attending the
Massachusetts Provincial Congress on April 15 in Concord
and were wary of returning to Boston. He summoned his
close friend and masonic brother, Paul Revere, along with
William Dawes to his home on Hanover Street in Boston,
and then dispatched them to warn Hancock, Adams, and
the countryside that the British regulars were out.

On the morning of April 19, Joseph received news of
fighting in Lexington. He slipped out of Boston and fought
alongside militia General William Heath in Menotomy,
where the bloodiest hours of combat took place. General
Heath and his men fired on the British as they retreated
to Boston, along what is now called Battle Road.

After the battles of Lexington and Concord and unable to

return to Boston, Joseph lodged at Hastings House in Cambridge. With John Hancock and Samuel Adams departing soon for the Second Continental Congress in Philadelphia, Joseph emerged as the de facto leader of what a militia captain described as "the intended revolution."

On April 23, 1775, succeeding John Hancock, Joseph was elected to the loftiest political position of the rebellion—president of the Massachusetts Provincial Congress. With little money or resources, he faced the challenges of a rapidly evolving revolutionary political and military climate. As a tireless and devoted leader, he responded to each new challenge with intelligence and courage.

With provincial military leaders, Joseph oversaw the initial phase of the Siege of Boston. Operating without formal legitimacy of either government or military, he strived to maintain a unified military command with civilian oversight. The Provincial Congress was about to offer him a directorship of medical service but instead proffered him a major generalship on June 14.

By June 15, it was clear the British were about to make preemptive strikes on Roxbury, Dorchester, and Charlestown. Joseph and the Committee of Safety decided the provincial army must make a preemptive move of their own, despite their shortage of gunpowder. At 9:00 P.M. on Friday, June 16, 1775, nearly one thousand provincial soldiers, under the command of Colonel William Prescott, assembled on the common in Cambridge opposite Hastings House. Joseph was not among them as they marched toward Charlestown.

Colonel Prescott and his men commenced building a redoubt on the Charlestown peninsula under the cover of night. The Committee of Safety's order was to build a redoubt on Bunker Hill, but by mistake Prescott and his men built the redoubt on an unnamed hill closer to Boston (later called Breed's Hill).

By daybreak, the British became aware of the presence

Map Title:A plan of the action at Bunkers-Hill, on the 17th of June, 1775, between His Majesty's troops under the command of Major General Howe, and the rebel forces. Contributor Names:Page, Thomas Hyde, Sir, 1746-1821. Montrésor, John, 1736-1799. Created / Published [1775]

of colonial forces and mounted an attack from British shipping on the Charles and Mystic Rivers, and cannon fire from a battery on Copp's Hill. At approximately 2:00 P.M., the British, under the command of General William Howe, began landing at Morton's Point on the southwestern tip of the Charlestown peninsula.

Joseph was nowhere to be found on the morning of June 17. There are speculative reasons for his absence. But what is clear was around 3:00 P.M., his former medical apprentice, Dr. David Townsend arrived at Hastings House and found Joseph suffering from a sick headache. David relayed the news the men on Bunker Hill were being fired upon by the British.

After Joseph donned elegant clothes, he and David made their way to Charlestown Neck. David stayed to care for men who had been wounded in the battle. Joseph went on to Bunker Hill. He encountered General Israel Putnam. Putnam relinquished his command to Major General Joseph Warren, but Joseph refused, saying that his commission was not finalized, and he had come to fight as a volunteer. When Joseph entered the redoubt, Colonel Prescott and his 150 exhausted men raised a cheer of *Huzzah! Huzzah!*

Like Putnam, Prescott relinquished his command to Joseph. Again, Joseph refused.

The rebels had, thus far, repelled two waves of the British advance. What ended the American resistance was neither lack of courage nor unstoppable British resolve. It was the depleted supply of rebel gunpowder. On a third advance, the British regulars, grenadiers, and marines swarmed the redoubt. The rebels tried to make their last stand by swinging their muskets or throwing rocks at the British. Colonel Prescott ordered a retreat.

Joseph was one of the last remaining men in the redoubt. There has been debate about what happened next. What is known was Joseph was shot, at close range in the face just below his left eye, probably with an officer's pistol and by someone who recognized him. His biographer, Dr. Samuel Forman wrote Joseph would have died instantly, unlike the scene depicted in John Trumble's painting, "The Death of General Warren at the Battle of Bunker's Hill, June 17, 1775"

The British stripped Joseph of his fine clothes, mutilated his body, and buried him in a shallow grave with a farmer. Exactly when and who mutilated Joseph's body is unknown. His youngest brother, Dr. John Warren attempted to find Joseph's body a few days after the battle, but he was stopped with a bayonet to his chest by British sentries at Charlestown Neck.

Joseph's body wasn't recovered until after the Siege of Boston ended in March 1776 and the British army withdrew. His brothers, John and Eben found his badly decomposed corpse. Paul Revere fashioned a false tooth with a wire for Joseph before his death. This piece of forensic clue did not surface until some years later as evidence that it was used to identify Joseph.

Joseph's remains lay in state at the Massachusetts Provincial State House in Boston for three days. The outbreak of the Revolutionary War dispersed the Masons, but, on the discovery of Joseph's remains, they returned to give their late Grand Master of the "Ancient Lodge" (St. Andrew's) the burial he was due.

On April 8, 1776, a large and respectable number of the masonic brethren assembled to attend his obsequies, and followed in procession from the State House to the Stone Chapel (King's Chapel). Joseph's eulogy was delivered by young lawyer Perez Morton. Morton met Joseph as a minor official on the Massachusetts Provincial Committee of Safety during the early months of the Siege of Boston. Morton's eulogy of Warren was well received at the time.

Joseph's casket was taken in funeral procession for interment at the Granary Cemetery. The Minot family offered their family's plot since the Warren family did not have one in Boston. His remains would lie in the tomb, lost to posterity for fifty years until his nephew, John C.

*Statue erected at his grave site in Forest Hills Cemetery, Jamaica Plain,
Massachusetts by the 6th Masonic District Massachusetts Freemasons
for the namesake of their Distinguished Service Medal, Most Worshipful
Joseph Warren, October 22, 2016. Photograph By: Salina B Baker*

Untold Stories

Warren, after much research, identified the body's where-abouts. Joseph was reburied two more times.

*St. Paul's Church in Boston in 1825

*Forest Hills Cemetery in Jamaica Plain, Massachusetts August 8, 1856

The Tory Peter Oliver's January 1776 newspaper address to rebelling colonists cited Joseph Warren's grisly end as just desserts for a scheming social climber and recklessly ambitious rebel against the king's authority.

In 1782, Oliver was quoted as saying, "Had Warren lived George Washington would have been an obscurity."

Joseph Warren shouldn't have been on the battlefield that day. The people needed him to lead the patriotic move-ment. They needed him as a friend, father, brother, and physician. At the time of his death, he was a thirty-four-year-old widower with four young children who became destitute and orphaned.

Dr. Joseph Warren sacrificed his life for liberty, and in doing so, became America's first martyr. His death encouraged the people of a nation yet to be born to keep fighting despite their grief. It's what he would have done.

John Adams in a letter to John Winthrop following the Battle of Bunker Hill:

> "Alass poor Warren! ... For God Sake my Friend let us be upon our Guard, against too much Admiration of our greatest Friends. President of the Congress, Chairman of the Committee of Safety, Major General...was too much for Mortal, and This Accumulation of Admiration upon one Gentleman, which among the Hebrews was called Idol-atry..."

Resources:

Forman, Samuel A. *Dr. Joseph Warren, The Boston Tea Party, Bunker Hill, and the Birth of American Liberty.* 2012: Pelican Publishing Company, Gretna, Louisiana. Print.

Philbrick, Nathaniel. *Bunker Hill A City, A Siege, A Revolution.* 2013: Penguin Books, New York, NY. Print.

Borneman, Walter R. *American Spring: Lexington, Concord, and the Road to Revolution* 2014: Little, Brown and Company, New York. Print.

Salina B. Baker

S ALINA IS AN AVID STUDENT OF Colonial America and the American Revolution. She is a published author with a historical fantasy series about the American Revolution called *Angels and Patriots* that has won twelve awards, including Shelf Unbound Best Indie Book, New York City Big Book Awards, Independent Press Awards, National Indie Excellence Awards, and American Fiction Awards.

Her lifelong passion for history and all things supernatural led her to write historical fantasy. Reading, extensive traveling, and graveyard prowling with her husband keep that passion alive.

Her ties to the US Military are her grandfather US Navy WWII, father US Army, husband US Air Force, and son-in-law US Coast Guard (active duty).

Salina holds a bachelor's degree in Computer Science. She lives in Austin, Texas.

Ruth Barmore

2

1989: A Christmas to Remember

I N THE SUMMER OF 1989, OUR family lived in Elkton, Maryland. My husband, Dennis, who was stationed at Aberdeen Proving Grounds in the Air Force Training Detachment, had received orders to Panamá. Yes, the Republic of Panamá, in Central America. When he told us about his orders, our sons, Russell, age eleven, and Patrick, age nine, were excited about what they perceived as a new adventure. Only one problem, Dennis' orders specified an "Unaccompanied Tour." In military terms, that meant only the active duty member, Dennis was going. His dependents, the three of us, did not have the authorization to travel due to ongoing hostilities in the country.

We dreaded his upcoming departure and hoped he would return to us safely. In September, we drove to Dover Air Force Base, Delaware to see him off. My heart sank as he boarded the Air Force shuttle bus headed for the flight line and a C-5 aircraft that would carry him to the Central American jungle. I tried to contain my emotions for our boys' sakes, and I would have been successful, too, had they not both wrapped their arms around me, sobbing. We all cried as the bus with their beloved father and my best friend pulled away.

Dead silence dominated as we drove home without him.

The next three months were hell. Our car broke down, someone tried to break into our home twice, and one of our neighbors suddenly began harassing me about the upkeep of our yard. Our problems did not stop there. The boys had run-ins with the neighborhood bully, Patrick fell and broke his front teeth, then Russell and Patrick began having behavior problems at school. Homework problems followed that stemmed from losing their math-tutor dad and gaining their flunked-every-math-class mom.

The support of friends kept me going. My boss, Roger and his wife, Mary picked me up for work when the car was in the shop and flexed my work hours around the boys' school schedule. Friends, Lou and Karen checked on us regularly and allowed me to vent.

We called Dennis weekly or tried to call. The phone lines in Panamá were prehistoric and controlled by the enemy faction there. In short, phones were turned off or on at the enemy's whim. On my end of the line, the phone continuously rang, allowing my imagination to run wild with war-time-disaster scenarios, including chemical weapons warfare and its aftermath. I had no idea the phones were inoperable.

As Christmas approached, I wondered how I could give Russell and Patrick a good holiday, especially if Dennis couldn't be with us.

Each time I asked what they wanted for Christmas, they answered in unison, "We want Dad to come home."

It was their mantra.

After a depressing Thanksgiving, Dennis called. He spoke with the boys and gave them the usual pep-talk. He asked them how they were doing, if they were keeping their grades up in school, and if they were helping around the house.

They were always happy to go out and play after they had talked to their dad.

Dennis had said he was trying to get orders to come home for Christmas. He hadn't wanted to share with the boys in case his request fell through. We made a pact to keep his homecoming a secret until he arrived on the doorstep.

After four months, Russell and Patrick were finally settling in. Their behavior had improved, and they were doing better in school Their nightmares and crying had stopped.

I, on the other hand, never got used to Dennis's absence. The loneliness weighed on me. But I was determined to set an example for our sons and didn't have the luxury of feeling sorry for myself. I stayed strong and encouraged them in every way possible. Until one evening when I experienced a weak moment.

After the first break-in attempt, the police had taken a report, promised increased patrols, and left. Russell and Patrick were safely asleep upstairs.

I could do anything *but* sleep, fearing the intruder would return. Tired, frustrated, and lonely, I went to the basement, sat on the floor, and cried my eyes out.

A week before Christmas, Dennis called. His orders were verbally approved but not cut—military jargon for printed out. Without them in his hands, he couldn't leave Panamá. He promised to keep me posted, and I prayed he would be successful.

That evening, he called again with good news—he had orders. But tensions in the country had escalated. If a conflict broke out, existing orders would be canceled. Hoping for a Christmas miracle, I prayed we would see him soon.

The next day, Dennis phoned from Pope Air Force Base, North Carolina. He had made it to the States. One problem—transportation from North Carolina to Maryland. Due to an impending Nor'easter from Fayetteville, flights to all points north were canceled. Determined to be home for Christmas, Dennis bought a bus ticket. If the weather held, he would arrive at the bus terminal in New Castle, Delaware, day after tomorrow.

I didn't want the boys to find out until we picked him up, but they were bright and suspected something. I made up a fish story about needing to go to New Castle to get a gift for my sister. They grumbled at having to go on the hour-long ride, but I bribed them with the promise of pizza.

As I pulled our station wagon into the parking lot of the bus terminal, I spotted Dennis through the gift shop window. He looked so handsome in his dress-blue uniform.

Best. Christmas Present. Ever.

Before I could completely stop the car, Russell saw him too and said, "Pat! Look! It's Dad!"

They flung the doors open, jumped out, and ran into the building to greet their father. My eyes filled with tears as they ran up and wrapped their arms around him.

It's a Christmas memory I will never forget.

And, one I will always cherish.

RUTH BARMORE

R UTH BARMORE IS AN AIR FORCE Veteran who proudly spent her enlistment as a Structural Repair Specialist working to keep the C-141 cargo aircraft mission-ready.

She is the wife of her career Air Force husband, Dennis, proud mother of two sons, Harley and Patrick, and a devoted grandmother of Cota and Jaken.

Ruth enjoys writing and is a contributor to the renowned *Chicken Soup for the Soul* publication.

Her other hobbies include sewing, quilting, knitting, reading, and traveling.

She lives in Arizona with her husband, Dennis and their cat, Brat.

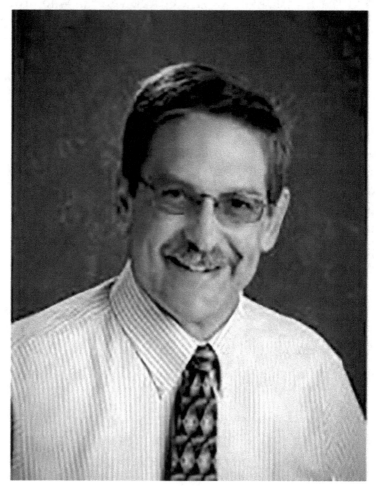

Rick Barram

3

INTERVIEW WITH JOHN FINCH

Transcription of interview with John Finch, late of the 7ᵗʰ New Jersey Regiment regarding the death of General Francis Patterson. Interview conducted by Percival Crandall, July 1, 1922, Veteran's Memorial Home, Menlo Park, N.J.

MY NAME IS JOHN FINCH, AND I was a private in the Seventh New Jersey in the spring of 1862 to August of 1864 when I was discharged for infirmity. I suppose I am about the only one still alive after all this time who can tell the story true—to tell the true story about how our poor General Patterson came to his end.

Now, I know books say he died accidental-like. Most don't even say how. But I know beyond any doubt he died by his own hand, with his own revolver, and that it weren't no accident.

Francis E. Patterson—Brigadier General Patterson was our brigade commander, that is, of the Second New Jersey Blues, as we was called. We was the Fifth through Eighth New Jersey Volunteers. We was officially the Third Brigade of the Second Division of the Third Corps, Army of the Potomac under General George McClellan, God bless 'im...

You know ol' Patterson was in the artillery back in the war with Mexico, a lieutenant. But once the war was over, he stayed in the army and came up to be a captain in the Ninth Infantry, U.S. I think it was in '58 that he left the army to go into private business, or some such thing.

But when the rebellion came, he was back in uniform. The general got himself an appointment for colonel of the Seventeenth Pennsylvania, I'm pretty sure, they was a ninety-day militia outfit. But in May of 1862, he was assigned to us, replacing Colonel Starr.

General Patterson came to us just as we moved to in-front of Yorktown and to start what y'all call the Peninsula Campaign. Of course, we had a little fight at Williamsburg first. Joe Hooker was our division commander at that time. He went all in when the Rebs retreated. Didn't hold nothin' back, but ol' Stoneman didn't see fit to send us no reinforcements. So, by the time the fightin' was all done, we had over five hundred killed and wounded just from our four regiments alone.

Sickles and his New Yorkers got even worse but with Williamsburg over, the general seemed to take ill a lot. I don't know if he was sickly before he came to us, but it did seem he was not seen much during the fighting. If I recall right, he was missing sick during the whole Seven Days, Malvern Hill and the like. Once we was holed-up at

Harrison's Landing we did see more of Patterson. Some say he was just the sickly kind, others say he had a fondness for John Barleycorn, but I can't say for certain. I do know he always did his best to make sure us soldiers had what we needed in the way of food and uniforms and such.

Anyway, at the beginning of August, ol' Hooker gets permission to lead our division and another division, don't recall which one, to try and retake Malvern Hill so as Little Mac can start back again toward Richmond. The attack was all supposed to be secret and we all had orders to be very quiet on the march but as we got closer, the general took it into his mind to blow his bugle of all things. Now a sober man doesn't go and do a damn-fool thing as that, do they? But anyway, the Rebels was on the alert and the whole attack was ruined. I cannot say for sure whether the general was in his cups, since I was not near to him at the time, but there can't be no other explanation I would imagine, that he was drunk.

It was soon after that all the Third Corps was moved and served under General John Pope at the Second Bull Run battle. Afterward, our corps was nearly used up, so we were placed into the defenses of Washington D.C. as the rest of the army went off to fight at Antietam. That's when Daniel E. Sickles became head of our division. During that time many of the regiments had time to send officers home to recruit men to fill some of our used-up companies.

How the getting-along was at first was between General Patterson and General Sickles, I cannot say. Sickles, of course, was a political general having been in congress and such, with very little in common with our Patterson, I would suppose. Sickles was a womanizer and lover of fine things. He and Hooker became friends but not 'til after Hooker tried to have him thrown out for being incompetent. But you know most of us New Jersey men were always wary of Sickles because of his great melodrama before the war when he murdered his wife's lover in Lafayette Park, right there in front of the White House, and then got off by pleading he was at that very minute, out of his mind with rage and couldn't have been responsible for his actions... but back to General Patterson.

At the end of October, in what would turn out to be the early beginnings of our great calamity at Fredericksburg, our division had been sent to begin a reconnaissance along the Orange and Alexandra Railroad in support of any other, bigger moves the army might decide to make in northern Virginia. Our job was to repair track and rebuild bridges and generally to keep an eye out for any Reb activity, of which they, particularly their cavalry, was always up to some mischief of one sort or another.

It was November first and our brigade made camp down the line of Warrenton Junction. Almost from the time we made camp, rumors came round of a large force of enemy cavalry operating south of us. But how these rumors sat with the general I cannot say. Some say he was drunk but others say he had lost his nerve, then one day he gave the order to retreat back up the line saying the position was too isolated. Patterson even telegraphed Sickles saying his position was untenable and he heard the whistles of cars coming and going—a sure sign of the arrival of more enemy. Of course we all heard whistles but who can say what weight the general gave that. Sickles was livid at the news of movement without permission and I think that must have been the last straw in his list of bad generallin'. So Sickles right then relieved poor Patterson from command. That was on November first.

On or around the seventh, with our brigade being out of position from where we was assigned, General Sickles ordered the Second Brigade, which was his old brigade, called the Excelsior Brigade, to move south so they could restore the line. Those poor devils had to move in the dead of night in cold and sleet to move where we had been. What I learned from some men in that brigade was when they arrived close to Warrenton Junction, the enemy had somehow withdrawn to below the Rappahannock River and where they weren't no more problem. Some say there was no evidence any enemy force had been there at all. But needless to say, the division was misaligned with the New Yorkers made to cover where Patterson was supposed to be.

I do know Sickles was very much enraged with our general and I had a chance after the war to read the published report of General Sickles in the Official Records of November eleventh, that he considered Patterson to be quite ill when he replaced him with Colonel Revere. Sickles also considered the whole affair to be a delicate one, even as he was requesting a court of inquiry be formed to investigate Patterson's behavior.

When news of our general's arrest was known, the men took a hard feeling towards it and towards Sickles, for I think deep down, the men liked ol' Patterson despite his love of the bottle.

About two weeks passed and Patterson had not had his day in court. The division moved around some and the boys even took to singing a little song we made up so as the New York men could hear it.

"Johnny stole and ham and Sickles killed a man" was how it went. We all thought it great fun but as for the New York men, who can say. On November twenty-second, we was camped near Occoquan, which was just a few miles from Fairfax Junction. I was part of the guard detail that day and night and because I had the cleanest rifle and the best brass, the sergeant detailed me at the company tent which was not far from where Patterson had his tent. The lieutenant told the sergeant who then told me the general had been acting strange all day and to offer him any help that he might require. I think any of us would have done that anyway and didn't need to be told as such.

That day and into the night was peaceful-like and I had been on watch when at nearly straight up two A.M. there was the bang of a pistol shot. Since all was so quite it was very startling and right away the sergeant and I and some other men who were not on duty but who had come out of their tents searched about for the source of the shot.

A candle was on in the general's tent. I went to check on him. I spoke through the flap and asked if everything was alright but there was no answer. I smelled burned powder so I poked my head in and there was the general laying on the ground with a bullet though his heart.

I right away called for the sergeant who ran in and told me to get the captain, which I did. Within a few minutes, all the staff officers and Colonel Revere were there, either in the general's tent or outside. Someone said they thought maybe he had shot himself by accident while cleaning his revolver. But everyone there knew even if you cleaned it with powder and ball in the cylinders you could take the primers caps off easy enough. I think it was only those thinking to save the general's reputation who said it was an accident, but the facts were plain.

Of course, I loved the general and I tell this not to ruin his good name but to make clear how a good man can be driven to such un-Godly actions. Me and all the brigade knew the general. He did not deserve to be under arrest and to live under such a cloud put there by Daniel Sickles.

It must be told true so there is no mystery as to what happened and how it happened and who was the responsible party. Since the general took his own life there have been, I wouldn't say a conspiracy or such, but those trying to politely avoid such a delicate subject of self-murder. I know the Philadelphia paper, the *Public Ledger*, even when all was known about the general's demise still didn't say it true and claimed it didn't know the cause of his death. Even years after the war, books about New Jersey's part in the war said that Patterson merely "died suddenly in his tent." Now what kind of epitaph is that for a soldier, let alone a general?

So I tell this, not to embarrass the man but to make the circumstances plain to all so every citizen can form their own judgments about this good man.

So, let me just say for me and the men, General Francis Patterson, a proud man, could not face the shame of an unfair inquiry, or worse, to be dismissed from the army, and so to avoid the disgrace, took his own life.

But for me and many of the boys of the New Jersey brigade, Francis Patterson was the second man killed by Dan Sickles.

RICK BARRAM

RICK BARRAM IS A SOON-TO-BE-RETIRED PUBLIC school teacher, having taught United States, World, and Military history at both the high school and middle school levels.

He is a long-time Civil War reenactor and serves on the board of two Civil War related non-profits.

His regimental history, *72nd New York Infantry in the Civil War* was published by McFarland in 2014. He has had five articles published in *America's Civil War* magazine with several more accepted and awaiting publication. He has served for more than twenty years as editor for his reenacting club's bi-monthly newsletter.

Rick has also given lectures regarding New York's Excelsior Brigade before the New York State Military Museum and before the Chautauqua County Historical Society.

He is currently working on two books. One, a collection of letters from Arthur McKinstry who served as a private in the 72nd New York. The second, a history of the 1861-1862 conflict along the Potomac River which pitted Confederate artillery batteries against U.S. naval and land forces trying to keep that important water route into Washington open to navigation.

Barbara Ellen Perkins Bazor, Ed. D

4

THE WAR NOTE

ONCE UPON A TIME A LONELY soldier fought in the middle of the war. One morning on his way to the chow hall, he saw a paper on the ground. Curiously, he picked it up and read:

I have been waiting for you to write me. This is my address: 1000 Holiday Boulevard, Eclectic, Alabama 36024. Sincerely, Marie.

For a moment, his eyes examined his surrounding for the rightful recipient of the note. No one was around. No one seemed to have lost it. After folding it four times, he tucked the paper inside his worn-out wallet.

The gloomy days of war continued. His weary heart grew tired. Then he thought of the *treasured* note. He started putting words on parchments and sent them off almost every day, yet never expected any answers. Surprisingly, he found joy in his new diversion. The unbearable days of war became endurable.

At last, the war was over. He had one thing in mind—to meet Marie. Finally, he found himself with a bouquet standing at the door where he sent his many letters.

The door slowly opened, presenting a lovely lady in her early thirties, inquiring about the unexpected guest. The soldier explained his presence and how he had been sending letters to Marie.

Delighted but sad, the young lady revealed to the soldier that Marie was quite grateful and had found comfort in those letters during her final days—her funeral was yesterday.

The unwanted truth pierced him! Speechless, he turned away in weighty steps. The beautiful lady caught up with him, carrying a ceramic trinket box that contained all Marie's letters for him but never made them to the mail.

Then she consoled with a smile, "I'm Mary, her twin sister. I knew you would come one day."

Their eyes locked at once.

Barbara Ellen Perkins Bazor, Ed.D

Barbara Ellen Perkins Bazor, Ed.D is a public educator with twelve years of classroom experience in Montgomery Public Schools (Alabama), and on her seventh year as an instructional leader in Bibb County School District, Macon, Georgia. She was recently nominated for the Georgia Association of Secondary School Principals (GASSP): *Assistant Principal of the Year Award 2020*—a program designed to recognize the outstanding leadership of active, front-line assistant principals. She was placed in the top five among all middle and high school assistant principals in Georgia.

Barbara served in the Army National Guard from 1997 to 2004. She earned her doctorate in Educational Leadership, Policy, and Law from Alabama State University in 2009.

Her latest book, *Subic: A Sailor's Memoir: Based on the Story of Bobby Earl Perkins* unveils a little-known account of her father and his fellow servicemen who endured racial discrimination in the military while stationed in Subic Bay Naval Base, Philippines, during the late 1960s.

Her works include *54 Poems for the Lord in 2 Days, The Joys Within*, and *In the Presence of the Ultimate: A Guide to Spiritual Inquiry*.

Barbara is married to James Kent Bazor, enjoying the southern lifestyle. They call Montgomery, Alabama home.

Tom Beard

5

Cap'm Mac

December 2020: This is a story about a man who failed to blow up a building, seaplane's demise, and helicopter's birth.

DONALD MACDIARMID HAD THAT CLEAN-CUT, NEXT-DOOR, nice-lad look. His hubris and the success it drove him to led both his admirers and rivals to elevate "Cap'm Mac"—if it was a friend speaking to him—or "Mac Dee"—if he was spoken about outside his hearing—to nearly a fictional character within the ranks of the Coast Guard in his lifetime and beyond.

"Cap'm Mac was cool and unflappable." According to a one-time co-pilot:

"Once, when we were tearing down the runway at Lindbergh Field (San Diego) in a PBY-5A, he dropped his cigar. He let go of the controls and started looking for the cigar under the seat. I completed the takeoff and had the gear up before he assumed command, with the cigar in its proper location."

A contemporary, who at one time flew with MacDiarmid wrote, "The colorful and charismatic MacDiarmid was a true 'legend in his own time,' and better known to the aviation troops than the [Coast Guard] commandants of those years. Like many pioneers, he was not only a dedicated man, but one of single purpose."

MacDiarmid graduated from the Coast Guard Academy in 1929, according to his statement, "through the Grace of God and somebody's mistake." He admitted later, his cadet honors at the Coast Guard Academy were meager. Prior to his Academy assignment, he served as a US Navy Sailor in battleships.

The newly commissioned Coast Guard officer, following a year at sea, entered US Navy flight training and *almost* completed. He failed his final flight. Speculation among colleagues overwhelmingly concluded his failure was belligerence rather than performance.

Following duty aboard two Coast Guard cutters, MacDiarmid commanded a 125-foot Coast Guard patrol boat in Seward, Alaska. MacDiarmid, admitting to excessive assertiveness, received four commendations. He was soon relieved, however, according to one admiral, because of a near mutiny by the crew over aggressive behavior.

MacDiarmid's next assignment as executive officer was aboard a 165-foot Coast Guard patrol boat. Two months later, he was acting commanding officer. Another unexplained, quick transfer came four months after. He shipped aboard a major Coast Guard cutter on a North Atlantic, wintertime ice-patrol in 1937 under more supervision as engineering officer.

The following summer, he returned to Navy flight training. And that time, as before, MacDiarmid washed out. Intervention by the Coast Guard liaison officer stopped his being dropped the second time. He finally got his Wings of Gold in April 1938.

MacDiarmid's first assignment as an aviator brought him to Coast Guard Air Station, Port Angeles, Washington. He served his first year as aircraft engineering officer. An early self-evaluation in an official report, Mac Diarmid wrote, in part, that Port Angeles was "the eight-ball station." His actions, later, assured and perpetuate his own observation.

The Coast Guard air station sat at the end of a three-mile-long narrow spit of sand and rocks, separating the

Strait of Juan de Fuca from Port Angeles harbor. In World War II, the base served as one small outpost in the defense of the Pacific Northwest. By the summer of 1942, Coast Guard amphibians flew from its runways searching for enemy submarines.

Not one with a career for starting at the bottom, Mac Dee filled out the remaining three of his four years tour as commanding officer.

When war manpower level bloomed, he commanded thirty officers and six hundred enlisted men—as a senior lieutenant.

Even with obvious opportunities MacDiarmid enjoyed, he had greater ambitions.

Immediately after the Pearl Harbor attack, Mac Dee flooded command seniors with letters, official and unofficial, requesting—demanding—combat duty of any kind.

MacDiarmid's wartime experience followed that of the fictional *Mister Roberts*, where both waged fruitless battles from the war's backwaters, trying to join the front. MacDiarmid fought with wartime bureaucratic bumbling, getting newly assigned men trained then saw them leave for the Great War—only to be replaced by more—in his terms: boots. He felt left behind. In one of many pleas exposing more of *his* feelings—again using a broad anonymous population for his voice—he wrote:

> "The pilots of this station generally feel that they have been pushed in a corner and forgotten or that their potential fighting value is held in very low regard."

MacDiarmid was the only one left behind.

MacDiarmid frequently quoted vague authorities in his official reports. Conclusions from the enigmatic references always provided hefty validation for his contentions. Emphasis depended on the point he wished to make at that moment, with facts sometimes conflicting.

For example, in the following excerpt MacDiarmid might be the only flyer meeting the description except he did not have thousands of hours at the time. No one did. MacDiarmid pleaded:

> "There are flyers available here with many years of sea service and experience as engineers and navigators and thousands of hours of experience in the air who are flying small obsolete ships on local escort missions—sometimes difficult enough considering the weather, but offering no possibility of earning credit or promotion—while young Army Air Corps and Navy pilots some of whom are practically boys (MacDiarmid was thirty-five at this writing) are flying long range attack missions on the enemy."

As the most experienced aviator in his command, Mac-Diarmid still had only about three years' flight experience. It was less time and familiarity than modern Coast Guard pilots today before being qualified for aircraft command.

MacDiarmid, being relatively high ranking, always commanded the aircraft regardless of his sagacity, or lack of it, if he met minimum requirements. Since he was also the approving authority as commanding officer, there was no question of certification. He signed them himself.

In one report, he complained about three PBY Catalinas allotted to his station already a month overdue and not expected for a year. MacDiarmid wrote,

> "[T]he officers at this station read the impressive aircraft production figures with considerable interest ... Our failure to get new decent equipment is surely not due to shipping difficulties. The popular explanation is that the new equipment goes to the new pilots [of the nearby Navy commands] who promptly smash it."

Mac Diarmid, in his conclusion, added further:

> "It is estimated that there has been enough beautiful equipment smashed through clumsiness or stupidity in this area alone in the last six months to have equipped this station with fine equipment five times over."

Typically, he trapped himself by writing contradicting statements in different letters. Earlier, in a series of reports, he declared most of his pilots were new and inexperienced, and most of the experienced were transferred after only a short stay.

The story of the Japanese bombing his command in Port Angeles six months following the attack on Pearl Harbor, resurfaced decades later from original records discovered in old file cabinets at the Air Station, and correlating interviews held with surviving participants.

The air station's main east-west runway ran parallel to the spit's north beach, as it exists today, and was at the time of the attack defended from air- or sea-attacks by six machine-gun emplacements—four at the corners and one along each side the near midpoint. Sheltered in each pit were two .30 caliber Lewis Machine-guns.

Standard navy depth-charges, fused with electrical detonators were located at each end of the main administration building to destroy it in the event of an enemy landing. The 1935 Works Projects Administration building with its period art deco frescos was located near mid-point along the runway on the south, or harbor side. It still is.

Early in World War II, the military on the US West Coast was tense to a possible Japanese invasion. And Captain Mac groused with displeasure over his unit's inadequate preparation for a defense. Therefore, he resorted to his typical bold actions to remedy his troops' laxness.

MacDiarmid took William Morgan, Ordnanceman Third-class, and "Red" Merril, Boatswains Mate First-class into his confidence. Morgan was directed to sneak around the barracks the night of MacDiarmid's planned drill and gather up all the rifle ammunition. (Each man had a Springfield rifle slung to his bedpost.) Also, during the night Bos'un Merril created shallow oil-puddles scattered about the station.

Then, early in the morning, Morgan crouched—holding

five sticks of dynamite—in the machine-gun nest across the runway from the admin building. Waiting.

MacDiarmid began his drill by taking off in early morning's darkness from the nearby Port Angeles municipal airport in one of the station's amphibians he had landed the previous afternoon. Shortly, the airplane screamed in over the base at low altitude in pre-dawn blackness on a mock attack.

The roar from the airplane's twin engines passing low overhead was the signal for Morgan to fling his dynamite sticks, then fire the machine guns into the open water north of the runway. Meanwhile, from this battle-noise signal, Merril set the oil puddles ablaze, simulating a realistic scene.

Men tumbled out of the building—through doors and windows—carrying with them empty rifles—dashing to safety in air raid trenches. One sensible sailor, like the fictional television character, deputy Barney Fife kept a bullet in his pocket—just in case. He was ready for the invasion. But his rifle accidentally fired as he fell into a ditch. The lone bullet to defend his country passed harmlessly between an ensign's legs, scurrying just ahead.

Meanwhile, tracer bullets from Morgan's machine guns streaked the dark sky creating a fiery display. Behind Morgan, across the runway and narrow spit, lay a Navy ship peacefully at anchor in the still harbor.

The slumbering Navy crew alerted by war noises immediately went to general quarters. The ship's guns were instantly ready—Pearl Harbor was not going to be repeated for the US Navy ship. Navy gunners commenced firing 20MM machine guns at the only obvious target in the darkness, the circling US Coast Guard—Grumman Goose.

Seeing tracers coming his way, MacDiarmid immediately abandoned his attack and hurriedly retreated north across the Strait into Canada.

Meanwhile, MacDiarmid's crew was more prepared

than he assumed. One junior officer, before abandoning his post for the safety of the air raid trench, sent a message indicating the air station was under enemy attack. An immediate wartime alert of an invasion spread down the entire west coast of United States, putting all military units on wartime alert.

MacDiarmid's crew was better prepared for war from the drill. However, he was partly correct in his assessment of his unit's un-preparedness. No one remembered to detonate the charges to destroy the admin building. Mac Dee, nevertheless, succeeded where the Japanese failed, by attacking the United States continent.

* * *

One more frustrating year passed before MacDiarmid got his wish to go to war. In July 1943, he was assigned command of a US Navy squadron, VP-6—an isolated patrol plane squadron located in Greenland.

The Navy awarded MacDiarmid the Navy Air Medal for aggressive Arctic Operations following his ten months' duty in Greenland, where the PBY equipped squadron was responsible for North Atlantic anti-submarine patrols. His unit did not get any submarine sightings or kills, however.

In the spring of 1944, MacDiarmid was next assigned to Coast Guard Air Station, San Diego—once again as a commanding officer.

Everlastingly the whip, MacDiarmid insisted on speedy responses to rescue alerts. When the alarm sounded to launch the ready aircraft, his men ran or used bicycles to reach the airplane fast. He expected even the cumbersome PBM seaplanes—rolled down the ramp and the beaching gear removed—with the plane in the air in five minutes.

A pilot slow in reaching the airplane could expect to find their commanding officer sitting in the pilot's seat.

Then, there was the time he flew into a rage when someone hid his bicycle.

MacDiarmid was a cockpit man. His mission, as he saw it, was to save lives and, moreover, prove the seaplane capable of that task. On that charge he proceeded with unparalleled vengeance.

MacDiarmid simultaneously held the newly emerging helicopter in open disdain. To one of his junior officers leaving for helicopter training, he said he would be "no good for the Coast Guard. The only thing you'll be good for is county fairs and hauling Santa Claus."

With victory in 1945 and a large inventory of modern seaplanes available, the Coast Guard returned to the task of rescuing victims of sea disasters. This meant attempting seaplane landings offshore, well beyond the sheltered waters for which the modern seaplane was designed.

MacDiarmid believed the PBM Mariner offered a far better service if it—using its long-range ability—could land at sea anywhere to retrieve downed aviators and shipping disaster victims. He set out to prove it.

Meanwhile, Captain Frank A. Erickson, also a former US Navy battleship sailor, a contemporary Coast Guard Academy graduate, and the Coast Guard's first helicopter pilot, became the original developer of the helicopter.

A longtime critic of seaplanes—though a seaplane pilot himself—Erickson wrote:

> "There were many aviators who still insisted that the Coast Guard's future in aviation required the operation of seaplanes from the open seas."

A clash of equals followed the close of WWII. One would win. Sides were taken with prolong fights between two groups of firmly held opposing beliefs.

The navy provided MacDiarmid with a modified PBM— instrumented to measure structural loads—assigned to his off-shore landing-test project in San Diego. For the following three years, MacDiarmid tested the airplane against the sea.

He discovered, even landing inline with wave crests,

his hypothesis to successful open-sea landings, keeping wing tip floats from submerging in a wave before the hull became buoyant was difficult. The situation led to a near disaster—concluding the program.

The seaplane skipped back into the air after striking a wave and stalled. The aircraft then smacked the water hard on its nose and right-wing, ripping the wing and its engine off.

According to the other pilot, the seaplane plowed ahead uncontrollable, still at high speed with MacDiarmid hanging onto his armrest yelling, "Whoa, Whoa, Goddamit whoa!"

The left wing then dropped into the sea, ripping off the wing-tip float. Unbuoyed the wing sunk, violently swerving the plane around to the left.

Once the plane stopped, the crew clambered onto the right wing's remaining stub, vainly trying with their weight to keep the left wing elevated. Despite their efforts, the seaplane slowly rolled over and sank. The airmen, flung into the sea, escaped unharmed. MacDiarmid reportedly told this tale on himself. (Open-sea landings required an admiral's approval.)

According to a former copilot.

"Some of Cap'm Mac's senior officers did not share his enthusiasm for seaplanes and open-sea landings. Once, when MacDiarmid thought some lives were unnecessarily lost, he went to the senior officer with a plea the admiral consider the hundreds of times that he had landed in the open sea and leave the decision to land to his own judgment. The admiral grinned easily, and after a short pause said, 'Mac, I don't think a man who would take an airplane into the sea hundreds of times has very good judgment.'"

MacDiarmid only proved the modern seaplane, designed for harbors, could not land in open seas successfully.

Despite the setbacks from proving offshore capabilities of seaplanes, he still thumped his thesis. His audience slowly vanished.

Mac Dee did accede—somewhat—to point out the helicopter's one ability was "excelling at the scene despite rough seas, or shoals or surf, all conditions unfavorable to seaplanes."

MacDiarmid then condescendingly agreed, "the records [of helicopter rescues] show occasional brilliant rescues accomplished under average command competence."

MacDiarmid, earlier, seeing the changes ahead—and ever the opportunist for rescue action—recognized helicopter pilots were beginning to get the important SAR missions, with accompanying notoriety.

In June 1953, he wrote (again with typical flamboyance):

"So many boys have been busting these mechanized Pogo sticks—and a few killing themselves in the operation that I decided inasmuch as I have to order people out in these things, I'd better learn to fly them myself."

This was predictable MacDiarmid hyperbole. At the time he wrote that, the Coast Guard had only one helicopter accident where two died. In a sense to depreciate his acceptance he continued, facetiously writing,

"I actually employ these monstrosities only to get across the [aircraft parking] apron to a real flying machine without burning my delicate feet on the hot cement."

MacDiarmid qualified in helicopters in 1953. As a result, he was also the target of attacks by contemporaries who lived many years under his visceral scorn over their acceptance of the machine.

"I hear by via the grapevine," Captain John Waters wrote to MacDiarmid in a flippant note, "that you are now a helicrapper[sic] pilot and have conceded that [Captain Frank] Erickson was right all along. We have heard rumors that the ready spot at the ramp is now occupied by a HO4S instead of a PBM."

The Coast Guard stopped using seaplanes in 1960.

MacDiarmid, even as commanding officer at yet one more air station—a forty-seven-year-old captain—volunteered to stand the search and rescue alert duty with the junior pilots, still racing them to the pilot's seat when the SAR alarm sounded. Now in helicopters.

MacDiarmid wrote in a report when he was still commanding officer at Port Angeles, "this station recently learned that COMINCH [Adm. Ernest J. King on 15 February 1943] has designated the Coast Guard to develop Helicopters for the use with convoys. Rumors of terrible losses suffered by some convoys offers a challenge to any belligerent spirit. All senior pilots on this station have volunteered for this duty," which might seem to indicate even he was an early volunteer for flying helicopters, or it may have been just one more ruse for him to go to war.

The depression-built building named for Captain Donald Bartram MacDiarmid still stands today, serving its original purpose as an administration building. Helicopters fly from the nearby runway. The seaplane ramp is permanently closed.

END

Tom Beard

Tom Beard is author, editor, and editor-in-chief of several books, plus writer of dozens of journal articles. Four books authored or edited by him received MWSA awards—three "Gold" and one "Bronze." Other awards: Admiral Arthur W. Radford Award "For Excellence in Naval Aviation History and Literature;" Voted writer of "2012 Best Article" by American Aviation History Journal readers, and "Meritorious Public Service Award," from the US Coast Guard Commandant for writings supporting Coast Guard history. Additionally, Tom did a stint as a documentary film writer and editor.

Tom holds a MA degree in history with additional formal graduate studies in American maritime history. He split a twenty-year military flying career as a Navy carrier attack pilot and a Coast Guard rescue pilot. Military aircraft types flown include prop and jet attack, surveillance, transport, seaplanes, and helicopters. In over 6,000 military flight hours, tens of thousands of take-offs were matched with the same number of safe landings. He holds FAA airline transport and commercial helicopter ratings plus a Coast Guard masters license for sail and power vessels.

Tom and his wife, as a team, sailed sailboats around the world almost twice over a sixteen-year period. Hobbies include rebuilding 100-year-old automobiles and writing.

Larry Duthie

6

THIN WHITE CASING

Non-fiction submission (A portion appeared in a different form in the memoir *Return to Saigon*).

F ROM THE SQUAWK-BOX CAME THE VOICE of a young sailor.

"This is a drill. Fire, fire, fire..."

He'd made an error. It was not a drill. He stopped and resumed with more urgency.

"This is *No* drill. This is *NO* drill. Fire, fire in the hangar bay."

I was in the ready-room waiting to head down the passageway for the 0730 mission-briefing. Nine minutes short, at 0721, the sailor's voice. Instead of the call I'd expected—to head down the passageway for a briefing in the air-intelligence room, it was the urgent, cracking voice informing us it was no drill.

I glanced around, wondering if there was to be some kind of action. No one moved.

"Happens all the time," one of the experienced guys explained. "Generators overheat, bearings lose their lube, electrical wires—they short and burn. Shit like that."

Another guy, who was in a flight-suit said a damage-control team would quickly have it under control. "Soon enough, a call will come to set Condition Yoke," he said, "and then normal activities can resume."

I continued sipping my coffee.

I was a nugget, the newest guy in the squadron, suited

up in flight gear that morning for a mission as wingman for our squadron's skipper.

A couple weeks earlier I had had a bad night of it, a rough time catching an arresting wire, and he let me know he wasn't pleased.

But lately flights with him had gone well, and on the previous day I'd flown wingman for the most senior pilot in the air group, the CAG—our skipper's boss. And CAG Carter had praised my bombing flight to the skipper. That buoyed my confidence—jazzed me up, even, so I anticipated another good hop.

That was in '66, beginning of the day. And the date matters: 26 October.

A few minutes passed, and then smoke filtered into the ready room. Soon it poured from an overhead vent. Jim, our intelligence officer, grabbed a chart and taped it over the vent's grate.

That worked for a few minutes, but then smoke curled up from under the door. Still no one seemed alarmed. I settled into my comfortable ready-room seat.

The smoke intensified. Someone suggested we go up to the carrier's flight-deck, where the air would be clean. When the ready-room door swung open, we confronted a solid wall of swirling brown smoke. The door was slammed shut.

Dick Perry, a lieutenant commander and very seasoned combat pilot said, "I know a quick route out the back, up to a sponson."

On older carriers like *Oriskany*, sponsons stuck out the sides of hulls like small balconies. Fresh air.

But the back door opened to another wall of smoke. A brown cloud gushed into the ready room. We choked on it, all of us.

"Get in a line," Dick commanded. "Grab the belt of the guy ahead."

He opened the door again and headed into the oily

brown miasma. I was about two-thirds back in a conga line of a dozen or so guys. We moved out at a good pace. I was a good swimmer—I could hold my breath a long time. Visibility was a foot or two, so I could only see as far as the stooped-over back of the guy ahead of me. We swiftly moved along, hunched over and hanging onto the belt ahead. Then our line stopped.

"The hatch. Dogged down!" Dick yelled.

The guy ahead of me turned around and spun me. The line reversed. I grabbed a new belt, and we rapidly back-tracked—which took us aft, down a long passageway. Knee-knockers were encountered at the expected intervals, but somehow no one tripped.

Someone coughed.

I, too, could no longer hold my breath.

"Down. Near deck. Better air," someone called through coughs.

I crouched lower, into a duck-walk. I felt vulnerable, suddenly aware that might be a way to die. A deep gulp of oily smoke set me hacking and gasping.

Our duck-walking gaggle kept going. The air, mercifully, became clearer the further aft we went. Until we could see again. Breathe again.

We stood, relaxed our grips on the belts ahead. Then we were up a ladder, onto the flight-deck, taking in good air.

But Dick wasn't with us. Dick Perry had fallen away from our line.

We organized into a search party and headed toward the bow, which was crisscrossed with fire hoses. A tall column of dark smoke billowed from the front of the ship. We looked for a source of OBAs—the oxygen-breathing-apparatuses we'd need to go back to rescue Dick.

And then, close to the bow, we found another cluster organizing a search for missing men. Heading up that party was Dick Perry.

He explained his call the hatch was dogged was merely

to give us information. He'd simply un-dogged it. He stepped into fresh air on the sponson, only to discover he was alone. He imagined the dozen or so men he'd been leading had all succumbed to the smoke. Our two groups huddled and briefly talked about what we had been through.

We then understood it was a serious fire. From the port side of *Oriskany*, a column of sooty brown smoke billowed hundreds of feet into the sky. The ship was dead in the water and listing.

Alongside, a destroyer had come in close. Her crew, manning fire hoses, shot high-pressure streams of water into our hangar-deck. *Oriskany*'s damage-control crews charged forward, dragging fire hoses, which all led down to the hangar-deck.

Four sailors on the corners of a stretcher came up from below to the flight deck. The man on the stretcher was partially dressed, wearing only his khaki trousers and an unbuttoned blouse. He had no shoes or socks. He lay lifeless with a very red face blankly staring at the sky. A corpsman put a stethoscope to his chest, then began CPR.

A sailor came over and leaned in with a camera, snapping a photo. A chief petty officer was immediately on the sailor, snatched the camera and flung it over the side. I walked away as the chief lit into the kid. The corpsman behind them continued heavily pumping with both hands, his arms stiff, on the man's chest.

The scene was surreal. I felt helpless.

A few yards away three young officers, who obviously had escaped the inferno up forward, lay side-by-side on the rough surface of the flight-deck. I spoke with one, who delivered the first details of the explosions and raging fire. I asked if he was hurt.

He answered, "yes," and pointed to his feet.

Like the lifeless man, he had no shoes, and his soles were blistered and red. A corpsman spoke with him. The man came to a sitting position. The corpsman gave him an injection in the thigh, then cut open the officer's t-shirt.

With a felt-tipped marker, the corpsman—a kid maybe eighteen years old—wrote onto the man's pale chest the morphine dosage he had injected, along with the time he injected it.

The corpsman then moved on to administer aid to the other two.

I spoke with others on the flight deck, and we exchanged what little we had learned of the fire.

It had started near the forward elevator and burned a helicopter and an A-4, like the one I was to fly that day. Fuel spilled and spread the blaze. And it was still burning.

The ship heavily listed to starboard.

I had been through fire-fighting training in boot camp, and again while in pre-flight training eighteen months later. Maybe I could be useful.

I wandered the deck looking for an OBA unit, asking sailors who had come up from the hangar deck if they knew where one could be found. A sailor handed me one, but it was fully expended and inoperative. I continued the search.

Three enlisted men manned the corners of a stretcher. I asked if they needed a fourth. They did, and they had an extra OBA. That one worked. We went down to hangar bay one, which appeared as if it had burned a long time earlier—as if it were some ancient war scene.

An A-4, partially burned, dripped water and foam. The canopy was shattered. Heat had fired the ejection seat's rocket-charge. The nose was partially burned away.

On the starboard side, near the forward elevator pit, the skeletal remains of a Kaman helicopter dripped water.

Sloshing through an inch or two of water were sailors in pairs and small groups. Some manned hoses, but most wheeled bombs to the portals—bombs still so hot they steamed. Water played on them until it was their turn, and then they were heaved over the side.

Other sailors pushed aircraft back to the number two

elevator to clear them from the hangar deck. Tangles of fire hoses, rock-hard with water pressure had been dragged into the two passageways leading to officers' country.

* * *

The fire started, I'd learn later, when an untrained sailor tossed a hissing flare into a locker stacked with flares. After ten seconds, its parachute popped free and then the flare ignited, converting the flare-locker into a bomb.

The inferno sent fireballs hurtling through the forward part of the ship. Heat cooked off the burned A-4's 20-mm cannon, and rounds ricocheted around the hangar deck. Fire and smoke raced up both sides of the ship and into living spaces for officers—which included my bunk room.

* * *

At the passageway on the port side of the number one elevator pit, the four of us, with our stretcher at an alarming angle, climbed steep stairs into dark officers' country.

We felt our way down the black passageway. I could hear my heavy breathing in the OBA. Electric power to that section of the ship had been cut. There were no lights, no ambient light. The further in we went, the blacker it became.

In total darkness, we came upon a group of sailors carrying a stretcher going the other way. We exchanged our empty litter for theirs, which was weighted with an unconscious man, and we worked our way back toward light. As we negotiated the dark ladder, we tried to keep the stretcher level, but the man's weight shifted.

His foot, which dangled over a corner, pressed against my wrist. It was wet, oozing from his burns. When we emerged onto the dim light of the hangar deck, we were directed to carry him aft toward the middle of hangar bay two.

He wore only his skivvy shorts. I recognized him: Pinky.

I knew him only by his nickname. And I saw then that some of his skin had sloughed from his foot onto my hand.

We carried Pinky to the officers' mess—the spacious wardroom served as a triage station for sick bay. It was well lit and mercifully clear of smoke.

Chuck Nelson was there, and he administered mouth-to-mouth to Pinky.

Chuck would tell me later that when he grasped Pinky's hand, the skin slid off. Pinky could not be saved.

* * *

It took more than three hours to extinguish the last of *Oriskany*'s fires, and far longer to locate and rescue some of the survivors.

Minutes after the fire started, John Davis realized it was serious and he left his stateroom. His roomie, Bill Johnson, was behind him, but turned back to finish dressing. Those few seconds cost Bill his life. John felt his way through the dense smoke. He thought he knew a route out—a left, a few steps, a right, a few more steps...but he got lost. Then, at the moment reality struck him he might not make it, a hand reached out.

"In here," a voice said. John was pulled into a stateroom.

It was the admiral. They hunkered down in that some-what protected space, sealing off vents and the crack under the door to keep the smoke at bay as the fire raged. The admiral's telephone still worked, and they let damage-control folks know they were alive. Yet, it would be hours before a rescue team reached them.

Barry Wood and some of the other guys I lived with in the bunk room had escaped by running forward and out through a space I didn't know existed—a place where the ship's anchor chains came into the ship. A chain locker in the forecastle.

Those who went aft and attempted to go down ladders on either side of the number one elevator—the only way

I knew—were found dead in bunches where they had been felled by the heat and smoke.

It took hours for the fires to be extinguished. Hangar bay one had been ravaged. The catapults were both ruined, warped by buckling plates, and the number one elevator was inoperable. Officers' country up forward was destroyed.

As we steamed back to the Philippines, crews cleaned up much of the debris, tossing it into the South China Sea. They tore away burned insulation which hung in ragged shreds from the overhead.

They hosed away soot. The hulk of the Kaman chopper, like bones, went over the side.

* * *

We docked at Subic Bay the morning of October 28, two days after the fire. *Oriskany*'s colors were lowered to half-mast.

A Marine guard, rifles at present-arms, honored the flag-draped caskets as they were carried down onto the dock. Two chaplains, the Catholic wearing vestments, stood side-by-side as bodies were brought down in metal boxes.

I stood on the flight-deck that morning surveying the perfectly aligned rows on the wharf, an American flag covering each, the corners folded military perfect.

Beneath four of those flags rested the bodies of fellow Ghostriders: Clyde R. Welch, our executive officer, a nice man known as a smooth and competent pilot; Dan Strong, our operations officer; Jim Brewer, a young lieutenant JG with an infectious smile; and Bill Johnson, who had bounced his tailhook off the water flying with Frank Elkins.

My first combat mission with Dan Strong seemed so recent. I had known him less than two months—from that first week of September when he and I went after a small bridge, until October 26. His death, two weeks after Frank Elkins disappeared, hit me hard.

Because his stateroom was adjacent to the flare locker

where the fire ignited, Dan was the first of the forty-four to perish in the unspeakable fire.

He had been asleep when his room spontaneously erupted in flames, ignited by the intense heat of hundreds of burning magnesium-packed flares roaring next to him.

In seconds, his room transformed into a retort, like a steel crematorium oven. His ashes were found in a position that suggested he had felt the heat, sat up, and managed to swing his legs over the edge of his bunk before he succumbed. That quickly, death had come.

Nothing remained intact in his stateroom except his wedding band and the cloisonné portion of one of his medals.

Under another of the flags rested the remains of Rod Carter, our air-wing commander—CAG—the good leader who had praised my flying.

Beneath other flags were the remains of guys I lived with in the junior-officers bunk room. I felt detached, gazing down on the rows of flag-draped aluminum boxes.

There was one other who had perished in the fire, but he was not under a flag on the wharf.

The remains of Lt. Cmdr. Omar R. "Whitey" Ford remained aboard *Oriskany*. He would travel part-way back to the states with us—he had requested burial at sea.

* * *

The ancient mariner's ritual took place the 5th of November, a clear and bright day. We were in the Pacific, riding on deep, glassy water.

Oriskany and her destroyer escorts slowed to steerageway. Most of the ship's company and the entire air-wing, wearing service dress whites, were formed into ranks on the deck near the island.

Whitey's remains rested on a small platform on the number two aircraft elevator opposite the island. He had been stitched into a white canvas shroud, over which was draped an American flag.

We were called to attention.

A chaplain spoke.

Marines fired a twenty-one-gun salute.

Then, taps—the mournful twenty-four notes from a bugle that calls up tears. Always, for me, calls up tears.

After that, six of Whitey's mates tilted the wooden platform. Lt. Cmdr. Omar R. "Whitey" Ford, inside that canvas, glided from beneath the flag, and silently dropped into the deep and glass-blue water burbling alongside our ship, the one with call-sign 'Childplay'.

I did not hear the splash.

A vision of that ageless rite, the chaplain speaking, the slim white canvas casing quietly tilted off a platform. It is one of the most heartrending memories I carry.

LARRY DUTHIE

L ARRY DUTHIE IS A RETIRED NEWSPAPER publisher who lives with his wife, Roz on a small hay-farm in Eastern Washington. In addition to writing, he spends his time rebuilding old sailboats, trucks, cars, motorcycles, and very old tractors.

As a naval aviator, he flew 137 combat missions over North Vietnam and Laos on three deployments, beginning in September 1966. He was shot down over North Vietnam and rescued July 18, 1967. He left the Navy in August, 1969. He continues to love aviation.

Over the years he's owned a series of light airplanes, including part-interest in a floatplane.

"There is nothing better for the soul," he will tell you, "than landing on the still surface of a clear mountain lake and then fishing from its pontoon."

James Garrison

7

A Soldier's Poems from the Vietnam War

On Going to War

They are alone,
       together in the kitchen;
He paces behind her,
Then stops in the shadows.

Beyond her white hair,
       bent over the sink,
The uncovered windows
       frame black holes
       into the night.

"Mother, I go December first,"
       he says.

The light in the hall is dim,
The TV stands blank and dark,
       a reflective eye behind him.
There is no sound
       except the ticking of the clock
       on the wall.

Her eyes are vacant,
And the wrinkles seem deeper,
        but she doesn't cry.
She says nothing,
Just turns away
        and looks
        out the window,
        into the night,
Dropping the ragged dish towel
        by her side,
 An old woman
        thinking that death
        would be kinder.

* * *

LETTER HOME

Yesterday,
just before sunset,
the short, round cook,
        who looks like Lou Costello,
tried to kill Captain Midnight
        with an M-16.

They carried him off,
        the little doughboy cook,
        in his dirty white t-shirt,
yelling, crying, handcuffed;
and there were bullet holes
        in the ceiling.

How's the weather now?
It's spring, isn't it?
But I guess not
since it's still February.

I keep forgetting
because it's always hot here.
But I miss mowing the grass,
      the smell of wild onions
      after they've been cut.

The Lou Costello cook is kept in a cell,
Eight-by-eight, with only a cot and a bucket.

He said, "Don't move."
I ran.

* * *

WAR'S CHILD

"Look homeward Angel now, and melt with ruth,
And O ye dolphins, waft the hapless youth.
Weep no more, woeful shepherds, weep no more;
For Lycidas your sorrow is not dead,
Sunk though he be beneath the watery shore ..."

From "Lycidas" by John Milton.

We all knew her—
the army and I—
called her Syphilitic Sandy:
war's sister, mother, and child,
a fusion of east and west,
bred by the last
      conquering horde,
      lusted for by the next.
A dark angel of desire,
soaring over a scarred earth
that left jagged tracks
      on soft, olive skin.

Untold Stories

"Hey man," she pleads,
      "I wanna be loved,"
there in the night,
   hot and clammy
      by the gate in the wall,
      paint peeling
      from the bullet holes.
"I need somebody
     love me."
"I love you," says the sailor,
   caressing her breast.
"I no think so," she hisses.
"I need somebody
     love me,
     no body,
        love me."

She embraces the sailor,
     and death,
on a sinking ship,
     a sacrificial bier,
in the murky water
     of the river primeval.
naked and clutching his watch,
     she drowns,
forsaken by the sailor,
     swimming for shore.

"Come,
     yield me your body,"
the water gurgles and sighs,
"I'll embrace your cool flesh
     and give you time's balm
     to heal and refresh;
come lie 'neath me,
     transfixed and transformed,

clutched tight
        to death's bosom,
                safe from the storm."

An urchin
        begging life,
        begs no more,
but beckons the sailor
        safe on the shore,
"Come,
        ride the dolphin's back,
            do not shrink
            from the deep,
come ... come here
        with me to sleep."

* * *

Sunrise at Boot Camp

We sit in the dark,
        clammy with sweat,
Backs against the barracks' wall,
        floors waxed,
        commodes cleaned,
Windows shining in a 60-watt glow;
Eyes unborn to the dawn,
        staring
        at rows of packs and rifles
        grounded between the wooden buildings.

The sky changes,
        light gray;
A lone pine tree struggles
Out of sandy soil
That bears ghost prints
        of men marching to wars,

Strides of those who came this way before.

Shit!
I forgot to fill my canteen,
        and the sinks are washed and clean.

High wisps of rose clouds,
        and I yearn to be free,
No more to hear the bone-death rattle of dog tags,
        the clang of metal wall lockers in the dark,
No more to taste the dust and hear the rasping orders
        that mean nothing to me.

Last week in the field, after chow,
The quiet kid from Indiana received a letter from his wife
        and slit his wrists with a P-38 army can opener;
Fifty push-ups and blood seeping through the bandages.
"You fail, you're fucked!" yells the drill sergeant.

The sun's slanting rays rest on the top of the pine.
"Fall in," the voice calls;
Not moving, I dream
        of different places and better times,
Of your body
        breaking the sparkling surface of the water.

* * *

DEPARTURES

Boarding trains, buses, planes
        up steps, ramps, and inclines,
        on tracks, wheels and wings,
        steam,
            diesel exhaust,
            and roar.

People leaving,
    faces and arms and feet,
    voices and laughs and silence
    tears and sadness
        and gladness.

Bags, coats, hats,
    briefcases and diapers,
    paper, pen, computer, phone,
    newspapers, books,
        dolls, toys and games.

Work, leisure,
    duty, pleasure.
Joy and fear,
    weariness
        and boredom.
Impatience,
    dread,
        drugged,
            drunk.

Waiting, hurrying,
    standing, walking, running,
        up steps,
    down ramp,
        through aisle,
            over knees and feet;
                seat,
                    sit,
                        sat,
                        sitting.
Going home,
    going away,
    going to work,
    going to school,

    going to play,
    meeting someone,
    leaving someone.

Alone in the crowd.

Alone.
Leaving.

Going to war?
Going to die?

Departing
    alone.

*   *   *

THE WENCH IS DEAD

(with apologies to Wm. Shakespeare)

It was a troubled time,
fraught with turmoil
and war in a foreign land.
So why should I care now?

A brief meeting of bodies,
nothing more than flesh pressed close,
lips and tongues touching,
breaths commingled,
laughter, sighs, and cries;
a matador twirling a bright red cape,
teasing a russet bull
pulling the room around (so she said).
Why should I care now?

Translucent oil, white skin, white sheets,
head thrown back, a pulsing vein,
honeysuckle scent on a sun-warmed neck;
a new dawn's light windshield reflected,
green spring leaves flashing by,
sun-yellowed in a fine new morning.
Why should I care still?

Lips, fingers, breath,
long past, long gone;
passion, sunlight, voice,
faded and dead,
never to engage the senses again.
All that remains are floating remnants
of a struggling memory,
lingering, tugging—
and those too shall die.
So why should I care now?

* * *

MICK

IN THE WEE HOURS OF THE morning, ghosts restlessly move through the old colonial villa. Most are flesh, blood, and bone with livers half-pickled by Jack Daniels. Private Becker, dead sober, has fire watch. It's easy duty—monitor the radio and phone, wake the tower guards, but mainly just stay awake.

The last night patrol has returned—long after its shift should have been over, and the next tower guard is clear of his bunk.

The light in the Operations Room, Sergeant Beadle's domain during the day, is dim and Becker huddles under a desk lamp to read. Kafka's *The Trial*, which the English major, a fellow conscript, shoved into his hands and said,

"Read this. You'll understand."

As he turns the page, light reflects from the thick lens in his black-rimmed glasses.

Short, squat Becker has a mop of unruly black hair that pushes the limits of military regulations even in these lax times. Times worthy of Kafka, to whom Becker already feels a strong kinship. Becker is a weigher of molecules, a watcher of turning wheels.

When Becker looks up, the reflected light plays across the bullet-shaped head and short-cropped hair of a big oval-faced sergeant, three stripes, a buck sergeant, just down from My Tho and pulling temporary night duty before moving on to his next post.

He sits on the other side of the desk, filling out a form report. He rarely speaks, doesn't joke.

One of the villa's ghosts bursts into the room from the hallway—the first sergeant, followed by his retainers: Sergeant Connors from the Motor Pool, Smithy the mess sergeant, and Hayes.

The first sergeant, red-faced, wearing fatigue trousers and an olive-drab t-shirt, looks around, glaring wild-eyed. Then he staggers over to the desk.

"Not one of those goddamn gooks is to bring a fucking bicycle in here," he shouts at the buck sergeant and Becker.

The buck sergeant nods but doesn't say anything. Becker just stares. Top must be talking about the old papa-san and the other Vietnamese who work in the compound.

"Never! You fucking hear me! Never!" the first sergeant screams and rocks forward over the desk, releasing a blast of foul air and producing a shadow monster across the ceiling from the lamp on the desk.

He's quiet for a moment, and then turns to his entourage, waves one arm back toward the desk.

"You can tell Mick to do something, and he'll fucking do it."

He starts to walk away, a big man with slightly stooped

shoulders—not a military bearing, but a man long in the military. He has small sharp eyes under heavy dark eyebrows focused down an aquiline nose. Narrow, truncated head, burr haircut, and puffy red face.

Then he turns back. "Don't ever try anything foolish with me, or I'll bust your ass—with this." He holds up his right fist and extends it toward the buck sergeant. He ignores Becker like he's not even there.

"You see these knuckles?" Top says. He drops his hand onto the gray metal desk, knuckles up—red, hard, and raw looking. "You see 'em, huh?"

"Uh huh," the buck sergeant says and slowly nods his head.

"Just don't ever go against me."

The first sergeant stands up straight, raising his shoulders and rolling them forward. "Know karate, huh?"

"No, I just—"

"You see that hand." The first sergeant's harsh voice cuts through the buck sergeant's quiet New England accent. He holds up his left hand and shakes it in the air. "Weak." He staggers and catches the corner of the desk with the hand he had held up.

"This one's the strong one." He holds up his right hand, clenched in a fist. He twists around and with his fist slams the side of a gray metal filing cabinet, a crashing blow, denting the side and rocking the cabinet back and forth.

"Two knuckles. That's all it takes. Two fucking knuckles." He pauses and glares at the buck sergeant. "Five more months and you'll make E-six, Mick. Just get rid of that goddamn bracelet." He points to a woven black bracelet on the buck sergeant's broad wrist.

"Top, I can't get rid of the bracelet." Mick shakes his head and stares up at Top. "I'll wear it as long as I'm over here. A Montagnard gave it to me when I was a roadrunner—"

"You mean ya bought it at the fucking PX."

"No, first sergeant, I didn't." He speaks softly but clearly. The only light comes from the lamp on the desk and the first sergeant looms above it. "It was given to me by a Montagnard when I was a roadrunner in the highlands. ... I won't take it off while I'm here."

The supporting cast hovers in the shadows by the door.

"Good!" The first sergeant booms, staggering backward. "If it was given to you, then you're authorized to wear it."

He turns and looks at his audience in triumph.

They smile and nod and move toward the door, Hayes in front. It's clear to Becker they want to leave.

Top is almost out the door with his crew when he turns and comes back. He stumbles to a stop beside the desk and leans over it, casting a huge shadow on the ceiling and the walls behind him.

He waves a meaty finger in the buck sergeant's face.

"Trim that goddamn moustache." Loud, but not quite a shout.

"I just trimmed it today, Top."

"Goddamn it, if you want E-six, trim it again. You're not authorized any hair below the corners of your mouth."

The buck sergeant doesn't say anything, but the muscles in his lean jaw work up and down.

Becker could be a speck of dust floating in front of the lamp for all the first sergeant cares.

"You'll be okay, Mick," Top says, "just don't try any goddamn foolishness."

Top straightens up, the shadows shrinking behind him.

* * *

Becker has lasting images of Top, a palimpsest with layers over this one: Top at his desk, head down, close-cropped red hair cut in an oval, ignoring him; Top shouting at him to get his head out of his ass; Top under his breath to the CO's back, "you fucking black-ass n***;" and Top under the stairs, during the mortar attack. On his knees, trembling, hands clutched over his head. Near him, Becker attempts to lace his boots, his hands shaking so hard he can't. Wrapping the laces around his ankles, he ties them and runs to get his M-16 and bandoliers of ammo, while Hayes puts his arm around Top and leads him off.

* * *

This time, Top reaches the outside hallway before he barges back inside—past his loyal troops, none of whom try to stop him.

The buck sergeant has lifted a small blue testament off the desk and started to open it.

"Readin' the bible, too," the first sergeant growls, standing in the middle of the room, his hands on his hips. "Caught ya." He shifts sideways in a slow dance step. "You scared or religious?"

"I'm religious."

"I'm fucking religious, too. Any goddamn time you feel like it, son, you just come on to my room, and we'll talk about the good Lord."

The buck sergeant doesn't say anything, nods his head, and lays the testament face down on the desk.

Top raises his hand, shaking his index finger in the air.

"But the next time I catch some motherfucking NCO runnin' to get some goddamn beads, I'm gonna court-martial the bastard." He stumbles to one side and drops his hand for balance. "You know who I'm talkin' about, don't ya? ... Don't ya, Mick?"

He turns without waiting for an answer and lunges through the door, held open by one of his retainers. He repeats as he exits, "Yeah, I'm gonna court-martial the bastard."

The room is silent. Neither Becker nor Mick, the buck sergeant, says anything.

Becker, his book open flat under the lamp, glances over at Mick, sending glimmers of reflected light across the other man's face, unremarkable except for its oval shape.

Mick shakes his head, his mouth drawn into a tight smile under his neatly trimmed moustache.

Becker goes back to reading, and the sergeant reaches into his fatigue pocket and takes out a rosary.

He holds it in one hand above the desk, in a gray edge of light, moves it through his fingers, clicking the beads together. Driving the ghosts away.

End

JAMES GARRISON

A GRADUATE OF THE UNIVERSITY OF North Carolina and Duke Law School, James Garrison practiced law until returning to his first loves: writing and reading good literature. His novel, *QL 4* (TouchPoint Press 2017), set in the Mekong Delta during the Vietnam War, has won awards for literary and military fiction, and it was a finalist for the 2018 Montaigne Medal.

His recent novel, *The Safecracker* (TouchPoint Press 2019), has won legal thriller awards, and it was a category finalist in the 2020 Eric Hoffer Book Awards. His creative nonfiction and fiction works and poems have appeared in literary magazines and anthologies. Sheila Na-Gig nominated *Lost: On the Staten Island Ferry* for a 2018 Pushcart prize.

His most recent novel, *What Seems True*, set for release by TouchPoint Press in the summer of 2021, was inspired by the 1979 murder of the first black supervisor at a Texas Gulf Coast refinery, a crime for which the shooter was never convicted.

Webpage: https://jamesgarrison-author.com/ - Twitter: @JimGarrison10 - Facebook: https://www.facebook.com/JamesGarrisonauthor/

Gerald Gillis

8

REFLECTIONS

T HOUGH THEIR TRIPS WERE NOW GREATLY limited, this one had proceeded with an unusually high degree of resolve. Earl Enslow and his wife Dorothy, each in their eightieth year, had come from Georgia to fulfill a pledge they had made two decades earlier.

It was April 2002, springtime in Washington, D.C.— when the District was at its radiant best in unveiling the new without diminishing the old. They walked along at an unhurried pace amid the many others—he in a dark suit, she in a beige dress, her arm gently interlocked with his. Earl stopped and took a moment to gain his bearings, wiping a thin bead of perspiration from his forehead. He wasn't fond of large crowds, never had been, and while his physical health had steadily declined as the years accumulated, he was determined to see it through.

They walked on further until Earl stopped again and squinted at a rumpled map.

"Do you see it yet?" he asked, his discomfort mounting.

"No," Dorothy replied.

"Are you sure we're in the right spot?"

"Yes, dear. We're in the right spot."

Several minutes passed before Earl finally breathed a sigh of relief when he felt Dorothy's tugging at his arm.

"Is that it?" he asked as Dorothy pointed ahead.

"That's it, right there in front of us. Do you see it?"

* * *

He arrived by Greyhound on a clear, crisp, autumn afternoon in November 1966. He wore an old leather jacket— dark brown, of the aviator sort—over an ash gray sweatshirt with the blue letters DODGERS arching across the front. His jeans were faded a bluish-white, more a reflection of use than a statement of fashion. His tan suitcase, streaked and scuffed with the hard miles of the road, was secured with a strand of nylon rope to keep its modest contents from leaking out. In the span of four months, the bag and its youthful owner had traversed the continent from west to east. Needles and Flagstaff and Tucumcari; Amarillo and McAlester; Ozark and Memphis, with several smaller places, to boot.

Now had come Decatur, just outside Atlanta. It was the end of the line for the moment—a far stretch from his distant West Coast origins and the life he had known prior to his self-appointed emancipation. All along, there had been a plan, a *hope,* of an eventual reunion with an uncle and aunt in faraway Georgia. Those relatives, the childless Earl and Dorothy Enslow, had not the slightest idea of whom, or what, they were about to encounter.

Their nephew, Torrey Alan Enslow was the only son of Earl's deceased brother Everett, and Everett's hopelessly broken, alcoholic wife Lenora. At the age of eighteen, Torrey was already a two-year dropout, a star-crossed underachiever in all the contemporary units of measure. Instead of earning a diploma, he'd held a variety of odd jobs—a cook here, a painter there—remaining in each long enough to acquire the means to move on to something else, something closer to his chosen destination. He had no vocation, no home, no father (and he often claimed no mother). All he owned, apart from his suitcase and his clothes, were a few *Holiday Inn* towels, three Hemingway novels in paperback, a cassette tape player with the music of Motown, and his late father's gold *Bulova.* Twenty bucks would have covered his net worth, with some to spare.

What he did have, however, was the cunning of a fox and an appealing, confident demeanor—a charisma, even—that belied his youth. A handsome face and a prodigious IQ didn't hurt, either.

* * *

Torrey blew into his cupped hands to ward off the evening chill. He watched as his breath vaporized in a steady rhythm, illuminated by the pale tan light of the brick home's interior. He smelled the pine straw in the flower garden and the odor of burning wood from the fireplace. Oak, he surmised as he watched the white smoke leave the chimney and twist skyward into the darkness.

Torrey was unusually tense as he stepped onto his uncle's porch, clearing his throat, and sensing that a misjudgment here might confirm his deepest, darkest fear that there were no more Enslows left for him in this life. He rang the doorbell and stood up straight, and when the slender, graying Dorothy opened the door and peered out, he judged from her tentative expression that the time and distance might indeed have become too long.

"Is there something I can help you with, young man?"

"Hello, Aunt Dorothy. It's me, Torrey," he said meekly, the trepidation seeping into his voice. "I'm Torrey Enslow."

Her eyes widened as she wiped her hands across her checkered apron. "Torrey? My goodness, is that really you?"

He grinned. "Yes ma'am, it's really me."

She pushed open the screen door and invited him inside. "Look at you! Look how you've grown."

He took one step inside before glancing back at his old suitcase in the same manner that a small boy might glance back at his waiting dog.

"Yes, Torrey. Get your bag and bring it in."

Dorothy warmly embraced Torrey and then called out to Earl, who was open-mouth asleep in his recliner near the fireplace.

"Earl, this is your nephew Torrey. Look at him, he's all grown up."

Torrey noticed the surprise on Earl's face as his uncle quickly emerged from his stupor, then stood and offered a firm handshake. Torrey absorbed Earl's slow, measured gaze that surveyed him from head to toe and then back up again. Finally, Earl's smile and brisk slap on the shoulder helped to dissipate the hot apprehension that had been lingering in Torrey's belly for hours.

"You've certainly changed, son. Look a lot like you father now. Like an Enslow."

Torrey smiled self-consciously. "Thank you, Uncle Earl."

The three of them stood in the den for several awkward moments, shifting their feet and making small talk, until Torrey eventually explained in an unemotional and forthright manner how he had left Southern California, and his mother, with no intention of ever returning. He would make a life for himself, he explained, without his mother's bedlam, booze, and boyfriends. When Torrey explained his plan of crossing the country to seek out his only known Enslow relatives, he correctly sensed Earl and Dorothy were deeply touched. To his great relief they promptly offered him the guestroom, indefinitely and with no strings attached, followed by his equally prompt acceptance.

Finally! Torrey thought to himself.

They settled in at the dinner table and discussed a range of topics—the escalating conflict in Vietnam; the election of Ronald Reagan as Governor of California; the retirement of Dodgers pitching ace Sandy Koufax; the music of the Beatles and other popular groups, all of which Earl described as "hard to understand and even harder to listen to."

Torrey grinned. He leaned forward with interest when Earl talked about Enslow Hardware, the Decatur store his uncle owned and operated. Torrey then offered a thumbnail sketch of the jobs he had performed and the skills he had acquired among his journeys. His uncle seemed impressed, and Torrey silently hoped that a job in the hardware store might be forthcoming.

"So, what can you tell me about your mother?" Earl finally asked.

Torrey wiped his mouth with the back of his hand and took a moment to collect his thoughts. He noticed his uncle observing him with quick, sidelong glances, but without staring. Torrey took a sip of iced tea and cleared his throat.

"Well, sir, she drinks a fifth of vodka every day, even on Sundays, and she chases it with orange juice and two packs of Luckies."

Earl stopped chewing and stared.

"She coughs a lot, doesn't eat much, and usually becomes either weepy or mean, and sometimes both. She passes out around midnight, gets up at noon, and starts drinking all over again. She steals the money I earn if I forget to hide it, and she explains that it's rent for the roof over my head. Her boyfriends came and went, and they were usually no more sober than she was. I had at least a dozen fistfights with several of them, grown men in their thirties and forties, and I was sure I would end up killing one of them, or being killed myself. I begged her for years to stop drinking, but she didn't because, well, she can't."

"So, you left," Earl said after a long pause.

"So, yes, I left," Torrey said, noticing Earl's glance at Dorothy. "Of course, my daddy died in 1953 when I was four, so the life I had was all I ever knew. I came to hate it, every single day and night of it, and I finally decided I was done with it."

The silence afterward became increasingly uneasy for Torrey. He noticed Dorothy turn away and wipe at her eyes with a cloth napkin. Earl mostly avoided looking directly at Torrey but otherwise said little else the rest of the meal.

"Anything else you need to know, Uncle Earl?" Torrey finally asked after a prolonged silence. "Anything about me?"

"No," Earl said, shaking his head. "I think you've told me what I wanted to know."

* * *

Enslow Hardware became a different place in November and early December, no doubt a result of Torrey Enslow's employment there as a store clerk. The arrangement had resulted more from Dorothy's insistence than Earl's beneficence, although Earl had finally concluded Torrey's efforts might prove useful.

As the weeks passed, Torrey seemed to grow into his role as a stock clerk. Earl provided training on many of the most commonly requested tools and parts, enabling his nephew to assist customers on his own. Young female visitors to the store showed up in larger numbers than ever before, hoping to attract the attention of Torrey. For his part, Torrey was a quick study whose value to the business steadily increased to a point where Earl viewed him as a possible successor.

In contrast, however, there were occasions when Earl became frustrated with his nephew. A tavern-owner friend of Earl's called to tell him that Torrey was drinking in his establishment on what he surmised was a fake ID. One night, when a burly college football player seated at the bar near Torrey made several insulting remarks about his youthful appearance, Torrey proceeded to knock the man unconscious with one swift punch.

"That kid's fearless, Earl."

On another occasion, a trusted supplier told Earl Torrey had requested several free samples from the supplier's tool line. Torrey had intimated he would soon be running the store since his uncle's health was declining. When confronted by Earl, Torrey admitted lying to the supplier to acquire the tools as barter for additional spending money.

On yet another occasion, a prominent banker stopped by the store one evening to inform Earl that his daughter, home from college in North Carolina, had been on several dates with Torrey. Earl resented the man's obvious condescension about his highly refined daughter going out with a high-school dropout, hardware-store clerk. Earl told the banker Torrey was old enough to decide for himself whom he should spend his time with, and suggested the father consider giving his daughter the same latitude. The meeting frostily concluded.

Whenever Earl's patience grew thin with Torrey, he took the time to provide his advice and wise counsel to a young man who had had very few breaks in his life, and whose blemishes often reflected the harsh conditions of his adolescence. He could also be firm and unyielding with Torrey, especially about lying and threatening the trust Earl considered essential to their relationship.

After one such teaching moment in Earl's office at the end of a busy day, Earl swallowed hard and asked Torrey to pay careful attention to what he was about to say.

"I've been thinking about this for some time, and I need to get this off my chest. So here goes: Torrey, I sincerely apologize for not having sought custody of you after your father died. I'm truly sorry that I failed you, son. I also failed my brother, and I failed our family. And it's the biggest regret of my life. I swear before almighty God, I will never fail you again."

Torrey sat quietly for several moments before clearing his throat, and said, "I appreciate that, Uncle Earl. I really do. But what you and Aunt Dorothy have done for me these past few months has given me a real sense of belonging I've been looking for my whole life. You haven't failed me. In fact, you've probably helped save me. Please, don't ever look past that."

Several days later, Earl was finishing a last bit of paperwork when Torrey knocked on his office door and peered inside.

"Uncle Earl, I need a moment of your time."

Earl motioned him in and noticed an air of formality he didn't normally associate with Torrey.

"I have something to tell you," Torrey bluntly declared, squarely standing in front of Earl's desk. "I've decided to become a Marine, just like you. I've enlisted in the Marine Corps, and I leave for boot camp in mid-February. I'll never be able to repay you and Aunt Dorothy for what you've given me, so I'll just say, 'Thank you,' and hope you somehow get my full meaning."

Torrey then reached out his hand to Earl. After hesitating, Earl moved from behind the desk to embrace Torrey. Earl held on to his surprised nephew for a long moment before finally releasing him. Torrey grinned, offered a "Right on!" and then left the office.

Earl sat at his desk for several minutes, reflecting upon all his nephew and he had come to mean to each other. He then softly wept for several more.

* * *

Earl and Dorothy Enslow, retired, had come to pay their respects. Fittingly, Earl wore a Marine Corps lapel pin on his jacket—a long-ago gift from his nephew.

Etched onto the panel to their immediate front, slightly below eye level, was the name TORREY ALAN ENSLOW. It was a single name amid an ocean of names—58,000 of them—engraved into the black panels of the Vietnam Veterans Memorial.

Earl and Dorothy spent nearly an hour in quiet repose as the memories of Torrey filled their heads and hearts. Earl finally braced a single sheet of white paper against the Wall's surface while Dorothy traced with a pencil the letters of their nephew's name.

Even though Earl's arthritis had greatly affected his mobility, he very much wanted to trace his nephew's name as a priceless keepsake. When Earl's fingers could no longer hold the paper in place, a bearded veteran in a bush hat stepped around Dorothy and kindly offered his assistance.

The long-ago letter from Torrey's commanding officer had told of a brave and selfless young Marine. His squad mates in Vietnam had been so touched by his life and so saddened by his death, several had felt the need to write to the uncle and aunt referred to by Corporal Torrey Enslow, USMC, as "the absolute finest people on the face of this earth."

Corporal Enslow had been mortally wounded while rescuing two members of his squad who had been hit and pinned down at Hue during the Tet Offensive of 1968. The Bronze Star citation had even used the words "conspicuous gallantry."

TORREY ALAN ENSLOW.

Earl thanked the veteran for his help and then stood back after Dorothy finished tracing the name. He carefully, almost reverently folded the paper and slid it into the breast pocket of his jacket. He then silently stood and once more took in the Memorial's breathtaking sweep and magnificent simplicity.

Earl turned and saw Dorothy's tears, and he felt the mist gathering in his own eyes.

Dear God, Earl kept thinking. *All those names, each joining collectively with the others in a gripping, powerful epitaph to their own ultimate sacrifice, their own ultimate promise, unfulfilled.*

When he remembered his youthful Marine buddies at Tarawa who had likewise given their last full measure, his own tears coursed down his cheeks.

Earl passed a handkerchief beneath his nose and then reached into his jacket pocket, producing a silver cross and chain.

It had been a Christmas gift to Torrey from Dorothy and himself, worn by Torrey at the time of his death. Earl had dutifully worn the cross every day since March 1968, when Torrey's personal effects had arrived from Vietnam.

Every day for thirty-four years he had considered the cross to have been on loan from Torrey.

Today, he was returning it.

Earl gently placed the cross necklace at the base of the Wall, directly beneath Torrey's name. He then stepped back and stood as erect as his old frame would permit. He presented a crisp Marine Corps salute, his right-hand slightly trembling.

As he held his salute, he noticed his own reflection returning from the Wall, as well as the reflections of several veterans standing nearby who had likewise come to attention and joined Earl in saluting.

They had begun to leave when Earl stopped and turned back for one last look. He was thankful beyond measure they had finally made the trip. The young man who had so changed his life with so short a visit those many years ago, that same young man whose life had been lost in service to his country, was still a part of Earl.

TORREY ALAN ENSLOW.

"My God, I couldn't be prouder of that boy," Earl said, taking Dorothy's arm in his.

Dorothy smiled and held tightly to his arm. "And I couldn't be prouder of you."

END

GERALD GILLIS

GERALD GILLIS GREW UP IN THE Atlanta, Georgia suburb of Decatur. He received his BBA from the University of Georgia and his MBA from the University of Tampa.

Immediately upon completing undergraduate school, Gerald spent three years as an artillery officer in the U.S. Marine Corps. After military service, he spent the majority of his business career in the medical-devices industry where he held executive-level positions.

Gerald has authored four novels: *That Deadly Space* (Mills Street Publishing, 2017), *Dare Not Blink* (Navigator Books, 2012), *Shall Never See So Much* (Booklocker, 2010), and *Bent, But Not Broken* (Sandlapper, 1986). He has also authored two eBooks entitled *How to Become a Successful, Effective Communicator* (Mills Street Publishing, 2017) and *Paige's Laws of Business* (Navigator Books, 2013). His books have been recognized with multiple awards.

In addition to his writing, Gerald speaks on a range of topics, to include leadership, service, effective communications, and business ethics. He has been interviewed on numerous radio and television shows and has spoken to business and civic organizations, schools, churches, and military associations.

Gerald is married and the father of three grown children. He and his wife reside in the Atlanta area.

Robert Goswitz

9

THE GIRL FOUND IN THE FOREST

October 7, 1965

WHIP-POOR-WILL. A MELANCHOLY CHANT REPEATED IN a circular rhythm. Native Americans called the bird's song an omen of death. Old New Englanders said the creature sensed a soul departing. *Whip-poor-will.*

Dawn arrived hesitantly. Luna sat up in her bed and looked out the window into the forest that surrounded the town of Saint Bernadine's Crossing. The silence of the northern forest had been disturbed during the night. A distant snapping and crashing of branches, the thud of impact had awoken Luna during the night. The whippoorwill had been unusually persistent since that moment.

"Sad bird," she said to herself.

A white fawn cantered out of the tree line, pink nose and ears luminous in the dim light. Large eyes alert, her tail twitched in anticipation.

Luna stood at her window. "Ohhh, you so pwetty."

She put on her hiking boots, troubling with the laces for a few seconds, her fingers fumbling in the dark. With a sigh, she gave up, put her coat on over her flannel pajamas, blew a kiss to the Frankie Avalon poster taped to the wall, and walked into the living room.

Luna paused under her parents' portrait hanging on the wall. A soldier dressed in Army green, with highly polished jump boots and a Special Forces Green Beret. He held a young woman in a white summer dress. The couple smiled confidently at the camera. An American flag folded into a glass-covered triangular walnut display case hung under the photo.

Luna went back to her room and picked the green beret off her dresser and put it on. Daddy's hat always gave her confidence. She quietly strode across the living room and closed the sliding glass patio door behind her.

The white fawn held her ground a few yards away. Luna smiled, treasuring the deep quiet of the forest dawn. The young deer trotted toward the tree line.

"Okay, here we go again." Luna followed the white fawn into the forest. "Hey, Pwincess! Slow down."

Luna's ankles pulled out of her untied boots. She stopped—there was enough light to secure the laces. The fawn patiently waited on the trail ahead.

With her boot laces secured, Luna stood and inhaled. The air she breathed emanated from a thousand trees: eastern hemlock, white cedar, aspen, pine, and the ancient ferns that covered the second-growth forest floor. The atmosphere bore a subtle balm, making a claim on her heart. It granted her passage from a world that labeled her as retarded, laughed at her mongoloid facial features, faulted her halting attempts at language, and mocked her short chubby body. The forest—a place between heaven and earth—freed Luna from that cage.

Striding purposefully, head erect, arms swinging, eyes shining, humming the melody to Frankie Avalon's "Surfer Girl," she followed the fawn up and down the boulder-strewn glacial hills, weaving between trees on the deer track. They passed out of the hardwoods entering the pinery planted in dense rows that blocked the sun. The fawn paused, seeming to know her companion needed a rest.

Luna was grateful.

"Let's take a bwake." She heavily sat down, resting her back against the base of a white pine. The wind hissed through the needles at the top of the trees. A dun-colored bird lit in the branch above her head and chirped out a cheery greeting.

"Hey, Gwama, how's it going?" Luna knew the forest and its creatures so intimately that she recognized the female cardinal's place in her family. The bird fluttered above her head for a second and flew off.

Refreshed, Luna got to her feet. "Where are you taking me, Pwincess?" The white fawn turned and trotted on through the pinery.

In half an hour, Luna noticed a break in the tree line ahead. Morning light pierced the forest canopy. Princess trotted into the clearing and stopped, alert, tail and head erect.

Luna tripped on a mangled chunk of aluminum at the edge of the clearing. Startled, she looked around. An airplane fuselage stripped of its wings had nosed into the forest floor at a shallow angle. Sheered trees were littered with white aluminum wing and tail fragments stretching back through the forest for several hundred yards. The door on the fuselage was gone, revealing a lifeless man and woman strapped into the two front seats.

A glassy-eyed, blond-haired girl dressed in sneakers, jeans, and a blue windbreaker stood in front of the wreck, a large red knot on her forehead. Dried blood fringed her hairline and her left arm bent at an unnatural angle.

Luna looked at the spot where Princess had been. The albino fawn had disappeared. Luna's feet carried her toward the girl. Her respiration increased. Tears came to her eyes. She stood, looking up at the unseeing eyes. Luna gently clasped the cool flesh of her uninjured hand.

"You got a bump on your head. I'm going to take you home. Wait 'til you meet Fwankie. He my boyfwend."

* * *

Flambeau County Sheriff Simon Plum, his deputy

Clinton Zweifelhofer, and county social worker Sonja Swenson stood over Luna and the injured girl as they clung to each other, seated on Luna's bed.

Signe Nordlander, Luna's grandmother, sat next to the girls. "Now, Luna, tell the sheriff what you told me."

Luna was frightened by the roomful of strangers staring at her. Their unspoken expectation stressed her limited facility with language. But when Grandma Sig reached over and patted her hand ever so gently, she decided to give it a go.

"Pwincess came to see me this mo-ning. She wanted me to follow her."

Sheriff Plum hitched his pistol belt and rocked on his heels. His deputy took out a notepad. "And who is this Pwincess? Excuse me, Princess."

"She a white deer. She got pink ears."

Grandma Sig looked concerned. "She tells a lot of stories about her animal friends."

Plum looked at Zweifelhofer, shook his head, removed his Stetson, took a knee, and smiled at the young girl. "It's okay, Luna, relax. Tell us where Princess took you."

Luna warmed to her task. "She take me a way out in a pinery. We saw da wreck. An I fine my little fwend." She hugged the injured girl. "Then, I bwing her home to meet Fwankie."

"Fwankie?" The deputy's pen paused.

"Frankie Avalon." Grandma Sig pointed at the pop star's poster taped to the knotty pine paneling behind the officials. "That's her Frankie."

Luna smiled. "Yeah, that's him!"

The Flambeau Falls hospital ambulance roared up the driveway, lights flashing and siren shrieking. Grandma walked to the front door to let in the ambulance driver and his assistant.

The sheriff continued his interrogation: "What's your little friend's name?"

Luna continued hugging the injured girl. "She hurt. She can't talk." Luna looked at the girl's vacant face. "It's okay, little fwend."

Grandma Sig led the ambulance crew into the bedroom. "Luna, these men need to take your friend to the hospital to see the doctor."

The ambulance driver and his assistant smiled as they advanced on the injured girl. She recoiled in fear and Luna hugged her tighter.

The social worker knelt at Luna's knee. "Luna, look at your friend's face. Can you see that she's injured?"

Luna drew back and looked. Her eyes watered. "Yes."

"She needs to see the doctor. Can you help us get her there?"

"Yes."

"You're being brave. Luna, would you stand and walk your friend over to the gurney so these men can take her to the hospital?"

"Okay, come along, little fwend." She stood and helped the injured girl to her feet. Her little friend was a head taller than Luna. "C'mon now, you can do it." Luna smiled up into the girl's distant gaze. "That's it." Luna helped her onto the gurney. The injured girl broke into tears and clung to Luna with her good hand.

"Walk with her to the ambulance," said the driver.

Sonja and Grandma Sig walked with Luna as she held the injured girl's hand. The narcotic injection administered inside the ambulance finally released her grip.

The three of them walked back toward the house as the ambulance zoomed away.

Back indoors, Sheriff Plum asked, "So, Luna, can you take us to the crash site?"

Her eyes got big because questions requiring a specific answer frazzled her. She hugged her grandma.

The kind matron rubbed Luna's scalp. "Luna, my dear child, the injured girl's mom and dad may be hurt. We need to find them."

Luna blinked out a tear. "Pwincess know the way, I fo-got."

Sonja Swenson knelt in front of Luna. "Now, darling, could we try a walk in the woods? Maybe your feet will take us the way Princess showed you to go."

"Okay."

Luna led the little search party out into the woods.

February 15, 1966

Tina Maples, head nurse of the Brain Injury Treatment Unit at St. Mary's Hospital, Milwaukee, Wisconsin made small adjustments to her winged nursing cap, while looking in the mirror on her office wall. Once nested properly atop her blond bouffant hairdo, she smoothed a few wrinkles from her white uniform, smiled at herself, and said, "I hope this works."

She snatched the manila file from her desk and marched down the long hallway. As Nurse Maples entered room number three, Sonja Swenson, Flambeau County social worker, stood and greeted her.

"Nice to finally meet you after all our time on the phone."

Nurse Maples smiled. "Thanks for braving the winter weather to drive all the way down here."

Sonja introduced her travel companions to Nurse Maples. "This is Luna Brunette, the brave young woman who found Angela, and her grandmother, Mrs. Signe Nordlander."

"Thank you for coming. You've done so much for Angela but we need your help again."

Grandma Sig said, "Sonja has kept us updated on Angela's progress. We got concerned when we heard she'd hit a roadblock."

"Can I see my liddle fwend?" Luna asked.

"Let me update you on her progress first." Nurse Maples opened the thick manila file. "Her broken arm has healed, as well as the other contusions and abrasions she suffered. Motor functions are normal. She understands what is said to her."

"That sounds good," Grandma Sig said, ever hopeful.

Nurse Maples agreed. "It is good, and luckily Angela did not have a skull fracture, but the severe concussion she sustained left her aphasic—unable or possibly unwilling to form words. This is what concerns us."

Sonja asked, "So, you think she might be able to speak but has chosen not to?"

"We don't know. Sometimes these issues are elective, sometimes they are organic to the injury. The poor girl has been through a lot."

"Luna and I would do anything to help." Grandma Sig dabbed a tear from her eye with a lavender-scented hanky.

"Yes, we need your help. Her trauma is severe. She literally fell out of the sky on her family's business flight from Oklahoma City to the Duluth Shoe Manufacturers Convention. The Davidsons had insurance so she will be cared for, but she lost her parents, was an only child, and has no next of kin in the area. The few relatives we've contacted have not been forthcoming. So, Angela sits among strangers in a strange land."

Luna grew impatient. "When can I see my liddle fwend?"

"I think we need you to see her, Luna. She has withdrawn into a depressed fog. Her response to anyone or anything is minimal. The psychiatrist thinks we need to present someone familiar to lure her back toward social interaction. Angela is in the dayroom. Let's walk down there to see her."

The four women walked down the hall to the dayroom for the Brain Trauma Unit. Nurse Maples ushered them into an observation room. She walked past several ping-pong tables. The television blared *The Price Is Right*. Two checker players, one wearing a plastic helmet, the other's head bandaged, greeted Nurse Maples. She briefly spoke with them, smiled, and walked toward the far corner.

Angela sat alone, sunk down in the couch, empty eyes staring ahead.

Nurse Maples knelt in front of Angela, briefly spoke to her, then returned to the observation room.

"Well, I told her she has a visitor. Of course, she didn't respond. Are you willing to let Luna visit her, Grandma Sig?"

"By all means. Luna frets over her. Don't you, child?"

"Umhmm...Can I go see my liddle fwend?"

"Come with me, Luna." Nurse Maples took Luna by the hand and walked her across the dayroom to Angela. "Go say 'hi' to your friend."

Luna knelt in front of Angela. "Knock-knock, anybody home?"

The glaze fell from Angela's eyes. She blinked. Her gaze fixed on Luna. A tear of recognition formed in the corner of Angela's left eye. Luna smiled. The two girls leapt into each other's arms and hugged for a long time. Angela was crying and shaking.

Luna looked up at her. "Don't cry now, liddle fwend, me an Fwankie are going to take care of you."

June 12, 1966

Sonja Swenson tried to ignore the chocolate chip cookies on the blue china plate at her elbow. She shared a smile with Grandma Signe as they sipped coffee in the widow's cozy kitchen. Music filled the living room. Two teenaged girls danced in front of a television. Angela, the injured girl, and Luna moved to the music of their favorite television show, *American Bandstand*.

Little Eva's soulful voice wailed from the television speaker, "D-o-o the loco-o-o-mo-shun with me-e-e."

Angela's long feminine frame swayed in easy rhythm with the thumping bass and the wailing saxophone, her feet chuga-chugging like a railroad train. She mimicked the dance moves of the *Bandstand* teens on the television screen.

Luna struggled to keep up, going through the motions,

smiling at her "little friend."

Sonja took a guilty bite of Grandma Sig's chocolate chip cookie and said, "It's amazing what Luna does for Angela."

"Yes, and I feel it's great that Luna has a companion, even one who doesn't speak." Grandma's voice was filled with approval.

Luna tired of the dancing and sat on the couch. Angela stayed in front of the television, long hair and limbs swaying to "You Give Me Fever," by The McCoys. Angela suddenly looked panicky. She located Luna, pulled her off the couch, and the two swayed hand-in-hand to the music.

"Taking care of Angela gives Luna a purpose in life. That's why I'm glad the courts awarded us foster care of this precious young woman." Grandma Sig glowed. "Thanks for your help."

"Lucky you came along."

"My husband left me with a good pension from the power company. When Luna's father was killed in Vietnam, her mother fell apart and drifted off. I adopted the poor child, which was good for both of us, but sometimes it got lonely. Angela is a nice companion for Luna and me." A tear formed in the corner of Grandma Sig's eye. "I'm so happy."

"Yes, and your success in adopting Luna made the court decide you were a worthy candidate for fostering Angela."

"You were my guide through the paperwork and courts." Flushed with happiness the kind matron dabbed at her tears.

"Grandma Sig, it isn't every day that my job makes me happy, but this is one of them."

Sonja decided she deserved another cookie.

June 14, 1966

Chee-er-ie—Chee-er-ie—Cheer-cheer-cheer. The cardinal sang in a loud clear voice. Dawn floated from the forest on birdsong wings. Luna sat up in her bed to look out into the woods. Angela rose from her bed and joined

Luna at the window. Princess stood just inside the tree line staring at them.

"Today, you go with me." Luna pointed at Angela then pulled on her hiking boots. Angela got dressed.

As the girls passed through the bedroom doorway, Luna blew a kiss to the Frankie Avalon poster. Angela touched her lips with her fingertips and pressed them against Paul McCartney's boyish kisser on the second poster. Luna would not share Frankie, so they found the Beatles' portrait for Angela.

In the living room, Luna paused under her parents' portrait. Angela brought the green beret out of the bedroom and smiled when Luna put it on. The girls hugged.

As Luna opened the sliding glass door, Princess stepped onto the lawn, tail twitching in anticipation. Angela hesitated inside the exterior door frame, as she had done the last few times, held back by past experience in those woods.

"C'mon, liddle fwend, Pwincess will protect us." Luna offered her hand. Angela accepted the offer for the first time, stepping down on the brick patio.

"Oh, you so bwave!"

Luna's smile was the key that unlocked Angela's heart. The two friends followed Princess out into the woods.

ROBERT GOSWITZ

ROBERT GOSWITZ IS A RETIRED, DOG-WALKING novelist who believes his best qualities will soon be discovered. He was a special education teacher for thirty-three years, working with cognitively disabled, emotionally disturbed, and at-risk youth. Before that, he was awarded a Bronze Star and the Combat Infantry Badge for his service in Vietnam.

Robert lives with his lovely and patient wife, Jody on the banks of the beautiful Bark River in southeastern Wisconsin.

He is currently represented by the Loiocono Literary Agency for his novel, *The Dragon Soldier's Good Fortune*

Joel Graves

10

A FIST FULL OF DEATH

I N MID-NOVEMBER 1990 DURING DESERT SHIELD, our unit was camped in Saudi Arabia (about sixty miles south of the Kuwaiti border) waiting for the call to move up. I was a newly promoted captain and the S-1 (Admin Officer) of 1st Battalion, 67th Armored Regiment—1st "Tiger" Brigade, 2nd Armored "Hell on Wheels" Division, and I had business at 1st Cav Corps headquarters. If we followed the hardtop road that wound around the mountain range, the 1st Corps headquarters was over forty miles away. But as I studied my map, I noticed if we drove cross-country, it was only ten miles. I got a compass bearing, and we took off.

My driver and I traversed rocky, desolate country. We passed nomads, all dressed in black, and camels and sheep munching on thin patches of grass. About halfway there, a large white snake shot across the front of our HUMVEE, and I told my driver to go after it.

I grew up on a cattle ranch. As a young boy, I managed to catch every kind of snake that roamed our part of Central California. I kept them in homemade terrariums in the barn and enjoyed feeding them insects, mice, and frogs. To me, the creature racing along the ground at almost twenty miles per hour was just another snake.

The snake was quick, but after a hundred yards it finally tired and stopped. I eagerly jumped out to see what it was. To my utter amazement, it rose up *and flared its hood.*

The snake was a beautiful, seven-foot-long white cobra

with a scattering of small black dots down its back and a creamy yellow belly. The snake watched as I retrieved the mattock handle from the back of the HUMVEE and slowly approached.

Although trembling with fear, I carefully pushed the snake's head down until I could grab it behind the neck. Yeah, I know...

The snake wrapped its body around my right arm, but I didn't think anything about it. Snakes do that. But this snake was big and powerful. It suddenly twisted its head to the right, working its jaws as it tried to bite my fingers.

Too much of the head was sticking out. I adjusted my grip, so less head stuck out. But to my horror, the snake slowly pulled its head out of my hand. In a few seconds, its head would come lose and I would be dead.

No matter how hard I bore down, the head slowly retracted into my fist until I could not see it. I reached up with my left hand and desperately squeezed my right hand. At this point, I decided to kill the snake by crushing its head, if I could, to keep it from getting loose. I had seconds.

My driver stood by, eyes bugging out, paralyzed. He hated snakes and never thought to ask if he could help.

I bent over and struggled with both hands, gripping as hard as I could. Then, the snake stopped pulling and loosen the grip on my arm. I relaxed my death grip on its head. It relaxed a little more on my arm. I took my left hand off. It loosened up more, so I reached around with my left hand and pushed the snake's head back out of my right fist, but not too far, to where it was supposed to be. Everyone relaxed. The snake closely watched me but stopped trying to bite or escape.

My driver let out his breath and whispered, "Damn, sir, you almost died."

I looked at him, smiling sheepishly.

Now I had a pet snake. Once the magnificent beast gave

up the fight, the struggling stopped, and calmness settled in. I petted the snake's head, examined the body closely, and finally got my driver to touch it with a finger, briefly. I unwrapped its body from my arm and gently laid it on the ground. The snake remained there without moving, head raised a few inches, intently watching us. I finally shooed it away and it sped out of sight.

My only regret—neither of us had film in our little cameras.

DRILL AND CEREMONIES—A COMMON LANGUAGE

D URING THE DESERT STORM ASSAULT INTO Kuwait, I was responsible for left flank security, maintenance, and medical assets. I rode in a HUMVEE immediately behind the last tank in the formation, followed by the maintenance and medical tracks.

Iraqi soldiers walked the battlefield, holding up white flags. Others were captured or surrendered as we overran their defenses. By evening, we had hundreds of prisoners. Word came down from headquarters to prepare the Iraqis for movement to the rear.

Before sending them out early the next morning, we needed a headcount. I told Staff Sergeant Smith to count the prisoners who were seated on the ground nearby. He came back thirty minutes later and said he tried but could not count them because there were too many, all jumbled together.

I was a non-commissioned officer for ten years. I had an idea of what needed to happen. I walked out to the mass of prisoners and stood in front of them. Many studied me with angry eyes.

I shouted, "Stand up!" and raised my arms up.

They stood. I was encouraged.

I shouted, "Dress right, dress!" and made a chopping motion with my right arm to indicate ranks and files. Then,

I stood with my left arm extended, repeating, "Dress right, dress!"

A short man suddenly leaped forward, rapidly speaking in Arabic. He nodded to me and shouted at the prisoners. He called them to attention, then had them form eight columns. The prisoners lined up, using their left arm to touch the shoulder of the person to their front and left, so they were evenly lined up. At the rear, they broke off to form even columns.

The little man, whom I later learned was a first sergeant, turned to me, stood at attention, and saluted. I saluted back and turned to Staff Sergeant Smith.

"Count the prisoners!"

Staff Sergeant Smith walked across the front then down the side, and in a less than two minutes returned with the count—267.

I indicated to the first sergeant to form two columns.

As they finished forming up, the HHC commander arrived in his HUMVEE and escorted the prisoners to the rear.

JOEL GRAVES

JOEL GRAVES JOINED THE U.S. AIR Force in 1976, and over eight years worked his way up to Tech Sergeant (E-6). In 1984, he switched to the U.S. Army, assigned to tanks (armor) and was stationed at Fort Irwin, CA with the Opposing Forces.

Midway through 1986, Graves attended Officer Candidate School at Fort Benning, GA and was commissioned a 2nd Lieutenant in Armor. After Airborne School and the Armor Officer Basic Course, he was stationed at Fort Hood, Texas and deployed to Desert Storm in 1990. After the war, the Army sent him to Fort Riley, KS and then Fort Lewis, WA, where he retired in 1997.

For six years, he worked in industry as an operations manager and logistics manager, then became a hospital and hospice chaplain, started an Anglican church, and retired completely in 2012.

After retiring, he concentrated on his writing, creating a book a year.

jim greenwald

11

TAPESTRY

within my mind
there exists a tapestry
woven over many years
filling my mind

an intertwined rainbow of color
filled with tears and remembered faces
faces of pain...silent faces

no pattern beyond chaos
my mind trying to quiet their voices

as tears make their final escape down my cheeks
my tapestry...cross...my internal prison

TAPESTRY REPRESENTS HUMAN EMOTION IN ITS many-colored threads. A spiderweb built of mixed experiences. A balance of needs, desires, wishes, and memories that haunt life. How many chances to learn have I ground beneath my feet? Have you ever looked into the mirror of your life to catch a glimpse of who you are, were, or became? Does war change a person, how can it not, when each night a parade of faces march across your mind's eye, words ringing out of what you denied them.

* * *

NO WORDS

you silenced my voice
placed me in this prison

you spoke of need...security
locked me away

emptied of words, devoid of solace
home but not, in a room with unknowing experts

they have seen "Saving Private Ryan"

they know what it is like to serve
having never done so

my voice remains silent, ever the good soldier

unable to share the dreams you left me

DEVOID OF WORDS TO SPEAK, I run to stand in the rain. Here I can hide my pain behind a false face. I cannot share much of my life, how unfair that would be, to see you suffer just like me.

JIM GREENWALD

J IM GREENWALD IS A MULTI-AWARD-WINNING POET/
AUTHOR, who likes to experiment with his writing.
He has authored fifteen books—his interests divided
between emotional, military, and Native American subjects.

A graduate of Saint Francis University (with four
degrees—he continues to take courses that interest him,
finding education far more interesting than what television offers).

He lives in rural Bedford County, PA.

Jim Hodge

12

Every Man a Rifleman

In 1965, I was among many young men who found themselves in the American Army. Some of us were there by choice. Some of us were there by draft. All of us were there experiencing a new way of life. Everything done by the numbers. Everything done in unison. Everything done in response to orders.

Our first indoor instruction class was a good example. We filed into the classroom in silence—dressed right, came to attention, eyes straight ahead.

It has been more than fifty-five years since that day, but I'll not forget the gist of what the NCO instructor said. He told us that on his command, "Ready seats," we would loudly say in unison: "Every man a rifleman," and only then would we sit. We went through that sequence a number of times, each time being told, "On your feet," so we could do it again and again.

The instructor was finally satisfied. He told us, "Every man a rifleman" would be our motto—our pledge. He then told us something I've not forgotten.

"People, whether you wind up as a cook, or as a medic, or as an artilleryman, or as a grease monkey in the motor pool...whether you wind up pushing a pencil or cleaning out latrines, I don't care who you are or what you are or where you are. First and foremost, above everything else in this army you are a rifleman. The chief of staff of the United States Army is a rifleman."

In the years since that day, I've no doubt violated that principle more than once, but I have tried to apply, "Every man a rifleman" to whatever level of employment I am. Knowledge, ability, and pride at the primary skill level should never be marginalized or abandoned.

BEER CONTRABAND AT 10,000 FEET

MY FATHER FLEW FIFTY-TWO MISSIONS AS a B-17 gunner in the Air Corps 483rd Bombardment Group in World War II. He is now ninety-nine years old. In his remembrances to his sons about those times in his life he has refrained from speaking about the ugliness of war, preferring to share the lighthearted experiences of those times. Thus, we have, *Beer Contraband at 10,000 Feet*.

One of his crewmates, George Stovall—a man he stayed in contact with until Stovall's passing—decided to smuggle a bottle of beer and an opener onto the plane as they prepared for another group mission from the airfield near Foggia, Italy. As the formation ascended over the Adriatic Sea on its way to its assigned target in southeastern Europe, each plane, in turn, dropped below formation to test fire each of its .50 caliber machine guns. With all planes back in formation the group continued its ascent.

Back in the canopy bubble of the tail gun position, young Stovall settled in. He was going to enjoy that beer before the inevitable engagement with German fighters as the group reached the Danube River.

A bomb run occurs somewhere between 18,000 and 30,000 feet. As low as 10,000 to 12,000 feet the atmosphere becomes thin enough oxygen masks are required. Whether the young tail gunner planned to drink his contraband before putting on his mask or he planned to nudge his mask over for a few well-timed gulps is unclear.

When he opened his beer, the pressure difference between the bottle's contents and the thin atmosphere in the wild blue yonder was enough to ignite an explosion of suds over Stovall and the plane's tail gun canopy.

George Stovall went on to become a school teacher in his home state of Oregon. He also became very active in the 483rd Bombardment Group reunions, eventually becoming chairman of the event.

When the reunion was held in Detroit in 2012, I had the privilege of attending with my father. When Dad saw his old crewmate, he greeted him with a pathetically amusing head shake.

"Stovall, how could they let anyone dumb enough to open a bottle of beer at 10,000 feet be in charge of the reunion."

George Stovall (foreground) and Harry Hodge at the 483rd Bombardment Group reunion in 2012.

A SPECIAL PICTURE REDISCOVERED

WHEN I WAS A YOUNGSTER OF seven years old in the early 1950s, my grandfather, James M. Irvine showed me a picture of his fellow soldiers and him from World War I. It made a stark impression on me when he said most of the men in the picture did not survive the war.

I wondered what happened to that picture and if it still existed. I thought I would never see it again. Then, in the spring of 2017, my cousin, Jim Irvine (who had lived in Colorado for many years) organized a luncheon at his sister's house in Michigan. He wanted to learn more about his family's formative years.

Our two aunts, Cathy Crawford and Elsie Morris (daughters of our grandfather) were among those there to share remembrances. Lo and behold, among the items they brought was the long-lost picture I thought I would never see again.

Enlarged, with imperfections removed, the framed picture proudly sits in my home office. My grandfather is seated, fourth from the left.

James Macqueen Irvine served in Scotland's Royal Field Artillery of the Lowland Division. I know he entered service as early as 1915 and served until the war's conclusion in 1919. Among his duties, he served as a forward observer for artillery. It has been reported to me he was wounded three times.

Jim Hodge

I HAVE ENJOYED WRITING FAMILY STORIES for many years. I am in the finishing stages of an historical fiction novel about a salt-of-the-earth Midwestern farm family as they make their way through the decade of the 1960s.

My wife of fifty-one years and I live in a semi-rural community northwest of Detroit, Michigan. We have two adult children and three grandchildren. I have been blessed to have been raised in the security of a close family. I revel we can be part of the American dream of owning our own home. In our case, that includes a couple of acres which allows us grow fruits and vegetables.

I entered the Army in June of 1965. I spent the majority of my time in the 2nd Infantry Division on the DMZ in Korea. My experience there was helpful in the novel I am completing.

Robin Hutton

13

THE DOGS OF SPECIAL FORCES

MPC BASS

LESS THAN A MONTH AFTER THE bombing of Pearl Harbor on December 7, 1941, Arlene Erlanger, a respected poodle breeder got together with her Westminster Dog Show and American Kennel Club friends and started "Dogs for Defense" (DFD)—an organization that launched America's war dog program. Operating on clear knowledge and appreciation for the abilities of their canine counterparts, DFD knew the role dogs could play in protecting our coastlines, forts, munitions, and power plants on the home front, and serve as scout, sentry, and messenger dogs on the war front.

Where did they get the dogs? People across America donated their personal pets to aid in the war effort. Forty-thousand dogs were donated to the "K9 Corps," and 10,425 went on to serve at home and abroad with the Army, Air Force, and Coast Guard. The Marine Corps started their own K9 program, mostly using dogs donated from the Doberman Pinscher Club. 1,033 trained dogs went on to serve with the Marine Corps, mostly in the jungles of the Pacific. The huge grassroots movement forever changed the role of dogs in war.

The Military Working Dog (MWD) program has come a long way from its humble beginnings in World War II. Dogs used by today's U.S. military are procured and trained by the 341st Military Working Dog Training Squadron at Joint Base San Antonio (Lackland Air Force Base), Texas.

There are different types of military working dogs, from the highly specialized single-purpose (explosives or narcotics, not both, and tracking) and dual-purpose dogs (patrol/scout and detection work), to the Multi-Purpose Canine (MPC). An MPC has all the major capabilities in one dog—because when the dogs are brought into the fight, it's usually with a Special Operations Unit. Their skills include explosive scent detection, tracking people, apprehending fleeing targets, and protecting the team through controlled aggression by entering target buildings to assist in clearing rooms.

The most commonly used breeds for MWDs are German and Dutch Shepherds, and the Belgian Malinois for dual-purpose work. Retriever breeds are preferred for specialized odor detection. However, the Belgian Malinois is the Marine Corps Special Operation Command's (MARSOC) choice for MPC because of its intense drive, focus, intelligence, and loyalty. These special dogs do not go through Lackland AFB. They are purchased separately from American kennels who procure the dogs from European breeders, and then trained.

MPC Bass served at MARSOC for six-and-a-half years before retiring in 2019. Born in the Netherlands on May 25, 2012, he was purchased by a kennel in Peru, Indiana that trained and sold him to the Marine Corps in fall 2013. He was given the identifier Whiskey131 (W131), was selected by MARSOC, and assigned to a handler who would deploy to Afghanistan in 2014. But before deployment, Bass and his handler had to go through intensive, non-stop training together.

MARSOC's training program was sixteen weeks long and divided into two phases. Phase One was an intensive eight-week basic course where the dog and handler learned to work as a team, one-on-one. The Marine learned how to be a dog handler. He trained his new partner in explosive detection, tracking, controlled aggression, building and area searches, bite work, and learned canine first aid. Most importantly, the handler learned his dog's *tell*— how the dog's behavior changed when it smelled a target odor, whether that odor be explosives, or an enemy combatant.

Meet MPC Bass.

Phase Two was even more intense, as the handler learned how to handle his dog in a Special Operations Team environment. This eight-week program included amphibious training, which consisted of both dog and handler swimming long distances, water insertion and extraction techniques, helocasting (jumping out of helicopters into the water) techniques, and boat raids.

There were also advanced explosive detection and advanced tracking work, more extensive shooting fundamentals to get the dog acclimated to live fire, close-quarters combat (CQC) training, fast roping and repelling (from helicopter) with the dog, and advanced canine medicine— anything they might be expected to do on a deployment when it was just the two of them.

Bass' 1st Deployment

After completing their training and certification, Bass and his handler were deployed to Afghanistan in early spring 2014. Even after all that training, the deployment did not go well for either of them. While Bass was a highly intelligent dog with a lot of energy and desire to please, he lacked the discipline and confidence to perform successfully. He soon developed one of the worst reputations in MARSOC. He lacked focus, had trouble finding explosives, and chewed up the Marines' water bottles and bite their gear. He was one of the problem dogs who showed great potential, but just couldn't perform to the elite standards.

But Bass' luck soon changed. Upon his arrival back to the states in December 2014, Bass was reassigned and paired with a different handler, SSgt Alexander Schnell. Schnell, originally from Rapid City, South Dakota joined the Marine Corps in 2012, and MARSOC in 2014. He had proven his incredible training skills with other dogs in his past, and Bass was in desperate need of a makeover. (Re)training for Bass began in January 2015.

A New Handler and a New Attitude

Bass found his redemption when he partnered with Schnell.

"I remember walking into the building the morning Bass returned to the kennels. I was excited, anxious, and slightly nervous to meet my new partner," wrote Schnell. "I walked up to the kennel run and looked in through the chain-link fence to see Bass. I saw a dark face, reddish fur, and two golden eyes staring back at me. As soon as I looked into those intense, predator eyes, I could tell he was a special dog. Anyone who locks eyes with his intense stare can tell there is real intellect, and that Bass is no ordinary animal."

No question about it, it was an immediate bond. Yet training took time.

"He was in pretty rough shape when I got him," said Schnell. "He just didn't have a lot of obedience or structure. I mean, he's still the same dog, right? So, his ceiling was always there. He just lacked the discipline and structure to be able to perform in that Special Operations environment, or even at a very, very basic level."

Bass and Schnell. Top, surface swim during amphibious training. Bottom, tactical obedience and CQC training.

Schnell quickly realized what an extraordinary partner he had been given. As training continued through most of 2015, Schnell and Bass developed not only an incredibly close bond, but Bass' true nature began to shine through.

"It wasn't just his intellect that impressed me," wrote Schnell. "Bass has always had a human-like ability to understand complex situations and feed off of the emotions from myself and members of his team. Bass was always a puppy at heart—trying to play with all of the team members' personal belongings, attempting to bait someone into a tug-of-war challenge with his toy, and having no awareness of how strong and destructive his tail was. The minute it was time to work, however, Bass' body language and personality would change."

Soon it was time to show his new team what Bass could really do.

IRAQ 2016—FIRST-TIMERS

In January 2016, Bass and Schnell deployed to Iraq with the 2nd Marine Raider Battalion, Marine Special Operations Team (MSOT) 8232.

During their first deployment together in support of *Operation Inherent Resolve* in Northern Iraq, Bass jumped from the frying pan into the fire with Schnell. Hard as it is to believe, they were the *only* dog team in Iraq for MARSOC at the time. They were supporting the Kurdish forces fighting against ISIS in the city of Kirkuk.

The pair conducted over 350 explosive detection sweeps during this deployment.

"Our team would set up forward staged positions to conduct offensive operations against ISIS forces," Schnell explained. "Before this could happen, Bass would search the entire area and any buildings for Improvised Explosive Devices (IED)."

Many of his searches were off-leash as he would search and find a safe spot for the MSOT to set up their headquarters.

Not only were Bass' detection skills a crucial element to the mission's success, Bass never flinched when the battle intensified.

"While under direct fire from enemy artillery and heavy machine gun fire," an MSOT member recalled, "Bass was still able to receive commands and search a clear area for explosives. While team members were being decisively engaged, Bass remained calm and awaited orders from SSgt Schnell. He took it upon himself to take cover in the bunker near the team element leader until SSgt Schnell could get back to Bass' position and clear an area for the mortar team."

Bass proved himself time and time again, and the admiration and respect from his team was mutual.

"Bass had extraordinary determination and love for his teammates," the MSOT member continued. "He would do anything and everything for those he worked with. His loyalty and dedication to his team contributed directly to the mission accomplishment and the safe return of the entire Marine Special Operations Team 8232."

After returning to the states in July 2016, Bass and Schnell prepared for their next deployment together. They were reassigned to the 3rd Marine Raider Battalion MSOT 8313 and deployed to Somalia in October 2017.

"Because this was a different mission set," Schnell explained, "there were different things to learn, and when working with a new group of guys ... I needed to make sure everyone on the team knew how Bass worked, operated, and knew how to work with him. So, you start the whole process over again, like going through your workup, pre-deployment training, and stuff to integrate with that team."

And training never stopped. Even after deployment, proficiency in explosives detection, controlled aggression, tracking, and mission rehearsals was a daily job. Maintaining team cohesion was crucial and took work.

SOMALIA 2017—ROUND TWO TOGETHER

During this six-month tour in East Africa, Bass and

Schnell conducted sixteen combat operations for High Value Individuals (HVIs) who were part of the Islamic militant group, al-Shabaab. The MSOT heavily relied on Bass during each mission for his explosive detection and personnel apprehension capabilities.

"Bass' ability to understand his environment and the threat combined with his ability to search and detect explosives and controlled aggression were some of the many traits critical to the success of the MSOT," wrote MSOT 8313's element leader. "[His] ability to work in the most stressful situations while maintaining the utmost discipline were a true testament to his steadfast, dependable and skilled nature."

Bass' competency and bravery stood out during one particular mission when the MSOT took small arms fire from their target (HVI). As the man fled in the dark toward an open field, he was wounded. Bass was called up. With the status of the enemy combatant unknown, Bass located him in the dark and was able to bite and hold him until his team members arrived and apprehended him.

"When given the attack command," the element leader wrote, "Bass moved on the threat with no hesitation and bit and held the HVI ... Bass' ability to work in highly complex and austere environments speak volumes to the type of animal he was and the capabilities he brought to the battlefield."

Bass and Schnell returned home in April 2018 after another successful deployment. After a short break and more advanced training, Bass and Schnell returned to the 2nd Marine Raider Battalion.

AFGHANISTAN 2019—A HERO IS BORN

Bass and Schnell were deployed to Afghanistan in February 2019 and were assigned to MSOT 8244. Bass' reputation had preceded him.

"[Bass'] versatility and proficiency made him one of the most valuable members of the team," the MSOT team commander wrote, "and despite often having to limit the number of Marines on a mission due to space available on helicopters, I ensured Bass came on each mission."

During the four-month deployment, the MSOT conducted thirty-four nighttime helicopter assault raids to capture or eliminate Taliban leaders. Bass was used to conduct explosive sweeps for IEDs, he provided protection where the team lived, and led the charge during dangerous building clears.

"Bass would enter buildings, rooms, crawlspaces, and tunnels before any team members, to check for enemy combatants," Schnell explained. "When there were known enemies barricaded inside buildings, Bass was sent in first to engage enemy combatants and give the team members an advantage when entering."

On the night of April 10, 2019, the MSOT partnered with an Afghanistan military unit, and together they conducted a helicopter assault raid targeting high level Taliban members in northern Kandahar Province, Afghanistan. Not quite knowing what to expect, there were more combatants in the fight than anticipated.

During the fierce four-hour mission, fourteen Taliban combatants were spread out across five buildings in a strip of compounds, some of which were guarded with IEDs. Close-quarters combat occurred as the team tried to clear each building. After securing the first building, Bass and Schnell located several hundred pounds of weapons and IED explosive materials inside a room.

The team moved methodically to the next building and continued the fight. Bass and Schnell led the way, searching for IEDs as they went along. At one point, Schnell had to fire his rocket launcher into the compound. After firing the rocket, the team was able to clear three more buildings.

When they reached the last building, eight Taliban

combatants trapped inside fought aggressively to maintain their position. Sadly, an Afghan partner was killed. Bass and Schnell remained outside the building, making sure no enemy escaped. After about an hour into the final stance, Bass was released and led his team inside to make sure all of the enemy had been eliminated.

What was truly incredible about the operation was the teamwork and symbiotic relationship of Bass and Schnell. During the chaotic and violent firefights with explosives, small arms, and hand grenades, Bass was tethered to Schnell's two-and-a-half-foot hip leash the entire time—including when Schnell fired the rocket launcher.

"I obviously didn't have time to tell him commands constantly, or make sure he was doing okay," recalled Schnell. "I'm in that moment, and I've got to take care of stuff. So, as I'm fighting and shooting, and people are shooting all around me and everything else, Bass is just there on my hip in the pitch darkness."

Really impressive about Bass' actions that night was while Schnell wore night vision and could see what was happening, Bass was in the dark.

"I'm sure I was stepping all over him in that moment, but he wasn't frantically trying to get away or trying to bite anybody. He's just following me around ... and then at the end of all of that, two-and-a-half hours later, I send

Bass in, and without hesitation he goes in and does his job. With all the crap he had gone through, he was still able to go do his job when I needed him to do it."

By the end of the mission, fourteen Taliban had been killed, hundreds of pounds of explosives seized, and over twenty enemy weapon systems had been destroyed.

Previous page: Much deserved rest after a multi-day operation in Afghanistan. Above: Afghanistan—after a day on the range training.

Bass and Schnell performed thirty-three additional nighttime helicopter assault raids during that deployment. In all of those missions, "Bass never faltered, never hesitated, and never failed to aggressively take the fight to the enemy when asked," wrote his team commander.

MSOT 8313's element leader perhaps said it best about this incredible team.

"The bond between Bass and SSgt Schnell went beyond training. Bass worked in a manner that showed there was no greater love on the battlefield than to lay his life down for his friends, and that ultimately is what led to the many successes SSgt Schnell and Bass shared ... and together Bass and his handler continued to work until their last day of active service."

LIFE AFTER SERVICE

Remarkably, there were no Marine fatalities on Bass' watch. Bass shared three of his four deployments (in three different countries) with Schnell. Bass was so integral to the team there was never a question if he would be included. They went on every single mission during their deployments, totaling over 100 missions together.

What a difference from Bass' early days and his first deployment.

On October 12, 2019, Bass officially retired from active duty. Schnell was also discharged that day. There was no formal ceremony, just a small gathering with friends and teammates at the kennels to pay tribute to Bass.

On November 14, 2019, Bass made history on a trip to the U.S. Capitol in Washington, DC when he was one of the inaugural recipients of the *Animals in War & Peace Medal of Bravery*. He received MOB #8, and stood in great company with Sgt. Reckless (horse, Korea); Cher Ami (pigeon, WWI); Chips (dog, WWII); GI Joe (pigeon, WWII); Stormy (dog, Vietnam); Lucca K458 (MWD dog, Afghanistan/Iraq), and Bucca (dog, FDNY arson detection). The medal was the highest U.S. award for animals who have served and sacrificed in war and peacetime, and was commensurate with the British PDSA Dickin Medal, known as the "Victoria Cross for Animals."

Bass stole the show as he mesmerized everyone with his piercing "predator" eyes.

Today, Bass basks in the sun and still loves to fetch his ball in Texas with Schnell, Schnell's new bride, Maddie, and a sweet Vizsla named Rooster.

Life is good—as it should be.

Sources

An interview and personal statement was provided by SSgt Alex Schnell in 2021. Witness statements on Bass' performance were provided by MSOT members from each deployment but could not be named for security issues. Source materials also include numerous online materials used to help gain a better understanding of the MWD program. They are too vast to list here, but are available upon request. Photos courtesy of SSgt Alex Schnell.

ROBIN HUTTON

ROBIN HUTTON SPENT HER ADULT LIFE working in major event productions and the motion picture business as a writer and producer. She is the author of the *NY Times* bestseller, *Sgt Reckless: America's War Horse*, and *War Animals: The Unsung Heroes of World War II*. She's President of Angels Without Wings, Inc. (AWW), a 501(c)(3) California corporation, whose DBA, The Sgt. Reckless Memorial Fund has dedicated six national monuments to the Korean War horse hero, Sgt. Reckless.

In 2014, Robin was named "Patriotic Citizen of the Year" by The Military Orders of the World Wars for her charitable work, as well as the Ambassador for Peace Medal from the South Korean government. In 2019, she was awarded the inaugural Sgt. Reckless Award, from the National Cowgirl Museum and Hall of Fame in Ft. Worth, TX.

In 2019, Hutton and AWW instituted the *Animals in War & Peace Medal of Bravery* in a ceremony in Washington, DC. AWW is also developing a museum to honor heroic animals. Visit https://WarAnimals.com and https://RobinHutton.com to learn more.

Ingo Kaufman

14

WATCHING

"THAT'S A BORING (EXPLETIVE) MISSION—SIT IN the desert sweating our (double-expletive) off for days, and hope we don't get our (expletive) blown up on the way there and back."

That was the general reaction when I informed my platoon of the battalion's new plan—over-watch convoys passing through our sector between Ramadi and Fallujah on Route 1, the main highway connecting western Iraq to Baghdad.

It was late spring of 2004, nine months into our year-long deployment. They would execute as always, but battle-hardened soldiers never liked receiving orders to guard infrastructure or watch traffic.

Although these missions *were* boring, Route 1 *was* perhaps the most preoccupying part of our sector on both a strategic and personal level. First, I found the area seemed to have its own otherworldly feel. Second, the events that led to that particular mission were tragic, and the work we did had real meaning. Finally, a strange thing happened late one afternoon I would never forget.

Route 1 marked the physical limit of the lush, green, irrigated agrarian strip that drew from the Euphrates a few kilometers south. From the air, I imagined the fluvial basin must have resembled a grass snake slithering through an arid country. Where we caught the highway, the desert began immediately north of the route and stretched to a horizon just beyond a ruined network of high-tension wires. The steel lattice transmission towers were toppled and melted—lifted from the background of a Salvador Dali landscape to form the border that was the northern edge of our world.

Every mile or so the access road abutting the highway branched off into worn, dusty paths that pierced due north to the skyline. An occasional car turned off and embarked upon one of them, shrinking to the size of a speck in the distance, and disappeared. I wondered where they could possibly be going.

It was a strange place with just enough topographical variety to make it mysterious. Who knew what goings-on of national interest quietly transpired in the vast and endless dusty wastes that seemed to be concealing some sinister secret? We couldn't see it, but we could sense *something*, and after such a long time in a combat zone we trusted our instincts.

Our shallow forages north of the highway had revealed so many traces and signs of life, both recent and distant, it was hard for even the weariest mind to indulge in restfulness. While we watched the highway, we had to be sure our backs were covered. We checked the ditches, collapsing mud huts, and small ridges that might hide an enemy.

Despite finding the occasional article of clothing, we never saw a living soul, save a group of friendly Bedouins who briefly lingered. Still, I could not quell the sensation there was something there, unseen, undaunted by our presence, haunting the endless, empty tracts.

Large, open wells pockmarked the landscape. Vestiges of a more prosperous time, they had once pumped blue water into the checkerboard of shallow irrigation trenches like a heart beating life-giving blood into thirsty arteries. In its prime, the grass snake had looked more like a plump boa. In that better age, families dwelled in the huts, farmed the land, and fed their children.

At some point, the pulse flat-lined, the trenches ran dry, and the agrarian ribbon contracted—probably along with the farmers' stomachs. The pools that remained were stagnant, moving only when a gust of desert breeze transformed the glass-like surface into scaly, greyish-blue ripples.

The grid of ditches stretched over a mile north. Its shallow, neglected furrows had partially filled over the years, but the ruts were still deep enough to wreak havoc on our Humvees' suspension systems the one time we were foolish enough to leave the dirt roads and cut cross-country.

The earth piled around the wells formed a barrier of hillocks that provided excellent concealment for our vehicles. In these shadeless oases, we occasionally amused ourselves by heaving large rocks into the pools. But these respites were seldom and brief—we had a job to do.

Our mission was to set up a screen to disrupt insurgents trying to place IEDs (improvised explosive devices) on the highway and protect the numerous coalition convoys daily passing through our sector. The only way to do so was to establish a permanent presence, positioning our small force in a way that allowed us to cover several kilometers of highway without compromising our ability to provide mutual support in case of trouble.

There had been countless attacks and firefights on this well-traveled stretch of highway, some of them fatal. As a Michigan native who grew up by I-75, I initially mistook the IED craters in the pavement for simple potholes.

The men of my unit were already intimately familiar with the highway long before I arrived as a replacement. They briefed me on the mission conduct for route clearance my first week on the job.

"It's easy, sir," one of my sergeants explained. "We drive like hell and keep our eyes peeled. If we find something suspicious, we set up security and call EOD (explosive ordnance disposal). If they're not available, we move out of the blast zone and shoot at it. If we don't find anything and no one shoots at us or tries to blow us up, the route is 'clear.'"

One tragic spring morning that all changed. Our platoon left Ramadi and headed east to clear the route to the other end of our sector. A long convoy was right on our tail. Riding on a tight schedule, we took our position at the head of the column to lead them through. When we reached the eastern limit of our sector, our four trucks crossed the median at an opening in the central barrier, reassembled, and started to head back west toward Ramadi as the lead elements of the convoy passed us and continued toward Baghdad.

We had not gone half a mile when an explosion ripped through the air. A plume of smoke, dust, and debris rose into the sky from the very point where we had turned around. Although every truck in my platoon had been a perfect target, the trigger-man had waited to deliver his payload. The open truck that received the blast was more vulnerable than our up-armored Humvees. I later learned a Marine lost his leg in the attack. It was time to improve our methods.

First, we honed our tactics, garnering more time for our missions to dismount and check problem areas—blind spots and potential hiding places north and south of the highway, culverts passing underneath, and behind guardrails. In many places the guardrails were missing, ripped up by individuals who hauled the metal away in small trucks and sold it for scrap.

Although considered an illegal act we should monitor, we quietly condoned it—the "looters" were depriving our enemy of a favorite IED hiding place. My own predecessor and three other members of his patrol had come fatally close to an artillery shell cunningly concealed behind a guardrail on another road to the south. When they realized what was happening, it was too late.

Our intensive sweeps bore fruit but remained inadequate.

Attacks dropped off but continued. We realized the only way to prevent them was to stay there, and our battalion established a permanent presence along the route to protect all convoys passing through our sector. It was more time and labor intensive but also more effective.

The best way to cover a large tract of road was to seek out the high ground. The region was slightly rolling with some hills, ridges, and draws from which two vehicles could command a view over miles of terrain. In some spots we were discernible from afar, while in others we were nearly invisible. Either way, the enemy knew we were watching, and as long as we ran those missions, attacks stopped.

Late one scorching afternoon as we languished in and around our vehicle, a white sedan approached the crest of the hill near which we sat. It slowed and parked at a distance where, were it a car bomb, we were barely outside the blast radius.

A middle-aged man wearing primarily western-style clothing got out, retrieved a shovel from the trunk, and dug a hole a dozen paces from his car. We watched, pondering what he might be up to and prepared to act. His behavior was definitely suspect, and we had to be sure there was no danger.

When he had finished digging the shallow hole, he returned to his trunk and pulled out something in a white plastic sack. One of my crewmembers approached the man, asked him to open the bag, peered in, and stood inert for a moment before slowly turning and heading back to make his report. The man stood waiting, holding his bag and scrutinizing our indecipherable murmurings and gestures from afar—waiting for an answer.

"It's a dead baby, sir."

Indeed, the few spots of high ground were also a final resting place for deceased locals—little makeshift cemeteries with chaotically dispersed shallow plots wherever the ground hid fewer rocks. We had always tried to occupy a parcel that offered the best panorama but was as far away as possible from the crude headstones. It was not just for personal comfort—the ghosts would tolerate our presence so long as we respected theirs. However, it was the remoteness of the hill upon which we had alighted that made the rare visit even more surprising.

"In a plastic bag?"

"Yessir."

The man stood there, cradling his bag and waited as we deliberated.

Our collective hyper-vigilance waned for a moment. Despite the persistent numbness that encapsulated my soul at the time, a lump rose in my throat. Nor were my fellow crewmembers unmoved. We were not mourners, but we had unwittingly become a funeral party.

As a baby who probably didn't have a name was about to be laid to eternal rest in a plastic bag you might get for carrying your Asian take-out or your Wal-Mart groceries, each of us dourly sought his own a way to be solemn, empathetic, and useful.

I opened the trunk looking for something...anything, thinking *even an MRE box would be better than a plastic bag*. There was no box, but I saw the thin scattered pile of pine-green sandbags. I took the newest, glossiest looking one. My driver returned toward the man to offer him our pathetic "gift."

The man turned and paused, seemed to mutter, "Shukran" and a few other words that conveyed gratitude, and took the sandbag.

My driver turned and headed back to our Humvee and left the gravedigger in peace to finish his solitary undertaking. Glancing intermittently from afar, we saw him make the upgrade. I felt confident we had affected the best possible intervention considering the circumstances. There was no self-satisfaction, but rather relief that we had minimized our degree of intrusion in such a way as to address any potential risk, convey a modicum of respect, and keep our distance.

No one spoke until he had left, and discourse was scant for probably a good hour thereafter before beginning its crescendo back to reassuring normalcy. The unceremonious interment seemed to force each of us to reflect upon the surreal scene we had just witnessed.

Where we come from, we are laid to rest in the cold ground. Here, just under the hellishly hot surface the ground was refreshingly cool. It seemed a comfortable place to repose in peace.

For some reason, I imagined the baby was a girl. Had it been a boy perhaps there might have been another family member or an iota of ceremony. My gunner and driver used to go on about how life seemed so much harder there for the girls, and they were right. I imagined her untimely exit from our mortal realm had spared her a life of hardship laboring the fields of the green snake.

There, six inches underground on the silent and lonely windswept hilltop, she would lie forgotten by all but the man who was most likely her father and a group of heavily armed foreigners who just happened to be there. Whether stillborn or newborn, she would sleep eternally in the humblest symbol of American adventures abroad—a bag designed to hold the very substance that enveloped it, nobly but futilely protecting her from the same.

Almost nothing grew in that parched waste. Unlike the rich, fertile earth of my native land that had its own bouquet of organic freshness, the dust was odorless. It penetrated the pores of our skin and infiltrated our nostrils with every breath. The longer we spent there, the less I wondered what lay beyond the horizon. That evening, I stopped caring altogether. I still peered over my shoulder because it was a habit, but everything was okay.

The ghosts were kind to us, for we now knew one of them, and like us, they had seen enough death. They understood that although we were not life-givers who would restore the land, nor would we be purveyors of its further destruction.

We were sentinels, perched on the high ground, our backs to the desolation and our gazes turned toward the green snake, watching over the living as they passed along the threshold between two worlds. Our .50 caliber machine guns challenged anyone who would disturb the stillness, but as long as we watched no one ever dared.

Dusk came on slowly. Amplified by the desert, the setting sun cast a vivid palette of pink and blue across the western horizon, engraving a permanent impression into my remembrance.

As the imminent darkness enshrouded us, we were still watching.

INGO KAUFMAN

I NGO KAUFMAN SERVED AS A REPLACEMENT Army platoon leader in 2004 in Habbiniyah, Iraq, with 1-34 Armor, 1st Infantry Division, and as the division's 1st Brigade Combat Team's HHC executive officer in Fort Riley, Kansas until 2006.

Following military service, the Michigan native worked in various logistical management, training, and engineering roles for two Fortune 500 companies on two continents.

Before enlisting, he worked countless odd jobs: journalist, American Red Cross authorized training provider, translator, substitute teacher, English assistant in France, industrial clean up, cafeteria worker, hotel night security, and many more.

Ingo enjoys nature, reading, spending time with his wife and two young children, and learning about autism and Asperger syndrome.

He is working on his first book—a series of interviews and personal accounts from his time in Iraq.

James Lockhart

15

WELCOME TO SUNNY ITALY

I N THE FALL OF 1974, THE 10th Special Forces Group at Fort Devens, MA was very busy. Eighteen months had passed since the last U.S. forces left Vietnam, and the 10th Group was deeply involved in individual and unit training for whatever was next. Soldiers, exhausted by extended service in Southeast Asia, were re-energized and the newer, untested men were anxious to prove themselves. The atmosphere was electric and a palpable urgency prevailed.

I arrived at Fort Devens on September 3rd from my previous assignment with the 1st Special Forces Group on Okinawa. As a captain, I was immediately placed in charge of an A Team—the classic Special Forces unit of twelve men; two officers and ten non-commissioned officers (NCOs).

My new team, designated A-236, had recently been formed by NCOs from other A-Teams in the company (formerly a B Team). Naturally, those teams sent their lowest ranking, youngest, least experienced men.

Two senior NCOs, newly assigned like me, helped form the foundation of the team. No lieutenant was assigned as permanent executive office and never would be during my tenure.

Recent arrival and inexperience did not exempt anyone from the relentless drive to improve and perfect mission capability through realistic training. My first taste of that came without delay in the form of a major overseas exercise.

Between 1969 and 1993, the U.S. and other NATO countries conducted annual military exercises which rehearsed plans to counter aggression by the Warsaw Pact nations. They were called Return of Forces to Germany or REFORGER. A-236 was selected to participate and we had to scramble to prepare for the September 25th departure. None of us had ever participated in such a major operation.

We flew to Germany in a C-5A transport plane, the largest in the Air Force inventory. The cargo compartment had been fitted with backward-facing, airline-style passenger seats attached to roll-in pallets. A comfort pallet provided a toilet. It was a vast improvement from the cold, noisy, slow propeller-driven C-130s, which were our normal transports.

We landed at Munich International Airport, some thirty miles north of the Bavarian town of Bad Tolz where one of the 10th Group's battalions was stationed. Such installations were normally referred to by the German term "*kaserne.*"

The Bad Tolz installation was called Flint Kaserne and had been built during the NAZI ascendancy in the 1930s as an SS officer training school (*Jagerschule*). It looked exactly like it had come from that era—it loomed. It didn't take much imagination to picture eager SS cadets goose-stepping through their drills in the expansive quadrangle. There, we received our mission assignment.

A-236 was surprised to find we would not be part of the large exercise in Germany. Instead we were slated to participate in a component exercise of Flintlock in Italy.

We were flown to the joint U.S./Italian air base at Aviano in the northeastern part of the country. There our team would be integrated with one from the Italian Special Forces and we were to conduct missions as a single unit. We never imagined what an interesting experience working with the Italians would be.

After pairing with the Italian team, we discovered a contrast between us in terms of rank and training. They were led by a first lieutenant. Their senior NCO was a sergeant major. Their lowest ranking man was a private, while none of our enlisted men was below the rank of sergeant (E-5). They were all trained in mountaineering and SCUBA diving, both of which qualifications we would eventually earn. But HALO (military free-fall parachuting) was a skill we would never achieve. They had very limited English and we virtually knew no Italian. Despite these disparities, we were all ready to work hard together to ensure our mutual success.

Our combined team shared a small barracks room with triple bunk beds. There was no place to store our gear, which made for a cluttered environment. We ate in an Italian Army mess hall and, therefore, the food was very tasty with the exception of some of the more exotic dishes.

A pleasant surprise for us were the casks of wine attached to several posts in the center of the mess hall. To the Italians, it was a routine component of their meals. But for us, it was free booze and we took more than our fair share.

While we waited for our part of the exercise to begin, we conducted a non-tactical parachute jump over the airfield at Aviano. The aircraft, parachutes, and jumpmasters were provided by the Italians. Their parachutes were much larger in diameter than ours, providing a slower descent and softer landing.

The doctrine for U.S. parachute operations follows a strict, rigid procedure to ensure efficiency and safety. After several time warnings, the jump master issued eight sacrosanct commands (not the least of which were "Check static lines" and "Check equipment"). The Italians, however, didn't seem to be so fastidious about their procedures. They condensed their jump commands to, "Stand up. This way to the exit. GO!"

On our team's jump, I missed the grassy areas and descended onto one of Aviano's concrete taxiways and, despite the Italian parachute, I had a hard landing. A-236's senior NCO was not so lucky.

In a standard parachute landing fall (PLF) the jumper landed toes-calf-thigh-shoulder in a rolling motion on one side of his or her body. This side landing was accomplished by controlling the maneuverability of the parachute in relation to the wind. However, the NCO somehow managed to perform a frontal PLF: toes-knees-chest. The injury he sustained to his knees prevented his further participation in the exercise. That impacted the team in several important ways.

As we were getting to know our new Italian team mates, they referred to themselves as *"Sabatotore"* which we assumed was the designation for Italian Special Forces. I later learned that it was a word that they felt most described their mission—saboteur.

When, at last, the combined team was placed in isolation to prepare for the mission, we learned we would be attacking an "enemy" ammunition storage facility and then "destroying" a bridge.

I don't remember many of the details of that preparation period except that the Italians were very confident in their ability to plan for a successful operation. Because they were so forceful about their ideas and the language barrier, we felt it was best for us to simply understand their plan without raising any major objections. And, with their familiarity with the area of operations, I decided to let the lieutenant lead the mission, although I outranked him.

We felt confidence in our preparation up to the point where we boarded the aircraft for our flight to the operational area. When we got to the airfield, we discovered our plane was an Italian C-119—a vintage model no longer in the U.S. inventory.

None of us had ever jumped from a C-119 or even been inside one. That was particularly meaningful for me because our injured senior NCO was supposed to be the jumpmaster on the flight. The Italians would be in another aircraft.

That left me as the only qualified jump master on the team. I hadn't served in that capacity since Jumpmaster School back on Okinawa.

The situation was highlighted when I climbed the steps to the aircraft and mistakenly started to make my way towards the cockpit instead of the cargo compartment. Although I knew the jumpmaster procedures cold, I was still apprehensive about my first live execution of them. I hoped the team would not sense my anxiety. We took off toward the drop zone with the Italians flying close behind.

It was a night jump and, as jumpmaster, I had to partially hang out of the aircraft's left jump door to identify the drop zone markings—an inverted "L" lighted by fire pots. All movement within the aircraft's cramped space was complicated by the heavy rucksacks suspended below our reserve parachutes.

When the Air Force crew chief notified me we were five minutes out, I initiated the jump command sequence that ended with the first man in the line poised at the jump door and everyone else close behind.

At the edge of the drop zone, the pilot changed the light beside the jump door from red to green, signaling that from his perspective it was safe to jump. It was my job to poke my head past the jumper in the door into the slipstream and await the moment when the short arm of the "L" was directly under the door.

When that happened, I slapped the first jumper on the butt and yelled, "GO!"

Since the entire team was exiting from one door, there was no need for an assistant jumpmaster covering the right door. When the last man was out, following procedure, I checked the rear of the fuselage to ensure no one was being pulled along outside at the end of a faulty static line. Then, I immediately jumped so as not to be separated from the team.

Despite the exceptionally dark night, we landed without incident, assembled, and easily connected with the Italians who had jumped on the same drop zone. We were happy to let them take the lead positions during the march to our first objective.

The plan, as we interpreted it, was to move during the night toward the objective, put as much distance between us and the drop zone as possible, find a suitable place to rest during the daytime, and then continue during the next night to our first target.

They chose to move alongside a set of railroad tracks. It had the advantage of ease of travel and rock-solid navigation.

A disadvantage was that the exercise's "enemy" could normally be monitoring such avenues if our parachute infiltration had been discovered. Another concern was it was an electric railway, which was quickly determined by the two bare wires suspended above the tracks.

Without a roaring diesel engine to signal its approach, an electric train could silently close on us from behind without warning. Although the Italians didn't seem to be worried about that issue, I volunteered to bring up the rear, often walking backwards. As it was, we moved along the tracks without incident.

Before dawn, we selected a remote barn to rest in during the day. It was a fairly small, isolated building. We chose an inside storage room measuring about eight feet square. It was filled to within four feet of the ceiling with dry hay in tightly strung bales. In our haste to distance ourselves from the drop zone, we had not eaten during the night so we dug into our rucksacks for some food.

As we were thus occupied, we didn't notice the Italian private had placed a heat tablet on a hay bale and ignited it to warm his meal. His sergeant major immediately detected the act and promptly administered several blows with his fist to the head and shoulders of the hapless private. While we thought this action was somewhat drastic, it also seemed appropriate, since the private was seated on the hay directly in front of the very small opening which was the only way in or out of the small space.

We had a much-needed rest that day in the cramped area despite the heat and dust. After nightfall, we began our march toward our first objective—the ammunition storage facility. Prior to our departure from the barn, the team met to review the plan of attack.

The facility was located at the edge of a small village, and both were served by the same electric transmission lines. We would approach the facility by following the transmission lines, which consisted of three bare wires, spaced about three feet apart and supported at a height of twelve feet by pylon-like towers.

Then, about fifty yards from the village, the sergeant major would throw a seven-foot length of steel chain up and over the bare wires and short out the electricity to the facility, leaving the security lights dark. Of course, it would also blackout the village.

We wondered what the Italians were really going to do since such an extreme action would be very difficult to simulate.

The next step was to approach the main gate to the facility and throw a smoke grenade into the guard house. That would simulate a tear gas grenade and we would disarm the guards as they fled the building. Having accomplished all of that, we would then be able to plant (simulated) explosives and "destroy" the stored ammunition. That part at least seemed fairly straightforward.

We moved out well after dark and eventually intersected the power lines. We followed them until we came within fifty yards of the village. We stopped while the Italians held a brief consultation among themselves.

We were still wondering what they were actually going to do, when the sergeant major took out his chain and heaved it up and over the bare wires. In an instant every light at the facility and in the village went dark. We were stunned at the audacity of the act.

Then, we ran toward the guard house to immobilize the guards. When the door to the guard house proved to be locked, our Italian teammates were not to be denied. At an order from the lieutenant, a soldier broke a glass window and threw in a smoke grenade which filled the guard room with acrid, colored smoke. Naturally, the guards immediately unlocked the door and came outside coughing and choking, eager for fresh air. They were restrained and we went about our business of planting simulated demolition charges.

A-236 was stunned by the incredibly destructive actions our Italian teammates had taken but felt we had to press on with the mission. As both teams were busy planting the dummy demolitions, I remained at the cleared guard house with our lieutenant, the lieutenant in charge of defending the facility, and a captain (who was an exercise evaluator from the Italian Army) whom we had not expected.

The two lieutenants were engaged in a heated argument which I could not exactly follow but seemed to revolve around who had prevailed in the attack.

As the evaluator stood silently by, voices were raised, gestures were flung, and passions ran amok. Finally, our lieutenant banged his head against a wall, literally. Although it seemed clear to me we had accomplished our mission, it was his bold gesture that won the evaluator to our side and the attack was declared a success.

We regrouped some distance from the village and the defeated defenders. Our next objective was the "destruction" of a highway bridge that spanned a medium-sized river. Still somewhat fazed by the recent remarkable events, we were glad to have our comrades again take the lead toward our next target. What, if any, surprises awaited us there?

Arriving while it was still dark, we left the bulk of our team at a distance, and five of us crept up to the bridge. Surprisingly, no one appeared to be guarding the top of the bridge. We silently moved closer and discovered an Italian Army soldier asleep on the riverbank under the bridge. It would have been easy to quietly approach and disarm him but the Italians had another idea. Unknown to us, they had brought a hand grenade simulator which exploded with a huge flash and bang.

They threw the simulator very close to the sleeping soldier and then rushed in to secure his weapon. I went along and saw that the poor fellow was laying on the ground, completely rattled, shaking and incoherent. The simulated demolitions were placed on the bridge and, for some reason, the lieutenant decided to wait there instead of melting away towards our extraction point. He was unable to articulate the reason for our delayed departure but I made some deductions from what happened next.

We were still under the bridge with the shell-shocked soldier when a vehicle stopped on the road above. Soon another Italian lieutenant clambered down and joined us. From what followed, I assumed he was responsible for the bridge's defense and, therefore, the commander of the unfortunate guard. The two officers stood on either side of the prone and whimpering private and another disagreement began, but without the passion of the one in the guard house.

It seemed to me that the crux of the argument revolved around whether the guard was negligent and whether our team had used excess force in achieving its objective. As each officer made a point that appeared to relate to the guard, he administered a nudge to the recumbent man's ribs with the toe of his combat boot. Naturally, that did little to calm the guard's shattered nerves but it didn't seem to be an unusual means of making a point to any of the three Italians.

Again, we were amazed by the inner working of their army.

I understood the issue eventually went unresolved and we moved toward the exfiltration point. At the conclusion of the exercise, we exchanged various badges and mementos with our new comrades and vowed to keep in touch.

For A-236, the exercise did not yield all of the experiences we had hoped for. However, it did give us a chance to work together in the field for the first time. We also closely interacted with the military of a foreign ally, which was a major component of the Special Forces mission. For those reasons, it was considered a successful—and eye-opening—undertaking.

None of us would ever forget our autumn getaway trip to the Italian countryside.

JAMES LOCKHART

J AMES LOCKHART SERVED IN THE U.S. Army for five years as a communications center specialist before being commissioned as an infantry second lieutenant in 1967. He served one year in Vietnam as an infantry platoon leader and company commander. His second tour of eighteen months was as a Special Forces A-team leader and staff officer. From March 1972 through December 1981, he served in Special Forces assignments including A-Team leader, company commander, staff officer, and reserve component advisor.

After retiring from the Army, he worked for AT&T as a technical consultant and in the AT&T indirect channel as a technical support manager. Subsequently, he completed seventeen years as an associate dean and professor in telecommunications/networking and computer information systems departments at DeVry University until his retirement.

He has contributed to the Military Officers Association of America magazine and the Military Writers Society of America anthologies in 2014 and 2015. He is the author of the memoir, *The Luckiest Guy in Vietnam*.

James holds a bachelor's degree in psychology and a master's degree in management. He lives in southern California with his wife, Suzanne.

Dr. Michael Lund

16

NEAR NEAR-DEATH EXPERIENCE

HE'D READ ABOUT NEAR-DEATH EXPERIENCES—THE MIND or soul or spirit floating out of the dying body, hovering above the scene, knowing all that had happened, was happening, would happen. He was angry because he had slept through it all.

"It's not fair," he told his wife, who was making a frittata. "A man goes through a traumatic experience, travels from this world to the next and back, he ought to at least have a cocktail party story to tell."

It was like war stories he wanted to tell about his time in Vietnam. He'd done such a good job of repressing the worst he couldn't recount them when an occasion arose.

She frowned. "That night is not something I want to relive." She pointed toward the refrigerator. "Get me the half of a yellow pepper from the crisper."

The late summer surge of Covid-19 cases had made everyone think about death. And seniors like Frank and Sharon thought about it a bit more.

He was at the kitchen table drinking a beer, one of the strange new brands their new neighbors had dropped off—a *Black & Tan*. He read the label: STOUT AND LIGHT LAGER. Why didn't they stick with the tried-and-true kinds like *Budweiser, Miller, Strohs*?

"What does your recipe call for?" he asked. "You're not flying by the seat of your pants again, are you?"

"I've made this a hundred times. Don't worry."

That told him Sharon was not only using whatever vegetables she had on hand but also measuring spices by "pinches" or "to taste." She was right, the results were almost always good. But he was irritated by her disregard for the precision of a recipe. That he followed the rules in his brief military career may have saved his life.

"I bet that's how the emergency room doctor treated me," Frank went on. "'Let's try this drug' or 'Hey, didn't some rep say we'd get vacations in Florida if we adopted their whatever.' 'Give me some of this and some of that.'"

Sharon pointed a finger at him. "You ought to be grateful you're walking around and...driving a car. And, you fell in love with her anyway."

It was true. The ER doctor had been too beautiful, he claimed, to be wearing scrubs and dealing with black-and-blue victims of domestic abuse, car crash injuries, bloody gunshot and knife wounds. She belonged on a movie set or in one of those television hospital shows where the staff is a stunning collection of tall, slim, talented individuals.

It had happened last fall but staying in during the pandemic he'd returned to the event more and more often, seeking some meaning in the close call and trying to connect it to previous experiences. The ER doctor had diagnosed him with a seizure, cause unknown. Virginia law required he not drive for six months. Thank goodness for the Veterans Administration. Who knew his (mostly) uneventful time in Vietnam would do so much for him in his old age?

On the night when whatever-it-was occurred, he'd gone to bed at his regular time (9:30 precisely). Sharon had been woken by his shaking in the bed, his mouth grinding. She couldn't rouse him and called the rescue squad. He gradually came to, lying on his side on a hospital gurney, staring at the movie star doctor who was telling him, through her mask, he was "just a little bit sick."

When she came by to release him, he saw her face—beautiful as he anticipated, but her jaw seemed slightly off center. He asked Sharon if she'd noticed. Sharon looked at him strangely.

Lately he'd decided he'd had an out-of-body experience in the ER, and it had been unjustly wiped from his memory. He wondered if he could get it back. Parallel experiences in his past gave him suggestions of what might have happened.

As he worked on the *Black & Tan*, he asked Sharon, "I've told you about the wreck I was in when I was five years old, haven't I?" It was unlikely he hadn't as they had been married almost fifty years.

"When some kind man helped you pee by the side of the road?" She reached up to the spice cabinet. "Did you like it last time when I used the tarragon?"

"Huh?"

Sixty-five years ago, he and his sister had been asleep side-by-side in the back of the family's 1952 Nash as they traveled east to visit relatives. The driver of the small truck behind them rammed the Lindblooms into a rocky wall bordering a motel driveway.

The Nash's back seats could be folded down to make a bed, so the children, sleeping side-by-side, weren't thrown forward at the impact. Frank didn't remember anything after being tucked in until he was relieving himself into a weedy ditch, an ambulance attendant at his side.

Sharon mused, "Maybe the tarragon was the time before last. Anyway, this is going to be good. I have leftover portobellos Elizabeth Khan gave me."

Elizabeth and her husband, William were new neighbors with whom they'd been social distancing across the fence. Frank couldn't fix their accent, but he knew they were part of that new class, "persons of color." He tried to keep up with such distinctions but privately mourned the loss of the few, clear categories he'd known in his Midwestern 1950's youth.

"Now that I rethink the car accident, it might have been my first out-of-body experience."

She turned to face him. "You've always said it was a blank in your memory."

He reached back to get another *Black & Tan*, pretending not to think of its hybrid nature. "Exactly. But now that I've had another blank, I'm reconsidering everything. My five-year-old brain probably couldn't take in that it had stepped over the thin wall into the afterlife."

His family had not been one to dwell on difficult times, and Frank would later tease his father about the car that saved him and his sister from serious injury: "Cars should be cars, not Airstream bullets." The Nash's unique aerodynamic body style was similar to the famous silver trailers with rounded coachwork.

"The eggs, please," Sharon said.

"Are you not hearing me? I going back and forth from this life to the next."

"Piffle."

"And I damned well don't like it."

She looked up to watch him open the refrigerator again, with more of a jerk than he'd planned. The light inside seemed brighter than usual. *Had his childhood self seen a shining light? Had he gone over to the other side? From light to dark or dark to light?*

Part of his experience of the accident had mysteriously come back a few years ago. He recalled an image from deep in the back of his mind he'd never placed. A man's face, very close, seen from the side, bloody and still, but sharply illuminated.

When he told Sharon about it, she asked him sharply, "A face? This isn't connected to your time in Vietnam, is it?"

"No," he'd protested. "No."

Breaking the eggs into a small bowl, Sharon asked, "Are you going to do a group letter to friends and family soon?"

"I'm going to try." He was distracted by the fact some of the eggs were white, some brown. If he'd done the shopping, they'd all be one color. "I'm going to try."

They decided during the time of restrictions, they would post a weekly electronic letter to close friends and family about their situation. Well, *she* had decided he was becoming moody and needed more projects.

In their annual Christmas letter, he took great pride adhering to what he insisted were restrictions everyone should follow—print (all black, no bold or italics) on white paper, no more than one page, equal spaces for each family member, no photos, no bad news. He recently succumbed to email and was having trouble meeting his own self-imposed deadline.

He realized decades after the event of his childhood, the bloody face in his memory belonged to his father, who rode in an ambulance after the wreck. His child's brain must not have been able to process his parents' vulnerability. His mother had broken both legs and was likely in the ambulance also, though he had no recollection of seeing her. As they raced to the hospital, the lights of other cars or streetlamps could have flashed across his father's face.

He told Sharon, "I'm pretty sure my soul went out of the car at the accident in Pennsylvania, returning to my body only in the ambulance."

She sighed. "What did you see? What do you remember?"

"That's the killer: I can't call up anything. Maybe a bright light. I may have to try hypnosis."

She shook her head. A reporter for thirty-five years, it was not likely he'd accept a reality not confirmed by witnesses or evidence. Clearly, the experience at the ER still troubled him. When he couldn't leave a subject like it alone, she knew to closely watch him.

His neurologist at the Veterans Administration hospital fortunately had reviewed his history, run tests (CT scan to rule out tumors), looked at his medical records. She declared Frank had had a severe reaction—not a seizure—from a stoppage of medication. Declared at no risk of another seizure, he was allowed to resume driving. In some ways, he might have liked a more exact diagnosis.

Sharon straightened up from putting the cast iron skillet in the oven.

He asked, "Did I ever tell you about the medical book of WWI injuries?"

"No. But it doesn't sound pleasant. Maybe I should be spared." She'd been a hospital administrator and had heard many medical horror stories, but grim pictures reached her second-hand, in words not pictures.

"This was when I was in college. A guy on the floor brought a book out of the medical school library. One of the contradictory studies about advances coming from tragedies."

"Scoot up a bit. I want to get a drink from the refrigerator."

His chair at the small kitchen table blocked access when he slid it back and crossed his legs. With their children out of college, married, and raising their own children, the kitchen served as dining room for the two of them, especially as they sheltered in place. Sharon said with resignation, "I guess I'm going to hear about WWI injuries whether I want to or not."

"It was on cosmetic surgery, the techniques they used for soldiers whose faces had been destroyed in battle."

"Faces again! Your father's, the doctor's. Well, that's not so bad if they were able to restore how the poor men looked before. And I'm sure they learned things that would help future victims."

Frank grimaced as he recalled the incident. "What I saw were photographs of the injuries, faces with no noses, eye sockets empty, jaws gone. There were series of some, each photo showing improvement but even the final one was scarred and disproportionate, parts stretched and pulled to approach...to approach what you would hope for the poor man."

"Oh."

"They passed the book around...and, and they laughed."

He sorrowed at the memory. "'Look at this guy!' someone said. Or, 'Hey, buddy, your nose isn't supposed to be
where an ear usually is.', 'I'm not sure this is a human or
a gorilla.'"

"That's terrible! What did you do?"

He looked down into his glass. "I guess...I guess I kind
of passed out or something. I was lying back against some
pillows on my bed when my roommate put the book in
front of me. I remember waving it away and then...when
I focused again, the group was heading down the hall to
show others."

"So, now you think you retreated from reality and flew
off to another world?"

"I think it's possible. Fortunately, they were all so
carried away with the novelty no one noticed. I must have
gone glassy-eyed. And, I don't know, I think I.."

Sharon reached across the table. "You're not going back
to what happened in Vietnam, are you? The door-gunner?"

He shook his head, "Of course not." But it wasn't true.

She'd lately been advising him to watch his alcohol
intake, but he really would like another beer. Since what
he had come to call the "incident," he'd had periods of
depression. Well, not as clinically defined, but feeling
down for no specific reason. And he knew he was more
irritable than he had cause, even with terrible stories of
Covid-19 he'd been reading about on the web. So, he
enjoyed extending their informal cocktail hour when he
could get away with it.

He'd been an Army correspondent in Vietnam, producing audio features about "Pacification"—the US strategy of building a more advanced society in the South
and thus reducing the appeal of the Viet Cong rebels and
North Vietnamese.

Near Tay Ninh, a city close to the Cambodian border,
he'd done a story about a hospital being constructed by
local workers and personnel from the United States Agency

for International Development. Like so many other projects, it suffered odd losses of material, unreliable labor, and bureaucratic holdups.

Frank had taken pictures, interviewed principals, gathered material, and knew he could knit together a positive feature, though he would have to withhold some key facts about the future—like the uncertain electricity supply for the hospital. He would weave a true tale that was also an unsupported optimistic projection.

It was the ride back that shook him. Like any good Midwesterner, he repressed the memory once he was home. But at times an image or a sound would call it up.

Huey helicopters can land when they lose power. They can land, but it's a tricky maneuver called "autorotation" and it involves the big blades, slowed by the dead engine, braking the descent and allowing the machine to glide like a plane toward a place to land.

The bird Frank was on got hit by small arms fire a few miles east of Tay Ninh. Frank's mind went out a second later when his head was thrown into the door frame beside him. He'd seen a flash of light from an explosion but missed the drama of a heroic landing in a small field outside a village.

"Have the beer," he heard Sharon say, putting a hand on his shoulder. Then she rose to take the frittata out of the oven. "But I want you to see someone."

"See someone?"

"It's time you got some help with these near near-death experiences. You're seeing too many faces out there."

The events were scaring him, too, especially that day.

He hadn't told her, but a package from a member of his old unit had been delivered the day before. It was a cassette tape with his audio story, *A Hospital Comes to Tay Ninh* on it. The son of his fellow Army correspondent, recently deceased, had found it in a closet.

It included a news release about the pilot being awarded

the Bronze Star for Valor. The son was sure Frank would want both.

What he religiously edited from his recollection of the helicopter's near crash on the way back to Saigon was that a door gunner had been hit in the head by shrapnel. Frank didn't learn about it until after he'd been checked out by the doctor at Long Binh, but the man had been bleeding out not three feet from him, his face erased.

Frank had been near death, but he'd slept through it all. Was he waking up now?

DR. MICHAEL LUND

D R. MICHAEL LUND, PROFESSOR EMERITUS OF English at Longwood University, is a native of Rolla, Missouri, and lives in Virginia. He is the Director of Home and Abroad, a free writing program for military, veterans, and family. He was a U.S. Army correspondent at Fort Campbell, Kentucky (1969-70) and in Vietnam (1970-71).

In addition to having published scholarly books and articles about 19th- and 20th-century British and American literature, he is the author of *At Home and Away*, a Route 66 novel series that chronicles an American family during times of peace and war from 1915 to 2015.

He has also produced two collections of short stories: *How to Not Tell a War Story* (2012) and *Eating with Veterans* (2015) as well as the novel, *Route 66 to Vietnam: a Draftee's Story* (2005).

Dennis Maulsby

17

WHUP-WHUP-WHUP

Outside the blanket, the hair
on my arms flutters
in the ceiling fan vortex.

Dream helicopter blades solidify,
slash at my eyelids. On the surface
of shallow rice paddies

scale-tailed alligator shadows
chase the gunships' reflection.
The land smells of copper,

iron—stench of viscera and blood.
Winking brass cartridges vomit
from ejection ports. Artillery rounds

geyser muck and water. I wake
sweat-smeared. The small snores
of a woman gentle my mind to earth.

Her warm, tranquil body an anchor.
And, I know as long as she keeps
me connected, I remain human.

DENNIS MAULSBY

DENNIS MAULSBY IS A RETIRED BANK president and military veteran living in Ames, Iowa. His poems and short stories have appeared in numerous literary magazines and on National Public Radio. His book of war poetry, *Near Death/Near Life*, and a book of short stories, *Free Fire Zone*, both published by Prolific Press, won a gold medal award and a silver medal, respectively, from the Military Writers Society of America.

His short story book, *Winterset, Stories of Pixies, Demons, and Fiends*, was released in 2019 by NeoLeaf Press and received an Eric Hoffer winner award and a Global Ebook Gold Medal award. His sci-fi/urban fantasy novel, *House de Gracie*, was released by NeoLeaf Press in March of 2020.

Maulsby is a past president (2012 – 2014) of the Iowa Poetry Association. He has memberships in the Military Writers Society of America and the Science Fiction Writers of America.

See www.dennismaulsby.com for more information.

Valerie Ormond

18

NEW BEGINNINGS

THE TERM "PIONEER" CONJURES UP IMAGES of early settlers venturing out West taking risks for new beginnings. I never saw myself as a pioneer but found myself among a group of pioneers as one of the first women to deploy on a combat aircraft carrier.

After the combat exclusion laws changed allowing Navy women to be assigned to combat aviation units and ships, I served on the USS *Abraham Lincoln* with Carrier Air Wing Eleven as a Fleet Air Reconnaissance Squadron 5 (VQ-5) intelligence officer. That first deployment turned out to be one of the most challenging, yet rewarding, periods of my life.

Air Wing ELEVEN Women Officers in 1995

Pulling out of port on a massive warship in1995, I stood on the deck watching the San Francisco skyline, reminiscing how my Naval journey began in the same city just eleven years earlier. I had wandered into the downtown Market Street recruiting office seeking an adventure. The adventure began, including experiences in Rhode Island, Hawaii, Korea, Virginia, Guam, Japan, Philippines, Hong Kong, Macau, Panama, and more all in the short period of growing from an officer candidate to a lieutenant commander.

Ormond on board USS Abraham Lincoln

The carrier deployment launched a new beginning as part of my first Navy cruise in an operational environment headed to a war zone. Approximately four hundred-fifty women left that day among more than five thousand total complement of the ship and air wing. It was the first time at sea for many of the women, other than the past six months spent in work up exercises getting ready for the cruise.

During the work up period, the air wing had already tragically lost a female aviator. On October 25, 1994, Lieutenant Kara "Hulk" Hultgreen crashed and died while attempting to land her aircraft aboard the ship. She was the first female to carrier qualify in the F-14 Tomcat and the first woman combat pilot to die in an aircraft accident.

Controversy followed Kara's death. A Navy flight instructor released training records to Elaine Donnelly who headed the Center for Military Readiness. Donnelly strongly opposed women in combat and saw the situation as an opportunity to prove her point. Someone also leaked Kara's accident report which resulted in a *Navy Times* reporter posting it online.

The 1991 Tailhook scandal wasn't far in the rear view mirror at that time, with its black cloud of sexual harassment of women still hovering over naval aviation as a whole. There were those who said the aftermath of the Tailhook scandal rushed pushing women to aircraft carriers to show the Navy's progress in treatment women as equals. The combination of the loss of a larger-than-life female aviator, the divisiveness of those still out to discredit women in aviation, and the national media attention over the incident had a chilling effect on the air wing.

The air wing also lost a well-liked male member of the crew during workups. Lieutenant Glennon "K-9" Kersgieter gave his life for his country when the flight deck's catapult shot his F/A-18 Hornet straight into the water instead of into the sky, due to aircraft equipment malfunctions. The air wing held a memorial service onboard, but it was back to normal flight operations as soon as possible.

Ormond ready to board ES-3A

I understood the reasoning for continuing with the mission, but it was difficult for me to process as someone who had not dealt with the daily realities of life and death situations in naval aviation.

Being the first to do anything creates learning for all. Men were not used to seeing women onboard, which often led to stares. Men were not used to women *being* onboard and still walked around in their skivvies. Port calls proved interesting since those had previously been all-male events—other than when wives or girlfriends flew out to meet a loved one at a port call destination. We worked our way through these events and grew as a crew from the first port call to the last of our cruise.

I experienced the ups of that kind of deployment, like a simple letter from home or learning new skills that would make me a better sailor in the future. I also experienced down times, like seeing others fail and leave the ship. I felt the disappointment of canceled port calls because the need to remain on station due to changes in mission and the needs of the Navy. But knowing you have been asked to support an important mission has its own rewards realizing you have made a difference.

Flight deck operations from the tower.

Most people don't consider being the new guy an enviable position. I was fortunate to have bosses, mentors, and shipmates who took care of me and made sure I learned as much as I could during that tour of duty. I got to stand on the carrier air wing platform during live night flight ops and see, hear, and experience the incredible evolution of human beings on the flight deck helping aviators land on arresting wires at night. I had the opportunity to fly with my squadron and take-off and land in an ES-3A Sea Shadow jet—experiences of a lifetime. I watched flight operations with the Air Boss and Mini Boss from the tower appreciating the orchestration of the most complicated and dangerous logistics operations in the world.

When an air wing deploys to the carrier, intelligence officers report to more than one boss. I worked for my squadron detachment Officer In Charge (OIC), the Ship's Intelligence Officer, the air wing Intelligence Officer, and the Battle Group Commander's Intelligence Officer (N2). Normally reporting to so many bosses, each having his or her own priorities, doesn't create an ideal situation. But in this case, it worked.

My OIC supported my initiatives to improve our unique air platform's intelligence reporting capabilities and to create standard operating procedures for all the squadron's detachments to follow in the future. The Ship's Intelligence Officer was also one of the females on her first deployment and proved to be a leader and a mentor I worked with again several times in my career. The two N2s during this deployment were as different as night and day giving me new insights into styles of leadership to emulate or not.

I learned the sailors, many of whom I still know today. I spent the majority of my working time in Supplementary Plot (SUPPLOT) as the Senior Watch Officer gathering indications and warning all-source intelligence information to pass to warfare commanders and the embarked admiral's staff. I managed a revolving cast of characters of intelligence specialists and cryptologists who were among the best of the best based on the demanding requirements of the SUPPLOT mission. We supported each other during interesting times when unexpected blips appeared on the screens in the middle of the night, and when we made hard analytical decisions about those blips and whether they posed a threat to our battle group or not. We would high-five after we'd completed the morning briefs which doubled as a quiz sessions of what we may or may not know about intelligence, analysis, world situations, or anything else on the N2's mind.

The Western Pacific and Arabian Gulf deployment's gender-neutral combat missions included Operation Southern Watch and Operation Vigilant Sentinel. Operation Southern Watch enforced the no-fly zone over southern Iraq in the post-Desert Storm era. Operation Vigilant Sentinel monitored Middle East operations in response to Iraqi threats against Kuwait. We didn't stand male and female watches or carry out male and female tasks. The men and women of the ship and air wing performed their jobs according to the plan of the day.

Miller and Ormond in front of TOMCAT

Many military folks hate to leave the service due to the bonds made while serving together in the military. While this can happen at any duty station or command, it becomes more pronounced when deployed, sharing sacrifices, and facing stressful situations. I will never forget my USS *Abraham Lincoln* shipmates and what they taught me. I became a better person for it.

Our crew made it back to the City by the Bay in October 1995 and we parted ways. The ship's company remained on the ship in Alameda, and the air wing personnel departed to their home duty stations in Whidbey Island, WA, Fallon,

NV, and San Diego, CA. We'd done our duty and stood the watch. We made it through without too many troubles other than an airplane fire on the flight deck resulting in a man overboard and minor injuries; two F-14 crashes with crews safely recovered; and a collision with the USS *Sacramento* (AOE 1) fast combat support ship during underway replenishment. Many of the crew had hoped to see more action, but that's part of Navy life and the timing of deployments.

The summer after that cruise, the Navy transferred me to the headquarters, Commander, Naval Air Force, U.S. Pacific Fleet (AIRPAC) as the Assistant Force Intelligence Officer. AIRPAC managed all aviation units in the Pacific but focused the majority of its effort on the carriers. My time with the squadron and air wing fortunately accustomed me to aviator humor, and I wasn't as intimidated as I would have been had I not had the experience of the previous tour. I was one of the two female officers on a 700-person staff, and the only one who had deployed on an aircraft carrier.

The male Navy commander I relieved at AIRPAC made a point of letting people know his opinion that I was not qualified for the job he had held. That news got back to me and took me a step backward. I understood not everyone fully embraced women in those kinds of assignments, but I hadn't expected that from a colleague in the intelligence community—a community generally supportive of each other. The thought stung, but I focused on what I'd always done—learn my job, find out what I could do better, and listen to those around me. I hadn't wanted the job to begin with, but it became one of the best jobs I'd ever had.

I became part of the AIRPAC evaluation team that certified aircraft carriers for the next phase of deployment. I evaluated intelligence operations and systems readiness. I flew with forty evaluators on two Carrier On-Board Delivery (COD) aircraft, landing on whatever carriers we inspected. I was the only woman in our group, and the first woman, officer or enlisted, to serve as a member of those staff evaluation teams. The men I worked with were utter professionals. My senior-level team members never asked me to look into "women's issues," and they never treated me differently than any other member of the team.

When I traveled to carriers during my AIRPAC days, I noticed how quickly situations had changed from my recent deployment, as if ten years had come between. One exception occurred on the USS *Constellation* when twenty-two female officers shared one single toilet and one flooded shower. After I waited in the passageway to take my shower in ankle-deep water, I asked women officers I knew if they had mentioned this problem to anyone. They said, "no," because they didn't want to make waves and complain. They wanted to fit in. I understood.

I brought the situation up to my seasoned Navy Captain team leader, mentioning that although it was not a direct intelligence issue, it impacted readiness and morale. He agreed. Not long afterwards, the Executive Officer (XO) of the ship pulled me aside and asked why I hadn't come directly to him with that issue. I explained to that captain I had my own chain of command to follow, but he shouldn't have put those women in that position in the first place. While visibly unhappy with me, he didn't argue my point.

One year later during an AIRPAC staff meeting, the Chief of Staff introduced the newest member of the team—the same XO. As I left the meeting that day, the former XO called out to me, obviously remembering me. I turned around, expecting hostility. Instead, he thanked me for doing the right thing. That captain ended up serving on my promotion board to commander and sending me a hand-written congratulations card after I was selected for the next higher rank.

Women don't join the military to be the center of attention. I don't have to be a psychologist to say this. I know it from being having been a woman in the military for twenty-five years. Women don't join to see their name in lights or to prove a point. That is something journalists seem to have had a hard time understanding. Many journalists wanted to hear how bad it was and how unfairly we were treated. I saw the frustration when certain journalists interviewed women, including me, who would not provide them the sound byte they'd hoped for.

During those mid-nineties years, I didn't think deployment and follow-on assignments were such a big deal. But as I talked to people who were not in the Navy, I realized it was. I especially enjoyed speaking with older women in their seventies and beyond who looked at me with longing in their eyes that they could have had the opportunities I had. I know my grandmother would have been so proud. I know my mom was. As women, we came so far, so fast, and it ended up truly paying off for the future of women in the Navy.

Any aircraft carrier today would not be able to get underway if it did not have its women onboard. I give men a lot of credit for helping change the laws to make it possible for women to serve in the same capacity as them in combat ships, aviation, and now ground roles. Each milestone has been part of a journey. We women on the USS Abraham Lincoln were among the first, but we had men along with us in our covered wagon train who helped make it happen—some more supportive than others. Those who helped know who they are. Those who didn't know who they are, too.

In 2021, the first female Commanding Officer (CO), Capt. Amy Bauernschmidt, will assume command of the USS *Abraham Lincoln*—the first time a woman will lead the crew of one of the Navy's nuclear-powered aircraft carriers. She also was the first woman to serve as an XO of an aircraft carrier—on the same carrier that first deployed women as part of its crew and air wing in 1994—the USS *Abraham Lincoln*.

Untold Stories

As we make headway with a positive future, I salute my early USS *Abraham Lincoln* shipmates. And I salute Capt. Bauernschmidt, and those who follow her, for continuing the adventure and pioneering more new beginnings.

VALERIE ORMOND

V ALERIE ORMOND RETIRED AFTER A TWENTY-FIVE-YEAR career as a naval intelligence officer and began her second career as a writer. She founded her own business, Veteran Writing Services, LLC, providing companies and organizations professional writing, editing, and consulting services.

Valerie's novels, *Believing in Horses*, and *Believing in Horses, Too*, won Gold Medals in the Military Writers Society of America book awards and six other first place awards in national competitions including the State of Maryland's Touch of Class Award. Her third novel, *Believing in Horses out West*, is scheduled for release in September 2021.

Valerie's non-fiction stories have been published in books, and her articles and poetry have appeared internationally in books, magazines, newspapers, and blogs. The Military Writers Society of America awarded her the 2019 President's Award for her work supporting the non-profit organization and other writers.

She lives in Maryland with her husband Jaime Navarro, a retired naval officer, their three horses, and two dogs.

One of her favorite quotes is Alfred Lord Tennyson's, "I am a part of all those I have met." Valerie thanks all those she has met for their rich contributions to her stories.

Patrick Potter

19

Benjamin Franklin Village

As an Army brat, I spent years shifting from post to post as my dad's assignments changed. Depending on how you count them, I lived in nine homes by the time I was twelve. My longest time in one place was an Army Airbase in Brienne-le-Chateaux, France. I was there for fourth grade through all of sixth. It was a great place for a kid like me. But then we moved during the summer before my seventh-grade year.

We moved into an Army housing area called Benjamin Franklin Village. BFV stood on the outskirts of Mannheim, West Germany and provided family housing for married soldiers assigned to several nearby barracks—like Coleman, Funari, Sullivan, and Taylor. BFV consisted of many huge, drab apartment buildings lined up in rows with little vegetation or vitality to be found. As I woke each day, I got the feeling living there was going to suck compared to my last home.

In our community in France, waking each day held the promise of new adventures. Depending on the season, my group of buddies and I spent all day outdoors, returning only for a quick lunch or when darkness fell. Our American housing area consisted of only thirty duplexes and our gang could quickly assemble for daily adventures. Our Boy Scout troop had been very active. Annual events included summer camp on the shores of the Atlantic with the local French scouts.

Many of us guys had also obtained motorbikes. Mine had been restored from a junk-heap with some help from a couple of mechanics in my dad's maintenance company. It had minimal power but good speed on flat or downhill stretches.

I had a newspaper route, clearing ten bucks a week with tips. And the weekday one-hour school bus ride for us third-to-sixth graders was a real adventure where we had a chance to carry on outlandishly, including with the girls. So basically, I had to leave France and move to Mannheim while I was at the top of my adolescent game.

We 'brats' were used to the sudden moves. But as it appeared from many articles in the *Stars and Stripes*, we had to leave France in 1966 because their president, General Charles De Gaulle decided he only wanted U.S. and NATO forces in France on his terms. Most of us agreed his decision stunk, given we'd bailed out the French in both WWI and WWII, but our opinions mattered little.

Among the dads and soldiers stationed at Brienne, some had completed their tours and were headed back to the states. Some of the luckier lower-ranking guys got an early ETS out of the Army. But most were reassigned to aviation maintenance units in the Mannheim area. Mannheim lay behind our front-line forces—the infantry, armored, and artillery divisions and brigades, so it contained mainly supply and support units.

My dad visited Mannheim and BFV before we made the move. He said we'd be moving into real nice quarters. He made it sound exciting. I looked forward to the move. We'd have a modern German-style apartment, furnished, with built-in closets and a kitchen nook—a rarity in Europe where many homes still used stupid *armoires* and old-fashioned stuff like that. We might even get a TV that could receive the one or two Armed Forces Network channels available in Germany.

My dad continued, "The apartments are modern, like in

the States. There's lots of carpeting and the government furniture is pretty new. I think your room might even have bunk beds, Patrick."

That last bit sold me. I'd never had a room with bunk beds. So, we were excited about the move at first. Plus, he told us about the huge PX and commissary nearby. And that my younger sister and I could walk to our schools, a change from the long bus rides in France.

Our mom didn't share in the enthusiasm. She and the other moms liked the little American village in Brienne, even though we lacked the amenities offered on big Army posts. They liked the sense of community, with families having to interact and depend on each other. We'd gotten to like most of the French people, we even knew some by name at the daily town market. Plus, the moms had already gotten the real scoop—the Mannheim military community had a bad reputation.

It consisted of dozens of units filled with thousands of rear area soldiers who were less than highly motivated. To top it all off, the U.S. Army, Europe confined its worst criminals at the Mannheim stockade. At that time, as Vietnam continued to simmer, crime and corruption appeared to be growing in Army units—especially drug crimes and increasing numbers of racial incidents in areas of big troop concentrations, like Mannheim.

Upon our arrival, we quickly saw BFV was no village. It consisted of row after row of huge apartment buildings with big parking lots, crumbling sidewalks, rusted and uninviting playgrounds, and a few scrawny trees. Most of the ground was beaten down and grassless, hard-packed from generations of Army dependents milling about. The rows of buildings gave it a depressing aspect—there were few prospects for fun or adventure.

Apparently, kids already living in BFV knew it sucked, and rarely ventured beyond their building. My friends who'd transferred from France were no longer readily accessible like they had been in our old tight-knit community, where we could meet up for adventures in the town, the woods and trails, the ponds and creeks, and on our bikes, motorbikes, sleds and so forth.

The BFV buildings were behemoths. They were rectangular with three stairwells, four floors and four apartments on each landing, so forty-eight family units in each.

There were nearly fifty of these box-like buildings, plus an adjoining area with about a hundred single family and duplex houses for higher-ranking officers and NCOs. There was plenty of space between buildings, but basically, as far as I was concerned, we lived in a high-density ghetto.

I spent a lot of time wishing things hadn't changed so much. Like, our active scouting program had continued, or I still had my old paper route, or we could still ride motorbikes or mopeds. Motorbikes were now *'verboten'*— rural France had few traffic laws for young kids. Not so in urban Germany—everything had to be by the book, and the *Polizei* kept a close eye on areas near U.S. bases and housing areas.

I rapidly developed a negative, disillusioned mind-set. I'd been forced away from friends and fun and dumped into a vast ghetto-land where kids seemed to be indifferent. They rarely came out of their homes and were satisfied with hanging out, talking, and getting into mischief. But even mischief seemed hard to come by in that boring, listless place.

Once school started, things got worse. Our junior high was much different from the elementary school I attended in France. Instead of one teacher for every two grades, we had a different teacher for every class.

None of my teachers showed much interest in their students—we cycled through, period-to-period, doing daily assignments. I knew few kids in my classes and became a loner, spending my spare time reading instead of interacting with the others.

I thought I'd enjoy the chance to walk to school. It could have been but from our apartment building you had to cross a huge area of dead grass, sometimes used for baseball fields. You then passed through two gates in a tall metal-mesh security fence to leave BFV, then crossed over a big sidewalk and two sets of streetcar tracks to arrive at the second gate. Then, you crossed a divided four-lane highway to get to another fence and gate that surrounded the junior high and high schools. Getting to and from school seemed like walking into and out of a penitentiary.

My worst day of school came on a pleasant September afternoon. A crowd of us departed school at the final bell and got through all the security fences, leaving highway, tram tracks, and sidewalk behind. A black kid I barely recognized gave me a couple of looks, then some glares. He was a slim dude, a little taller than me, and dressed fairly nice. He came closer. After another glare, he gave me a shove. The exodus toward home slowed and a crowd formed around us.

His shove was unexpected. "What the heck? What are you doing, man?"

"What am I doing? What the hell are you doing, you dumb shit?"

"I'm not doing anything. I'm going home." I indignantly stated.

"Yeah, you just going home to Mommy. How come I always see you walking around like a dumb shit? Looking around at everybody? You don't know nothin' or nobody? What the hell's wrong with you?"

With that, he gave me a real shove. I stumbled backward and my books flew from my left arm, strewn across the ground. He came toward me with fists flying.

I reacted fast—lifting my arms and hands but a punch or two had already come through, rocking my head. Another swing went past my eyes, a miss. I grabbed at his arms. Then I swung wildly a couple of times.

I'd never been in a fistfight before. I failed to get any good hits on him. He jabbed at my face a couple more times, then hit me with a hard right, causing my nose to flash hot and wet.

I stumbled sideways, then tripped and fell. I jumped back up, aware of the pains in my head and hot liquid streaming from my nose.

But he'd already half-turned and was moving away, along with most of the crowd.

"Yeah, remember that, you dumb-ass," he called back at me.

"What the hell," I mumbled. "What the hell was that all about?" I shouted to his back.

A couple of kids helped pick up my books and handed them to me, quickly looking away.

A girl with a concerned look said, "Your nose is bleeding."

"Yeah, I know," I replied, fumbling with my books as I searched my pockets for a handkerchief or a tissue, anything to clean up the mess. I didn't have any, so I used my hand and top of my shirt to clean up as best I could.

As I came into our apartment, my mom came out of the kitchen. Her smile turned into a shocked look.

"My God! What happened to you? You look terrible. Let's get you into the bathroom. Oh my God, your face is a mess!"

"Some kid picked a fight with me. I got him a couple of times, though," I exaggerated, wishing it were true, and not feeling good about the whole thing. "I didn't do anything to him, he just started hitting me. I'm gonna get back at him."

"A fight! Why? No, you forget about getting back at him. You just keep yourself out of trouble," she said, wiping my face with a wet hand towel.

That evening, after consulting my dad, my parents arrived at Judo as the solution for the problem. They thought it could be the best way to increase my strength and self-esteem. The local American Youth Association on BFV offered classes twice a week.

I started classes there, hoping they'd be useful. I quickly realized that, unless you were incredibly motivated, it was a joke. Besides, most kids knew that AYA classes weren't cool. Basically, nothing was worthwhile about the AYA Center unless you were there with some of the cool kids. My dad tried to raise my spirits, joking with me about Kung-fu kicks, but it didn't help much.

I spent my time thinking of how to get back at the guy who'd beaten me up. I learned his name was Melvin and his dad was the Sergeant Major of one of the nearby support battalions. Many nights before going to sleep, I imagined giving Melvin a low punch to the stomach, then an uppercut to the face as he helplessly bent over. I imagined blood spewing from his nose as his body straightened and he fell to the ground, unconscious. Other nights, when I'd had a good day at the Judo lesson, I imagined flinging him heavily to the ground, then standing over him as he begged me to let him get up.

But I rarely saw Melvin. We were both in seventh grade but in different classes. My schemes to learn his vulnerabilities never came to fruition. I occasionally overheard his buddies during classes. It appeared that Melvin and some of the others lived in tough, authoritarian households, with dads who were harsh and demanded lots from their kids. It also seemed their dads were heavy drinkers and not in a sociable way, either. My thoughts strayed away from getting revenge.

I slowly came to realize maybe I was at fault to some degree. Maybe I carried a chip on my shoulder, angry at my new surroundings, the loss of my good buddies and my newspaper route, the lack of camping and scouting activities, even angry at De Gaulle for kicking us out, and at the stupid BFV kids who never wanted to do anything adventurous. Deep in my mind, I wondered if I was partly at fault.

My year got better but not by much. I never liked the school or my teachers. I stuck with scouting even though the program was lame compared our adventures in rural France. Reading turned out to be the easiest outlet, especially when I discovered Funari Barracks, adjoining BFV, had a big Army Recreation Services library. The library proved ideal for a seventh grader with good reading skills. I got into Army and military history books, historical novels, and a few books of romance with descriptions of sex. My adolescent reading appetite knew few bounds.

I joined in with my dad in a couple of new activities, like selling off our '57 Chevy station wagon and buying a new Studebaker Lark from the big PX (it was so big, it had booths for car dealers at the entrances). I went on jaunts with him in support his new hobby—buying old German grandfather and grandmother clocks.

We came to know several older German couples around their kitchen tables, trying to converse and bargain using our pocket German-English dictionary. We saw a side of the locals that seemed much different than when they hustled snobbishly past Americans, seemingly looking down on uncouth GIs or young Army wives or sloppy-dressed dependents. The Germans could seem rather uppity on the streets of Mannheim and its suburbs but were nice folks when sitting around their kitchen table.

I stumbled into another activity of note. It took until almost the end of the school year, but I caught on to the secret the basements of BFV buildings—with storage bins for each apartment, and the washer-dryer rooms—could also offer privacy for young couples. Many kids slipped down there for privacy away from the prying eyes of adults. The dimly lit basements with pleasant detergent smells proved ideal for those seeking touchy-feely action.

I had the good fortune to make it down the basement

steps with Marcia, a cute girl with a full figure and long, brown hair. She lived two stairwells over. She'd taken notice of me on the walks to and from school.

We often talked about our history or social studies class, our favorites, or our lunch box contents. Among other things, she mentioned kids she knew who'd told her about their nice times in the basements in a way that made it seem cool and fun. I felt awkward talking about it but she spoke in a jaunty and confident way.

One afternoon, as I sat on my apartment's steps, she came up the sidewalk, merrily chatting with two of her friends. She stopped at my stoop, confidently confronting me as the other girls continued on, whispering, glancing back and flirtatiously laughing. I sensed something good could be happening.

Marcia sat close by me for a second, gave me a nudge and said, "Let's go downstairs."

"Sure," I said.

She grabbed my hand as we entered the doorway. As we left the bottom step and turned into the quiet dimly lit hall, she turned a pouty face toward me. Her dark hair brushed my face, and her lips brushed my cheek and the corner of my mouth. I felt electrified.

It came naturally for me to put my hand in the small of her back, discovering soft, warm curves. My other hand slid to her side, as I felt soft sensations on my chest, through her blouse as she pressed briefly against me.

Sadly, the experience quickly ended. We heard a housewife slowly clomping down the steps. Marcia's lips brushed past my ear, "We'd better go," she whispered.

We quickly separated and started up the stairwell, passing the woman—the wife of a SSG I knew from the third floor—who gave us a not-friendly squint over the top of her clothes pile as Marcia and I passed her. Excited and giggling, Marcia waved and raced off to catch her friends.

I looked forward to spending lots of time with her. A

few days later I saw her passing by on the sidewalk holding hands with a ninth grader. She briefly waved but I knew she was running in a different circle. I tormented myself with what might have been.

My dad finished up the European tour as his DEROS date neared. Being a senior NCO in a helicopter maintenance unit in 1965, the writing was on the wall. He received orders to Fort Benning, Georgia to the 1st Cavalry Division as the unit re-organized and prepared for a stint in the ever-growing Vietnam War.

The *Stars and Stripes* and other papers trumpeted the 'Airmobile' concept as an amazing new strategy that would surely turn the war in our favor.

Our family departed Rhein-Main Air Base on a big charter passenger jet in mid-summer, headed for a new place. Likely Fort Benning, maybe not. I hoped for a better place, but I knew I'd miss certain things from each of the old places and that I'd have to make the best of each new one.

PATRICK POTTER

PATRICK POTTER IS A NOVICE WRITER but not a novice to the U.S. Military. After eighteen years as an Army dependent, he entered the U.S. Military Academy at West Point, graduating with the Class of 1974. He served over six years on active duty as an Armor officer, mostly in Germany during the Cold War.

After active duty, he joined the Army Reserves, mostly working in Psychological Operations and Civil Affairs units. He commanded a battalion of an USAR Training Division. As a civilian, he pursued a thirty-five year career as a defense contractor in Northern Virginia, working a range of projects including operations research, acquisition, risk assessment and threat analysis, and tasks to enhance unit training and readiness.

Pat and his wife live in Vienna, VA where they raised four sons, one of whom is active duty Army and another is in the Army National Guard. They have a dog, Boomer, and have frequent visits from their two grandchildren who currently live at Fort Campbell, KY.

Pat is improving his writing skills through the MWSA as well as the Mighty Pen Project sponsored by the Virginia War Memorial and VCU.

Joan Ramirez

20

DIGNITY

"I'M NOT SHARING MY ROOM WITH a gambler," Jerome Bigelow said, his fist pounding the dining room table.

"Son, you know better than to talk that way about your grandfather," Franklin Bigelow said. "He's a decorated war hero. He fought with dignity to defend our country in the Vietnam War."

"I need to study for my history exam, Mama," Jerome said, pushing in his chair.

"I'm not going to listen to you denigrate your grandfather, even if he isn't your blood relation," his father said. "With his pharmacist background and medic skills, he saved many American soldiers' lives over there."

Jerome moved past his father toward his room.

"Don't turn your back on your father when he's talking to you," Gladys Bigelow said. "Your grandfather came home from the war with PTSD. It affects each person differently. I'm not making excuses for him, but everyone who served their country overseas deserves to be treated with dignity and respect."

"Each morning when I ride the bus to class, I see the same homeless veteran wheeling himself around the neighborhood. I'm not heartless, guys, but grandfather not only lost the family farm in Kansas, he gambled away the jade ring his friend gave him as he lay dying on the battlefield. I remember him showing it to me when I was a kid. With all the gold and diamonds surrounding the jade, it looked like a miniature crown. A sane person would've held onto such a valuable piece of jewelry."

"I'll clear the table, Franklin. You talk to your son."

"Come into the living room, Jerome."

"Dad, I have to call Tammi. She and I are working on our final papers for that history project. I can't do it without her. Her parents are real strict. If I don't call her before nine, I'm on my own."

Franklin pointed to an antique clock in the living room. "It's only seven. You have two hours left. We need to talk."

Jerome sat on the edge of a chair. "Okay, I'm listening."

"Son, this is your last year of high school. Then you go to college where you'll be expected to deal with higher levels of thinking. No time to start like the present. I know how much Tammi wants to be an investigative reporter. As a child, she'd walk around this apartment with a magnifying glass and a flashlight looking for anything your mother had lost."

Jerome chuckled at the memory. "She was a character."

"My father knew he wanted to be a pharmacist when he saved a local kid from choking. He was about your age. It turned his life around. He stopped hanging out with gangs and started studying medicine. His father didn't have money for that kind of degree, so Gerald chose pharmacy school.

"He told me he paced back and forth with a textbook in his hands studying to gain the knowledge to practice his craft. He opened his own store with a loan. Just when he was building up a customer list, the Army sucked him into the Vietnam War. He went without one word of complaint."

"I know the story, Dad. You've told it to me a dozen times."

"Maybe so," Franklin continued. "But what you've failed to remember from our talks are the traumas and horrific war conditions that American soldiers had to endure in that country. Do you have any idea of what your granddad went through or what it took to survive?"

"Well, I read some stuff when Tammi and I studied for a test on Indochina."

Jerome smoothed his mustache. "Here's my suggestion to you, son. Get into a good study groove now. Write that final history paper as though it were a college mini-thesis."

"That's a great idea," Mrs. Bigelow said, carrying a bowl of fruit to the table.

Jerome thought about his parents' conversation the previous evening. His mood turned somber. "Come into my room for a minute."

He pointed to airplane models hanging from the ceiling. "The other night you talked about grandfather coming here to recuperate from his heart attack. His eyesight is failing. If he breaks one piece in my collection, I can't replace it."

Mrs. Bigelow stiffened at the remark. "He's seventy-seven years old. What do you want from the man?"

"Let him get a pacemaker. Then he can live on his own and have the veteran's hospital monitor it." Jerome reached up to a shelf and gathered his DVDs. "I'll have to hide these."

Mr. Bigelow felt the heat rise to his cheeks. "What would he want with your music? He's generations removed from you."

"Well, if he's going to share my room, don't turn it into an infirmary. He can sleep on a futon next to the closet. I'm not giving up my bed."

Gladys Bigelow put on her prune face. "What happened to the boy who helped me pass out food to the homeless on Thanksgiving Day?"

"I was a child when you adopted me, Mama. I'm a grown man now. What will my friends think if they find out I'm babysitting an old man who gambles away his money?"

Mr. Bigelow threw his arms in the air. "I give up. Son, I'll always love you, but you need an attitude adjustment. I'm going back to my office to check on inventory for the boss."

"Dad, you're smart. You should return to college and get your Bachelor's. You're only missing one semester."

"It's too late for me, son. I'm too set in my ways. You pick up where I left off and then some."

Jerome saw the sadness in his father's eyes. "I'm sorry, Dad. I didn't mean to offend you. It's just that you have so much to offer. I hate to see you wasting it on selling kitchen appliances."

"Son, your grandfather raised me to hold my head up and be proud, no matter what I do. As long as I'm not stealing or cheating anyone, I conduct myself with dignity and expect equal treatment from customers. You'd better call Tammi."

"Right."

Jerome picked up his cell phone and started to punch in his best friend's number when he heard a knock at the door.

He opened it a sliver.

"Yes, Mom?"

Gladys Bigelow pushed her way in and pulled on his ear. "Maybe your father is a softie, but I'm not."

"Ouch, what was that for?"

"I got a call from the veteran's hospital on Long Island. Your grandfather will be released this Saturday," she said, pointing to her heart. "I think it would be an act of caring if you came with us to bring him back to our house."

"You're always telling me to think of someone else. I promised to coach Tammi's brother and his little friends in soccer. You don't want me to let them down, do you?"

Gladys laughed. "Spoken like a politician. Okay, you win this time, but remember, your grandfather deserves to be treated with the same dignity as you're giving to those kids."

"You have to earn it. The last time I saw Granddad he did nothing but complain about how his apartment was falling apart. Well, whose fault is that? It serves him right for drinking so much, losing that valuable ring, and being a pain in the butt to everyone around him."

"Gerald drank to forget the devastating memories of war. I overheard you talking to your father. It might be a good idea to do more research on Vietnam for your final paper. Knowledge is power. Read about how it really was for soldiers in that war."

"Hey, Mom, you told me Granddad was living in Florida before his heart attack. I haven't seen him since I was five. That was thirteen years ago."

Jerome didn't like to see tears coming from his mother's eyes.

"It took so long to receive an answer to my cousin's inquiries. We were told your grandad went down with the ship. Government officials called it MIA, Missing in Action," Mrs. Bigelow said. "My cousin refused to believe Gerald was dead. He kept the faith for both of us. After our only child died in a motorcycle accident, you were our miracle adoption. Don't let misguided anger keep you from honoring a war veteran."

Jerome's cell phone chimed.

"I'll see you later," Mrs. Bigelow said, closing the door behind her.

"*Jerome*, I've been waiting," Tammi Johnson said.

"I'm sorry."

"What's the problem?"

"Me."

"What do you mean?"

"Mom made me see my grandfather as a different person."

"How so?"

"He's an old man, Tammi. I'm punishing him for being human and making a mistake."

"So, what you told me about his gambling isn't true?"

"It probably is, but two wrongs don't make a right. He was decorated for being a hero in combat. Mom says I should read more about the Vietnam war and the effect it had on returning American soldiers. I did, but I forgot about my grandfather's courageous actions during the war as a medic to help wounded soldiers. I had this idealized image of him."

"The perfect warrior who could do no wrong," Tammi said.

"Something like that."

"I'm glad you realized how wrong that kind of thinking is, Jerome. Instead of telling me, you should talk to your parents. They've been good to you."

"Meet me before class in the library tomorrow morning to go over everything."

"You got it, and, Jerome, you're doing the right thing in helping your grandfather. I wish mine was still here."

* * *

Jerome tapped the side of his father's door. "Can I see you for a minute?"

"Sure, son."

He did the same with his mother who was finishing up in the kitchen.

"Meet me in the dining room."

"Okay, son. Why have we been summoned?"

"Mom, Dad, I owe you an apology. I had no right to judge grandfather the way I did. He's suffered a lot. So, when he comes to stay with us, I'll be respectful. In fact, I might interview him for the school newspaper. After all, he is a war hero. He probably has a lot to say."

Mr. and Mrs. Bigelow grabbed hold of Jerome's shoulders. "We're proud to call you our son."

Jerome shook his head. "Thanks, guys. I'm grateful to you for pointing out how important it is to honor our veterans and what they did in battle to keep our country safe. Each of them, Grandfather most of all, should be treated with dignity."

End

Joan Ramirez

J OAN RAMIREZ LIVES IN THE NEW York metropolitan
area, is a published photojournalist, has short suspense
stories online, and has taught English as a Second
Language to students around the globe.

This story was inspired by her respect for war veterans. She has also published *Jamie is Autistic* and *Go for It Leadership Handbook* and is crafting a historical suspense set in World War II. Her latest endeavor is *The Write Rules* for her company, JL Regen Enterprises LLC.

Kathleen M. Rodgers

21

THE MOVE THAT CHANGED MY LIFE: OUR TREK NORTH TO ALASKA!

—Three companion poems penned decades ago in a travel journal I kept on our trek North to Alaska. The poems have never published and are the simple observations of a twenty-six-year-old mother-to-be, married to an Air Force fighter pilot. We were on the journey of a lifetime over land and sea that took about three weeks to arrive at our destination at a remote Air Force base twenty miles southeast of Fairbanks.

THE ROAD

4/10/85

Wheels Keep on rolling
down the asphalt highways,
charcoal-colored
ribbons
stretching out across
a sea
of rolling hills
and flowered meadows
where horses graze
beside old barns and
creeping vines.

We travel on
day by day
and stop to sleep

in roadside beds
and eat from
menu meals
prepared for weary travelers.

It's our life
on the road for now
no tv or telephones
the drum of the tires—
the hum of the engine,
the static
of the C.B. radio...

From truck to ship
over rolling seas
far into the North
where polar bears
and whales
travel the cold surf.
From road to sea,
then back to land.
Alaska!
It can't be far!

THE FERRY (FROM SEATTLE TO HAINES JUNCTION, YUKON TERRITORY)

4/13/85

They board
from all walks of life
carrying the belongings
for a long voyage
to the far North.

Some are just visitors
who won't stay long
but others,
like us

are modern pioneers
on a journey
into the
"Last Frontier"

But all are passengers
with one thing in common.
Whether young or old
rich or poor,
each on a journey
headed North!
Somewhere in Alaska.

Some, like the old ones
are on package tours.
But the others,
the majority,
married couples, babies
single men
women alone
are on an adventure
into the Great Unknown.

THE COLUMBIA

ALCAN Highway Circa 1985

Untold Stories

4/13/85

She takes us
across
to another land.
Her decks loaded
with many faces.
All eyes
fixed on the view
of mountains
where pines reach
high into
the sky
smothered in clouds
of white and gray.
Old people
play cards
and drink cocktails.
Young men
with beer cans
stand over the rails
others read
and shoot loads
of film,
their cameras
capturing a scene
in time.
Passengers on
"The Columbia"
clumped together
for this
one voyage
Up a channel
hugging the shores
into the lands
of infinite Alaska.

KATHLEEN M. RODGERS:

ATHLEEN M. RODGERS IS A NOVELIST whose work
has appeared in *Family Circle Magazine, Military
Times*, and in several anthologies. A professional
writer for more than forty-five years, her novels have garnered many awards and favorable reviews from readers.
She's been featured in *USA Today, The Associated Press*,
and *Military Times*.

The *Flying Cutterbucks* is her fourth novel and was
released June 2020 from Wyatt-MacKenzie. She's repre-
sented by Diane Nine, President of Nine Speakers, Inc.
Kathleen is the recipient of the 2020 MWSA Founder's
Award and was a 2019/2020 Writer of the Year Finalist.
She's been a member of MWSA since 2008.

Photos:

With a headful of dreams and a bellyful of baby on the back of the ferry, Columbia, Inside Passage, Circa 1985
(Photo by Tom Rodgers)

On the Alcan Highway, Circa 1985 (Photo by Tom Rodgers)

David M. Snyder

22

Danger Close

THE TERM, *FRAGGING* (THE MURDERING OR attempted slaying of a fellow soldier) has been around since war's beginning. The term itself first entered the lexicon of the soldier in Vietnam since many such killings involved the use of the fragmentation grenade. But many means—including gas, smoke and physical assaults—are common. In Vietnam alone, the estimate for such attempted murders topped 1000 and led to over 100 deaths.

Why have I chosen to write about fragging? As the XO (Executive Officer) of a helicopter company, I was fragged with a hand grenade shortly after our maintenance officer was assaulted with smoke grenades. Just before those incidents, three men in my unit (a company commander, his first sergeant, and a mess sergeant) were killed by a hand grenade as they discussed their unit's grievances about the mess hall's food. The men were assigned to 1st Cavalry Division, Headquarters Company.

The maintenance officer of E Battery, 82d Field Artillery (AVN) slept in his tiny room in the officer's hooch when unknown assailants threw a dozen smoke and tear gas grenades into his room. They blockaded the door to his room to prevent his exit. The other officers in the hooch saved him and treated him for smoke inhalation and other injuries. We could not identify the perpetrators but believed them to be enlisted soldiers from the maintenance crew.

As the XO of the unit, it was my duty to ensure the unit's enlisted men followed the unit's rules and regs, and to mete out disciplinary actions when required. I did so, but I admit I had my favorites. Soldiers who did not want to be there showed their anger in every way.

Of note were a group of five young soldiers from the maintenance crew, who were heavy marijuana users. Almost every night, that small group of men sat around a fire pit (a short distance from the unit area) and smoked pot. Their personal sign of rebellion was the black, red, yellow, and green *Rastacaps* they wore as they enjoyed their smokes. The first sergeant and I knew they were smoking pot, but it was difficult to catch them with a joint in their hand (a prerequisite for disciplinary action). We did, however, find it in their rooms and on their persons more than once.

I disciplined the five men often. They suffered loss of rank or pay, or both. They hated the first sergeant and me, and we were aware of how they felt. They said it with their eyes each time we passed.

* * *

My room as XO was in a hooch next to the officer's hooch that comprised the orderly room, the office (shared by the company commander and me), and two sleeping rooms—the CO's and mine. I entered my room either through the door to the orderly room or from an outside door. I never locked the outside door. The orderly room door remained locked when not occupied.

It was 0100 hours when the attack came.

I was asleep on my cot and a loud clanging sound woke me, as something metallic hit the floor of my room. The outside door to my room slammed shut.

Sitting up, I grabbed my flashlight and scanned the floor. Three feet from my cot was an M26 series grenade. I balled up on my cot and waited for the explosion, but none came. When I examined the grenade again, I realized the culprit had not pulled the pin. Shaken, I left the room and woke the company commander. He was incredulous and glanced into the room before we went to the orderly room and called the MPs.

The MPs got the grenade and questioned me, the CO, and 1SG as to the culprit. I had not seen the thrower, but we told them about the group of five who had been angry about their disciplinary problems, and about our suspicions regarding the maintenance officer's attack. Together we came up with a plan to catch them.

The next morning at 0700, I called a company formation to tell the unit about the attack. I also told them the grenade was a dud. The MPs had retrieved the grenade and were going to fingerprint it. In the meantime, it was being kept in the company safe in the orderly room.

Of course, it was not in the safe and the MPs doubted they could get any usable prints. But we hoped someone would try to recover the grenade and the MPs would arrest them.

That night, two MPs and I waited in my dark office for someone to enter the orderly room to retrieve the grenade.

At around 0100 hours, an explosion rocked the company area. Not at the company headquarters where we were, but elsewhere. The MPs and I ran out of headquarters and saw a crowd running toward us. My gut tightened. A crowd formed on the other side of the officer's hooch, near the ammo crate hooch. As we approached, we saw someone on the ground.

We forced our way through the crowd and found the ripped and torn body of a young soldier lying face-down in the dirt. He wore only his shorts and his *Rastacap*. I recognized him as one of the five young soldiers who smoked marijuana around the fire pit.

The young soldier was alive. He was attended by a medic from a nearby medical unit and was air evacuated to Saigon by one of our crews. He suffered grievous wounds to the back of his head, back, and legs.

The explosion did not injure any of the officer hooch's

occupants. The ammo crate hooch suffered very minor damage. There were no witnesses to the incident.

MPs investigated as best they could. They concluded the victim had attempted to toss the grenade over the hooch next to mine to land it on my roof. His arm was not strong enough. The grenade hit the nearest hooch and rolled back down its sheet metal roof. It landed as his heels as he tried to run away.

The Army MEDDAC flew the young soldier to Japan for treatment, but he died of his wounds.

After the incident, we covered over the fire pit and forbade the wearing of *Rastacaps* outside the hooches. An inventory of our grenades showed the grenade had not come from our small inventory. There were no more attacks on our company by unit personnel during my tour.

DAVID M. SNYDER

D AVID M. SNYDER WAS BORN IN Syracuse, New York in June 1945. He was educated at the United States Military Academy at West Point. He graduated in June 1967 and was assigned to the Army's artillery branch. Snyder attended flight schools at Fort Wolters and Fort Rucker, where he qualified in UH-1, OH13, and OH 23. Assigned to E Battery, 82nd Artillery, 1st Cav Division, and stationed at 1st Cav base camp at Phuoc Vinh August 1969-August 1970, he provided aviation support to all artillery battalions of the 1st Cavalry Division. While assigned to E Btry, Snyder served as a pilot, Operations Officer (OO), and Executive Officer (XO).

After combat tour, he served as a Personnel Management Officer (PMO) responsible for assignments of officers in grades O-3 and below to units of the Aviation School and Center. Snyder achieved rank of Major.

Following military service, Snyder attended Cornell University and earned an MBA in 1972. For forty years as a civilian, he served as a healthcare executive in hospitals and other healthcare organizations around the U.S.

He now lives in Louisville, KY. He is single and has three children and three grandchildren.

He writes for fun and has one published story. He is currently working on an historical fiction novel set in the Civil War.

Vic Socotra

23

BOONDOGGLE

THE TERM "BOONDOGGLE" IS DERIVED FROM the Middle English "boon," or pleasant flavor, and "doggle," or pack of slavering wolves.

Santo Domingo, Haiti, Ships at sea

ARTESANIA CRAFTS
CASA VERDE
ISABEL LA CATOLICA
N 152 STO. DOMINGO

I have had that particular word slavering at me for years. Particularly as life's little foibles have allowed me to look both forward and aft. There were old wars and new ones, and I was part of the vast machine of the American Empire of its time. I was lucky to have been part of that big one, the one that collapsed seventy years of Soviet life, and a few others.

As I type this, we may be seeing our own machine teeter on that brink. Since it is so big, I thought you might be interested in how part of it worked—and works still. Regardless of who is in charge.

I got back from a deployment to the Med in 1990 on USS *Forrestal,* first of the supercarriers. She was great gray beast of a ship, named in honor of the first Secretary of Defense. Along the way, and while in Homer's *Wine Dark Sea,* the Berlin Wall fell. There was a lot that followed—things that make me dizzy still. In the tumult, I found myself back in Washington with all the other Cold War crew. We were looking for how the new world and its strange new order might work.

In the process, I wound up working for some great people who attempted to figure it out—only a few of whom are threatened with indictment these days. There were those who thought a peace dividend might be in order. I didn't disagree but thought we ought to keep some of the old machine that worked to deal with the new world that didn't. In so doing, I began to understand how it worked for military intelligence—or what my Army pals termed "MI."

The agency where I was assigned at the time managed money and process in the military intelligence area, and I often found myself attending meetings, often at cross-purposes with the representatives of the service I served. It was about budget and money and how to craft a future with it. Being at odds with people who wore the same uniform was tangibly surreal.

To my surprise, I found the impenetrable classified mysteries of the Intel world were assigned by Big Navy, as a second duty, to communications specialists assigned to the Office of Legislative Affairs. They held the clearances necessary to discuss the issues, but no particular skin in the game encouraged advocacy of any of it. I was finishing the tour with the defense intelligence folks and had wangled a sea duty job down in Florida to stay competitive for promotion.

When we prepared to pack up the house again and head back to sea, I mentioned the situation to the Director of

Naval Intelligence on the obligatory out-call that signified my departure from the DC swamp.

RADM Mike Cramer was an unconventional and bold officer. I told him Big Navy was eating his lunch, since he was unrepresented in the meetings that mattered about allocating money to Fleet Intelligence. He took the news from that vital but unrecognized bog in the swamp with interest, since it never made its presence known outside the corridors of power. We shook hands and I did the long trudge out to north parking with a lightened briefcase and drove back down south on the painful I-395 corridor to my house to continue packing things up.

There, the phone rang and notified me my orders had changed. Instead of the bounding waves, I would report to the Navy's Office of Legislative Affairs, post-haste.

It was nothing grand—in case that's what you were expecting. It was a tired old office on the 4th deck of the Pentagon, third ring.

The *Dragon Lady* I came to love ruled the access desk and the handful of civilian workers. She managed the captain in his cubbyhole. There was a large room to starboard with a dozen desks of varying vintage and some people who seemed good-looking enough to have speaking parts, though no one was doing it. Instead, the faces were bunched up in concern or wearing wan smiles of minor accomplishment. I won't tire you with the variety of tasks and assignments associated with the office. Liaison, services, and briefings to the House and Senate intelligence committees were the mainstays. And of course, favors given with the expectation of others being received.

The one task I found most astonishing—I was the travel agent for the House and Senate intelligence committees looking at naval issues or Navy places. It made sense to the office, since that was how things worked for major mission areas. And travel was good.

As a senior staffer once told me, "You know you can trust people if you travel well with them."

Whistling up jets and cars and hotels was a major part of the turf.

This is an account of boondoggles of the congressional variety, arguably one of the most spectacular of the breed. In real life, the term is normally used disparagingly by co-workers.

"Oh," they will say. "You are off on a *boondoggle*." Normally, a scurrilous descriptive adjective went along with it. The clear connotation was you were shirking work, frittering away the taxpayer's money, and generally tip-toe-ing the line of propriety with at least a toe. I'll grant you there was some basis to that thesis. I'll not deny you get free headsets on jets.

But I didn't know what was coming. At that particular moment, Haitians landed in Florida on home-made rafts, and a humanitarian crisis built. Congress needed infor-mation. I was the *New Guy* in the shop. The rest of the crew were front runners from aviation, surface, submarine communities. They wanted nothing to do with the trip or escorting it to the area in trouble.

"Welcome aboard," said the captain on a peremptory in-call. "Pack your bags. You leave in three days."

Over the course of the next two years, I discovered there was also trouble in the Caribbean, Yugoslavia, Vietnam, China, Taiwan, Burma, and North Korea. In the process, we boondoggled a Nobel Laureate out of house arrest, negotiated a doomed nuclear deal with the other Koreans, helped upgrade refugee camps on sun-drenched islands and normalized relations with Vietnam. So, you have to take things in context.

A congressional boondoggle worked like this: a member, senator, or staffer decided they need to go somewhere to investigate some issue. Working conditions at the *Louis Viton* luggage plant in Paris, for example. Arms control issues in Geneva. Prisoners of old wars. Trade issues any-where. They then took the issue and a proposal to the chairman of their committee. The chairman signed out a letter to whatever office or agency happened to have responsibility for the issue area in the executive branch. The agency handed the request over to its congressional liaison shop, which assigned a middling senior specialist to arrange the trip—tickets, reservations, state department clearances, the whole shooting match.

It's really quite elegant. Congress doesn't have to cough up the money for the trip. It all comes out of the individual budgets of the agencies or departments. And you will love this: the appropriations committees, the ones who *really* dole out the dough, insist on having a **separate** system to handle their needs and ensure the authorizers don't know what they are up to.

But, I won't go into that—it would seem to make this byzantine system cumbersome and duplicative. LOL.

There are a lot of moving parts to this grand democracy. One example is where the money started. A huge chunk of the resources that support congress is buried elsewhere and invisible.

For example, if all the military folks who were detailed to work on *The Hill* were directed to wear their uniforms to *The Hill* one day, it would look like a coup. We wore plain clothes, for the most part, and of course our salaries were paid by the defense department. All the agencies had people up on *The Hill* on detail. That kept the staff off the congressional books. It's part of the same loopy but compelling argument that has people spending millions to get elected to jobs that pay $178,000 a year.

There are strap-hangers and horse-holders, too. Which would be me, and people like me.

There were five of us on that particular trip.

All citizens know the government cannot lobby itself. That would be wrong. But it is entirely appropriate *to provide timely information* to decision-makers to ensure the fact-finding trips indeed find the *right* facts. There is nothing quite so unsettling as knowing there is a congressional delegation out there somewhere, talking to other disgruntled bureaucrats about things that might show up in a funding bill and screw up your program. Drastic changes to the budget can result, and the time spent trying to correct impressions warrants having someone along to provide damage control on-the-spot. Perceptions are everything. And in that town, if you have to explain something in the *Washington Post*, you've already lost.

There were perks, of course. When not directly requisitioning military airplanes, ships, and helicopters, we made the best of it with commercial platforms. Boondogglers travel business class, not first but only on flights outside the continental United States so it isn't quite so visible. It's all legit, and it is right there in the *Government Travel Regulations*. Shouldn't even feel guilty about it.

An example: Going west, we would usually leave Dulles at ten in the morning and get into Tokyo the following afternoon. Upon arrival, the senior boondogglers were expected to attentively listen to some folks from the embassy in Tokyo. Industry recognized the importance of a little extra comfort in long distance travel, but let's face it—it's a guilty pleasure. If we were paying for it ourselves, us horse-holders would be in the back with all the other main-cabin trash. But since we are actually ***providing timely information,*** or at least had the potential to do so, it was important to be right there with the members of the delegation.

Guilty pleasures aside, they usually are actual working trips. Like the one above, we hit Tokyo for twenty-five hours on the ground. We then slogged back out past Tokyo Disney World to the fortress airport and jetted off for Shanghai. We got in late, hit the hotel, and rose relaxed and refreshed for meetings beginning at eight. We were back on the way to the airport by two that afternoon, discovering DC was not the only major city on this green earth to have two major airports. We had found the wrong one first. We swore we would be in Seoul Korea that night, and I recalled the raised voice—that seemed to sound like mine—insisting Pan Am delay for the staff.

This was a sub-species of boondoggle, or what is known in the trade as a "bag-dragger." The senior member of the delegation is another key factor. Some are known as bears for work, and not afraid to request formal briefings in the evening if that is what they desire when regularly running the traps overseas. Sometimes it might be Saudi and Bahrain. Africa after that. With all the interest in the looming China threat and the unsettling prospect of Korean unification, it naturally was time to re-visit. Something might be up. The itinerary might wind its way through Hawaii ("Let's see: It's January in Northern China. Then Waikiki. Do I have galoshes *and* flip-flops in the bag?").

Onward, flying northeast then through the Pacific Northwest before finally running out of steam in Alaska. Never in a hotel more than one night, so it was pointless to unpack. Return to Dulles International around midnight on day eleven, ready to start generating point papers for those whose dreams we might have blown up.

The places sound glamorous in the planning phase, but looking at packing lightly for tropics and arctic, and realizing I was actually going to be spending my time looking at the back of somebody's seat, I often felt the onset of last-minute travel anxiety. But at least the headsets were free, and the bar was open on overseas flights. Has to be that way—somebody might have a question. ("Another Magnum!" shouted the senator. "And keep them coming!").

I finished packing. Passport was at ready. The mukluks and sunscreen were stowed away in the luggage and was ready for the taxi to Dulles. In the coming weeks, I knew we would be talking to many people about significant issues involving your taxpayer dollars, you can be sure. And if you are well positioned and have the chairman write the

Navy a letter, you could be absolutely confident we'd be available to provide timely information to whoever might need it. And if you needed a favor or help in beating back a pack of slavering congressional wolves, **this was just the boondoggle to do it.**

So that's how that trip went. The first one—three days away—had most of the scut work done. The air transportation was ticketed, ships at sea notified, the embassy warned what to expect. All I had to take on was collecting the three members at their residences and head for the Caribbean in search of *truth*.

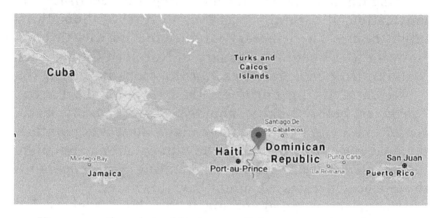

Here was the gist of it, in careful non-partisan language:

"Between 16-19 July, a congressional delegation headed by Representative Bill Richardson (D-NM) visited Port au Prince, Santo Domingo, Guantanamo Bay, and Grand Turk Island. While in Cuba, the delegation visited the headquarters of JTF-160 and inspected the migrant camps on the base. On Grand Turk Island, the nearly complete but unoccupied refugee facilities were inspected, and the delegation dined with British government officials. In the Dominican Republic, Congressman Richardson consulted with the Embassy Country Team and President Balaguer. Traveling by helicopter to the Haitian border at Jimani, the delegation was escorted

*by Haitian government officials to Port Au Prince where
Rep. Richardson met separately with Ambassador Swing
and members of the de facto government, including a five-
hour dinner hosted by acting head-of-state Gen. Raoul
Cedras. Rep. Richardson characterized Gen. Cedras as
'not altogether intransigent.'"*

That was the summary, proper. At the end of that cas-
cade of shows—suitably loaded with all sorts of righteous
facts—we roared around a potholed corner, swerved around
one big enough to eat a bus, and with emergency lights
flashing went hell-bent for leather out of Port Au Prince.
We had to meet the helicopters in the desolate country
near the border with the Dominican Republic.

The Peugeot spun wheels on the soft gravel of the new
road. The young Haitian man at the wheel held his arms
rigid, but the beating the front end had taken made his arms
shake like he had Saint Vitis Dance. Beside us, a slate-grey
lake was placid, the low hills beyond them barren. Small
boats smuggling fuel down towards the city made a brave
profile in the morning—triangular sails bright in the low,
soft light. The lake was lovely from that vantage. You saw
no poverty, nor pain, nor even a mounting international
imperative. It was just a place, and a pretty one, where
the light reflected against the green and gray hills that ran
away to the northwest.

We saw the Haitian border checkpoint to the right—low
crude cinder block buildings that once might have been
pastel. Brett pointed over the ear of our FAH'D security
escort into the rosy light of the dawn over the dark green
Dominican mountains that loomed before us.

"Look!" he said, leaning forward against his lap belt, "the
Agency helos are here! They are landing at Jimani!"

I squinted into the dawn and saw clouds of yellow dirt
rising against the sun, just as they had the morning before
as we plunged down out of the 21st century into the 19th.
It seemed an eon before, as though life had undergone a

fundamental alteration. For one, the vision before us meant almost certainly we were going to live, and, absent some mischance associated from the armed men around me, we would be home later the same day. The knot in my stomach unwound a bit. There was just one border crossing to go and then we could leave the island of Hispaniola and return to our own larger one.

It all worked out, the meetings with the general and the helter-skelter transits through the Haitian night had passed. Soon the headlong high-speed Haitian motorcade, headlights on and blinkers flashing would be history we could talk about with the Eritrean ladies who run the *Starbucks* down on the second floor of the E-ring back at the Pentagon.

I wondered if Pierre Cardin (*nom de guerre* of our FAD'H officer guard in the front right seat) saw it the same way. They had done exactly what they promised. They were professional and mostly prompt, even if their jackets did not button well across their pistols. How did that all square with what we had seen? And the threat of invasion that loomed as a very real possibility?

So that was part of it. My job was to make up the story of it, filled with useful information. And invasion or not, we needed to have the cars waiting for us back at Dulles. There was a hearing coming up, sworn testimony about whatever I could present with any coherence, and hopefully good not only for my programs, but for Navy. And the nation, of course.

That is a boondoggle. You ought to try one. Try to avoid the bag-draggers, though.

Vic Socotra

V IC SOCOTRA IS A RETIRED NAVAL Intelligence Officer. Entering the Navy in the Carter administration, he had a chance to marvel at the big machines that defended the nation on four or five oceans.

Travel was always a passion, and in the tumult following the Vietnam War, he decided to go see what he could. His first book was written on the USS *Midway*(CV-41)as installments in the ship's newspaper and published as *The Adventures of Nick Danger, Third Eye*. It may be the only detective series distributed by Navy electronic message to other ships in the battle group.

After the Cold War, he learned the Intelligence community by working for its leaders. One of his good friends was RADM "Mac" Showers—last surviving member of the Station HYPO code-breakers and as a CIA civilian, helped set up the FISA court system. The recent changes in the IC reflect some of the old stones being rolled around again.

Now in Virginia's piedmont horse country, the extraordinary vantage back to *The Swamp* and how the bog works remains a vivid palate for literary fun.

Editor's note: J.R. Reddig, writing as his long-term pen-name "Vic Socotra."

Ted Spitzmiller

24

Time Well Spent—My Army Experience

Three years in the military provided a foundational education and outlook that shaped and focused my career and much of my life.

WITH THE CUBAN MISSILE CRISES OF October 1962, the possibility of being drafted loomed. In those days, most young men were obligated to serve in the military. I interviewed with the Air Force and the Navy, who required an enlistment of four years—an eternity at the age of nineteen.

The Army required a three-year tour and was the only service that would guarantee the specific school for which you enlisted. I took the Armed Forces Qualification Test (AFQT) to determine what career paths might be open. I was leery of the testing process as I had not done well in high school and graduated at the bottom of my class. However, I was more than pleased to discover I could choose any program in their several hundred-page catalog.

Having had difficulty in high school, I was leery of any extensive schooling. In my job as a draftsman, I had been exposed to those squiggly electrical symbols called schematics. I had been told by many *in the know* that the future was in electronics. I didn't have much confidence in my intellectual abilities—the AFQT scores notwithstanding. One Military Occupational Specialty (MOS) (as military jobs were called) was a fourteen-week school that led to

an MOS of '250'—*Guided Missile Electronics Technician.*
It became my objective.

MAKING THE COMMITMENT

I passed the military physical and signed the enlistment
agreement. I received a legal-looking letter from the Army
guaranteeing the school. But it ended with the phrase "...
and will then be assigned in accordance with the needs of
the Army." They would provide the schooling but then do
with me what they wanted. Fair enough. I was starting a
new life at that fork in the road. It was an exciting prospect that held many unknowns. It was to be one of the best
decisions of my life.

On March 14, 1963, I arrived at the Induction Center
in Newark, New Jersey, where another physical was the
first order of business as a series of lines and forms moved
about fifty of us slowly through the day. It wasn't until
late afternoon that we took the oath.

The poked and prodded survivors gathered at the exit
to board a bus to Ft. Dix. Although only about seventy
miles, the bus ride was probably the longest and loneliest
of my life. I reflected on the irreversible decision made but
saw it as a new life as we rode through the blackness of
the night. There are few times where irrevocable choices
will take you on a mostly unknown path.

We arrived at the reception center and were issued our
first article of clothing—a heavy olive drab overcoat. I
guess they understood that some of the 'boys' getting off
the bus would not necessarily have the proper attire for the
season. As I lay awake that first night, I recall mentally
multiplying 365 by three—1,095 days to go.

The first week was called Zero Week. It consisted of
all the things to be accomplished before starting the Basic
Training cycle. There were twenty-four different items
of clothing issued for an overall count of seventy-two,

222

including the duffel bag in which it was packed. Total value was $205.40. The most expensive was the overcoat ($23.00), the least expensive was the dog tags ($.05 each). How do I recall the trivia? I still have the paperwork. Soon, we were all looking like soldiers rather than the ill-groomed and eclectically clothed rabble of the first few days.

During this period, I occasionally reflected on the process itself and the thousands of guys who had preceded me (the soldiers of WWII and Korea) and who had passed through the same barracks relatively few years previous.

As the first week ended, we were anxious to be assigned to our training unit to start the real work of becoming soldiers. A role we were often reminded was our primary responsibility—regardless of the MOS that we would be working towards.

Basic Training

The two-story wooden barracks, built during WWII, housed our platoon of forty-four soldiers (four squads). Our Drill Instructor (DI), named Smith, joined the Army during WWII and had taken part in the Normandy invasion in 1944.

We came to respect and value our *cadre,* as they were called. This was especially true when we saw them in Class A uniform wearing all their ribbons. Each had earned the Combat Infantryman's Badge (CBI). This award is given only to those under hostile fire while serving in primary infantry or Special Forces duty actively engaging the enemy in ground combat.

Each platoon was assigned a Platoon Guide and four Squad Leaders from among the recruits. Those who had 'prior service' (to include ROTC, CAP, etc.) were preferred. My CAP experience was enough for me to get one of these coveted positions. It exempted me from other tasks such as KP, Fire Watch, and latrine duty during Basic Training.

While several recruits resented being drafted, most applied themselves to the training. As I had spent a part of my youth in the woods playing soldier, I looked forward to testing myself. I had to temper my foolish pride with the fact that several million other guys made it through Basic before me.

Interspersed with the combat training were sessions on the Uniform Code of Military Justice, the Code of Conduct (which had to be memorized), and the various aspects of the Geneva Convention that governed the rules of warfare.

There was plenty of Physical Training (PT), which began before breakfast. Typically awakened at 5:00 A.M., we had fifteen minutes to shave and shower. Of course, the beds were made to military specifications. Spending a week sleeping under the stars was a challenge as it rained (no stars), was cold, and the tent was barely big enough for two. The food was excellent—even when we were 'in the field,' which we often were. With all the activity, the metabolism went into high gear. I began Basic weighing 154 pounds with a twenty-nine-inch waist. Within eight weeks, I was over 180 pounds and had to exchange my pants for a size thirty-three.

Three weeks into the *cycle* (another word for the eight-week ordeal), we were issued our WW II .30-06 caliber, 8-shot, clip-fed, M-1 Garand Rifle. We learned to disassemble, clean, and reassemble the weapon. Each day for two weeks, we went to the firing range and learned how to "zero in" and shoot this high-powered rifle. This phase, called *Train Fire*, was enjoyable. Safety was a key aspect that was always impressed on us—and enforced.

Following this, we participated in an exercise called the *Infiltration Course*. This was about as close to actual combat as Basic training would come. We were taken out into a trench and, on command, went over the top and crawled forward with our combat gear. We went under and around obstacles (such as barbwire) while a line of machine guns (about a hundred yards away) fired over our heads, and explosive charges went off in craters nearby. It was neat during the night session because every few rounds from the machine guns were tracers, so you could see them flashing by a few feet above your head.

Following *Train Fire*, we had to *qualify* with the M-1 by demonstrating one of three degrees of skill—Marksman, Sharpshooter, or Expert. For this exercise, the upper torso of a man appears at intervals from twenty-five to 300 yards. These targets, electrically raised, were set into foxholes in an area of shrubbery, so they were not obvious. The recruit had to spot them and fire within so many seconds, or they went back down, and you missed the opportunity to score. The target had a sensor that recorded being hit by the bullet.

Sunday was the only day off, and that was typically spent at church in the morning and then the Enlisted Men's Club with pool tables and card games—or catching up on a little sleep.

The weeks went by quickly for me, and soon, it came to an end. We received our orders for our next phase of training, which for me was Guided Missile Electronics in Huntsville, Alabama. They gave generous travel time (250 miles a day) and full airfare. This allowed me to go home for three days and get a half-fare flight using military standby.

While Basic was an important milestone, it didn't establish how I might react under combat's life and death conditions. Only the real thing can reveal that aspect of a person's character. I sometimes wonder if I could have earned the CIB.

REDSTONE ARSENAL

I remember my trip to Redstone Arsenal vividly as it was my first flight on an airliner. I flew out of Newark

Airport on a four-engine Capital Airlines Vickers Viscount, a British built turboprop. We went first to Washington DC, and then Knoxville before arriving at Huntsville in the late afternoon.

I immediately began the electronics class per the schedule the Army had given me before my enlistment. I knew little about electricity and found the course difficult, although exciting. As in high school, I was a poor student and struggled through the long hot, and humid summer.

I barely made passing grades. There were some math and physics, which I was able to comprehend, but some of the more complex concepts gave me problems. There was no textbook, but lots of hands-on experimentation. Our final exam was to build a super-heterodyne radio receiver. It was a fun and practical application of our new-found knowledge. The last two weeks were a new addition to the curriculum—transistors! The essence was how they functioned to replace the vacuum tube.

What occurred at the end of the fourteen weeks was nothing short of a miracle and would have a profound effect on the course of my life. Those in the bottom half of the class went out to work worldwide as electronics technicians (MOS 250). Those in the top half went on to advanced schooling and learned the systems of the missiles.

For some unknown reason, when they split our class to send the top half to advanced schools, I was included. It could have been they were holding the list upside down—putting me at the top. The new assignment for eight of us was an obscure school in New Mexico at what was then called Sandia Base.

SANDIA BASE

The TWA 707 flight out of Idlewild Airport (now Kennedy) took me to Chicago to change planes. The gate agent said she had some good and bad news, which did I want first. I asked for the bad news—all the coach seats were full. I had a moment of terror as I would be in some trouble if I missed signing-in to the base by midnight. As the cold wave was sweeping over me, she smiled and added the good news,

"So, we'll have to put you in first class."

I was assigned a window seat requiring me to squeeze past a lovely and well-dressed young lady. We exchanged a few pleasantries on the two-hour flight. As we landed at Albuquerque, the Stewardess (that's what they were called in those days), said to the young lady,

"You would like to be the last off?"

So, after everyone had exited the plane, I squeezed by her again to get off.

In those days, passengers used stairs rolled up to the plane. As I emerged onto the top platform of the stairs, a crowd of people were below. Someone in the throng called out,

"Hey soldier, please come down out of the way?"

I turned to the Stewardess and asked, "What's going on?"

She replied, "Oh, we have Anita Bryant flying with us today."

She was a famous singer of the day. I had spent over two hours sitting with her and had not asked her name or what she did for a living.

The course was a five-month-long *Nuclear Weapons Electronics Maintenance* class (MOS 304).

Those waiting for school to begin we would start each day with a formation in the company quadrangle. The First Sergeant assigned a variety of busy-work details that included KP, and other menial labor-intensive tasks. I resigned myself to this—not knowing that it would be almost two months before my class would commence.

However, one morning not too many days after I had arrived, the good sergeant, in assigning the daily duties, asked casually,

"Can anybody type?"

Well, I had a typewriter in my early years to pound out my aviation stories. So, one finger on each hand was intelligent enough to find the alphabet and the numbers, and a thumb that knew how to do a carriage return—I raised my hand. Somehow typing sounded a lot better than KP. Of course, if asked, "How many words a minute?" I would have been hard-pressed to give a number, but ten might have seemed doable. Fortunately, he never asked.

Told to change into Class A uniform and given an address a few blocks away, I reported to an office where clearances for important visitors attending nuclear weapons briefings were processed. Given a desk in the corner, I was taught how to fill a variety of forms. Yes, my typing was slow, but most of the typing was only a word or so in each blank space, so typing speed was not a factor—whew!

NUCLEAR WEAPONS TRAINING

I finally began a class in November 1963, and the content was fascinating. The first two weeks, called *Weapons Familiarization*, described how nuclear weapons worked, including some elementary physics. It involved a lot of safety for radiation and high explosives and an overview of the Army's tactical nuclear missiles.

The second phase was a hands-on disassembly of a typical weapon—the Mk. 31 warhead used in both the *Nike Hercules* (surface-to-air) and the *Honest John* (surface-to-surface) missiles. The remainder of the five months was devoted to the various electronic test equipment used to verify the weapon's functionality.

We needed a good understanding of how the weapons worked and why various safety procedures had to be used. We maintained the weapons and the test equipment that verified their operational condition and the radiation instruments for monitoring the safety aspect.

On Friday of the second week, I was finishing lunch at the mess hall when someone put the radio onto the PA system. President Kennedy's motorcade had been shot at in Dallas. At first, I thought the bulletproof glass would prevent any injury. Returning to class, we learned that the President had been riding in an open-top car and was dead. It was a real shock.

AN EXCEPTIONAL OPPORTUNITY

Just as 1963 had brought significant changes to my life, 1964 would do likewise. The course went well, and I was slated to go to Germany following graduation in March 1964. However, the unit did not form, and I was given another extraordinary opportunity. As I finished at the top of my class (That upside-down list again), they asked if I would like to remain at the school and become an instructor. I was to compose a fifteen-minute presentation on a topic of my choosing to be given to a selection board. I chose the *Redstone* missile because I had significant knowledge of its role in our space program—and it was an Army missile.

The audition (as they called it) went well. I was assigned to the Electronic Test Equipment Repair Phase and began preparing for my first class. Before I would be allowed to teach, I had to make the presentation to a group of officers and senior NCOs. I spent two weeks preparing for the appointed day. It was difficult, probably because of the pressure of having some high-ranking officers standing in judgment of a Private First-Class E-3 for such a prestigious position. Over the next twenty months, I typically taught a two- or three-hour class each day.

To bring the reader up to date, I married a young lady in July 1964 who I met on a blind date, horseback riding along the Rio Grande.

The Decision to Leave the Army

I considered making the Army a career when my enlistment was up in March 1966. Because the Vietnam War was taking a toll on helicopter pilots, I was hopeful the Army might not insist on uncorrected eyesight. When I went for my exit interview with my Commanding Officer, he asked what it would take for me to re-enlist. I told him if I could go to rotary-wing training (helicopters). He picked up the phone, and within a half-hour, I was over at the medical center, getting a flight physical. Unfortunately, while they would waiver a lot of conditions, eyesight was not one of them.

I had also passed the Officer Candidate School (OCS) exam, and Donna and I talked about that prospect. Having interviewed with IBM a week earlier and having a strong indication that they would be offering me a job, I decided to leave the Army. It was a fork-in-the-road that I occasionally wonder how our lives would have changed if I had chosen otherwise.

As it was, the electronics training and the opportunity to be an instructor in the nuclear weapons field provided a foundation for a thirty-five-year career in computing that culminated in my retirement from the Los Alamos National Laboratory in 2001.

As I reflect on the opportunities presented to me, I believe the decision to end the draft in 1972 has noticeably changed our culture. Young men are no longer required to serve our country and experience the discipline and responsibility of that privilege—likewise, the exposure to a wide variety of career paths. I wonder too, how much Basic Training has changed to keep pace with technology.

Ted Spitzmiller

T ED SPITZMILLER HAS HAD A WIDE range of opportunities over the past half-century. Early in his career he taught electronic maintenance of the Army's tactical nuclear weapons. Then it was on to the internals of computer hardware and software, while employed by IBM. At the Los Alamos, National Laboratory in New Mexico (from which he retired in 2001), Ted taught and documented super-computer operating systems. Along the way he managed to pick up a BS and MS in Computing Information Systems.

While all this was going on in Ted's professional life, he was also deeply involved in his first love (second only to his wife of 56 years)—aerospace. He holds a commercial pilot certificate and is a flight instructor.

Ted has had seven books published on aviation and space-related topics as well as scores of articles in popular aviation magazines. He has made numerous presentations on a variety of aerospace topics in a wide range of venues. He was the editor of *IFR Refresher* magazine for more than eight years, Ted appreciates opportunities to share the wealth of skills and knowledge acquired over the years in the realm of aerospace history and technology.

Caution: The accompanying photo is ten years old!

FE Taylor

25

My Purple Heart

T HIS ACCOUNT OF THE INCIDENT THAT qualified me for the Purple Heart is being written almost 54 years later, on Memorial Day 2020. Like so many other recipients, very few people know of our award and even less know the details.

I have had time to reflect upon what went on that night beyond the basic, loud explosion, bright light, one-eighth-inch-diameter (3.2 mm) steel balls passing through and lodging in my body, severe leg pain, medevacked to MASH hospital, forwarded to in-country hospital for surgery, and rehabilitating in a Japan hospital.

Until our grandson's soccer team played in a tournament in Hanoi, Vietnam (he lived with his expat parents in Singapore), memories of November 14, 1966 had been stored on the bottom shelf of my mind. Realizing the Army sent me to Vietnam to kill the grandparents of our grandson's opponents, I reflected on my service.

Among the first replacements for soldiers no longer in combat, my assignment to the 5th Battalion, 7th Cavalry, First Cavalry Division (Airmobile) began on October 4, 1966. The 5th Battalion trained together in the U.S. and joined the 1st and 2nd Battalions in Vietnam in April 1966. Based in the Central Highlands (where volcanoes once bellowed and created 9,000 feet peaks), Camp Radcliffe, 240 miles northeast of Saigon, became a bedroom for 16.000 First Cavalry soldiers who transformed the village of An Khe's into a city. The cavalry's horses had been replaced with 434 helicopters. Subtropical, raining one out of three days, lows of 68 and highs of 82 created fog for breakfast and dinner and scattered sunny days. Camp aromas ranged from rotting jungle organic matter to aviation fumes mixed with wafts of fecal fragrances emanating from latrines, to mess hall odors and diesel fuel exhausts.

Joining Company B in the boonies on a dark and rainy night, I spent the night sleeping in a building gutted by fire. A gunshot broke the rhythm of the falling rain, waking me from a light sleep. Out of the dense vegetation surrounding the building, a sentry appeared.

He wore a dripping wet poncho and a helmet. His M-16 hung from his shoulder and his right hand gripped a 45 pistol.

Illuminating the sentry's face with his flashlight, the platoon sergeant asked, "What was that round about?"

"My 45 accidentally fired when I got tangled up in some vines," replied the sentry.

When the sergeant's light focused on the sentry's right boot, I saw blood coming from a hole drilled by a bullet. A million-dollar wound, the self-inflicted injury was a ticket home.

I'll always remember the look on the sentry's face as he glanced down to see the red flowing from his boot, a fearful look of apprehension and embarrassment that indicated he was not sure of what the future would bring but he knew this war was over for him.

Constantly on the go for thirty days, Bravo company experienced muggy days, chilly nights, and periodic showers. Sleeping on the ground, eating C-rations, sloshing through rice paddies, and trudging mountain slopes covered by sun-blocking jungle canopies left little time for personal cleanliness. Most of the guys had given up wearing underwear.

Loosening the laces of my boots after walking through rice fields all day, I pulled my fatigue's legs up to see what appeared to be cigars attached.

"What's this on my leg?" I blurted out, suspecting all along they were leaches but trying to block out the grossness of a creature sucking blood from my body.

"They're blood-sucking leaches," came the response.

"Squirt some bug juice on its butt, he'll come out," a voice of experience replied.

Soaking the leeches with Army-issued insect repellent worked.

You're not in Kansas anymore, Taylor, I thought to myself.

During my initial weeks of combat, Company B incurred casualties from booby traps, firefights as well as another self-inflicted wound. Dickerson, a fellow replacement, shot himself in the ankle with his M-16. Our first sergeant and six other men were killed by enemy fire. I avoided being injured when our platoon leader, Lieutenant Bronson tripped a booby-trapped grenade as I followed ten yards behind carrying the platoon's radio. I did not see Lieutenant Bronson again after his medical evacuation.

"Chinooks will pick us up at 0900 hours tomorrow," our platoon sergeant announced.

Company B boarded helicopters and flew to a forward support outpost, Hammond—located in Binh Dinh Province, fifteen miles west of the coastal city, Qui Nhon.

"It's been sixty-five days since we've been in camp," muddled one of the men.

"Showers at 1500 hours," announced by the company commander was like hearing your named called in a raffle.

Stripping naked, the 112 men of Bravo company huddled together waiting for each man's turn in the portable showers.

"Scrub in a hurry men. Give your buddies a chance before the hot water is gone," extolled the CO.

Vietnamese mama-sans sold us Coca Cola through the base's perimeter fence as we waited our turn to shower. Each of us asked the other, "Where do they get the Cokes?"

No one knew.

"Formation at 1700 hours," ordered the CO.

Two by two we were assigned foxholes, located on the perimeter of Hammond, to guard the artillery battery. After setting up housekeeping in a foxhole the bartering began,

"I'll give you my beer for your cigarettes," my foxhole mate offered.

We were allowed two cans of warm beer on occasion. The cigarettes came with our food rations. Eating and sleeping on a conventional basis was like visiting grandparents, meals were served separated by down time.

The following day the company commander barked "Formation 1200 hours."

Strange, I thought, *formation in fifteen minutes when the mess hall opens.*

Wasting few words, the CO began," The next one of you who shoots himself should save one round in his weapon so I can put in it through your head."

Incidents with self-inflicted wounds clouded his command record.

Continuing he said, "Going home with a self-inflicted wound will disqualify you for VA benefits."

Proving a shooting as intentional would be difficult, I thought. Battlefield chaos veiled the credence of war.

At 1000 hours on a sunny day with few clouds to block the blue sky, Bravo company assembled to honor the company's men killed in action. Bayonets pinned seven M-16 rifles erect into the red soil. Crowned with helmets, each rifle stood like a sentinel beside a pair of empty boots.

The chaplain prayed, "...and by giving their lives for their country they are now in heaven."

New path to salvation, I thought.

Raised "right" in a small Southern town found me in church whenever the bells rang. Qualification for salvation did not include dying in battle. "Thou Shall Not Kill" did come to mind.

236

I remembered Bible battles were fought for "God's King-dom" from which our chaplain must have concluded that killing Buddhists and atheists qualified us for salvation.

I wondered, *Did atheists killed on the battlefield have to go to heaven?*

LBJ told us we were fighting for Vietnamese freedom. Dying for Vietnamese democracy made some sense at the time, but promising salvation seemed Machiavellian.

Freedom gives one the right to believe anything they want to believe, including not believing. The memorial ceremony made a powerful impact on me. One of the sketches I made while in the hospital recuperating depicted that memorial service. By that time, I had really become wary of the war.

In one of the greatest graveside memorial speeches in American history, President Abraham Lincoln said that those who fought and died at Gettysburg were rewarded by the cause for which they fought and died. President Lincoln made no reference to salvation as an extra benefit of dying at Gettysburg.

Spiritually is embraced very effectively by the military. It was not by accident Emperor Constantine (272-337AD) converted to Christianity and incorporated Christians into his legions of warriors when fighting to consolidate the Roman Empire. Christians were magnificent warriors, tri-umphant in battle. Giving of your life while fighting for a way of life so dear is powerful motivation for a winning Army.

Christians remain omnipotent warriors. The preponder-ance of engraved gravestone insignias in our 131 National Cemeteries are a mixture of seventeen Christian crosses. My dog tags worn in combat had PRESBYTERIAN stamped into them. The sword came first in spreading Christianity around the world, followed by missionaries. Seeds of that war were sown one hundred years earlier when French priests arrived in Vietnam.

Not wanting us to become too relaxed while at Hammond, we conducted night patrols of the surrounding area on a rotating basis. Our company had four platoons with each one having four squads. Each night, two squads performed sweep-and-destroy patrols that never worked. One squad went to a predetermined location and set up in an ambush on an existing trail. A Claymore land-mine would be set up with a tripwire strung across the trail. Sitting in position for several hours, being quiet while thousands of mosquitoes attacked inflicted pain. Our Army-issued insect repellent did not come with a 100% guarantee.

The squad not performing blocking duty walked a predetermined course in an attempt to flush out the Vietcong and drive them into our ambush. We had men who could lead our squad on a compass bearing but no one ever knew exactly our location on the map as we did not know the distance traveled on each bearing. We could not find our destination coordinates in the darkness due to our inability to see landmarks.

My injury happened on a night I volunteered to count steps while following the point man, Jasper Catanzaro. He used a compass (received from home that glowed in the dark) to keep us on our assigned course.

My forestry work required determining distances by pacing when taking sample plots in the forest on a predetermined grid. Our platoon sergeant, a career soldier with a made-for-Hollywood face, followed me. A low-key NCO, Sergeant Morehouse quietly and efficiently performed assigned tasks. Behind him, in a single line, the rest of our partrol followed—including a replacement who arrived with me, Luther Mahon, and our new platoon leader, Lieutenant Reber. Our CO, Captain Hitti ordered Lt. Reber to follow along to see how an experienced NCO lead a patrol.

After walking for several hours in pitch-black darkness, our point man activated a landmine—he'd tripped a wire that ran across the trail. The simultaneous bright light and loud explosion erased the blackness. As I lay on the ground, I saw and smelled smoke as our medic and uninjured squad members shined their flashlights on us to determine the nature of our injuries. An intense pain radiated from my right leg.

Medevac helicopters arrived around 0300.

Remembering that night now, it seems as if the air ambulances were there in a very short period of time.

Vivid memories remain of the rhythmic thumping sound made by the arriving Huey helicopter rotors and the bright lights which shone from underneath the choppers—used to assist the pilots in finding a place to land.

The dust-off pilots who risked their lives to fly us to medical treatment and for their ability to find us in the dark will always have my deepest respect.

Those with more serious injuries filled the first medevac. Placed on a stretcher, I flew out on the second medevac. By being closer to the landmine when it exploded, the pellets did not hit me above the waist.

The pellet's path originated at ground-level, and as they spread, they rose ever higher. By the time the pellets reached our platoon sergeant (walking behind me), they were at eye level. He lost an eye. Mahon, walking behind him, received pellets in the head. All the wounded were flown to a MASH hospital at Hammond.

The TV series, *M*A*S*H* accurately portrayed my experience.

At the MASH hospital, I saw six others who had been wounded. We were in one tent, lying on gurneys in close proximity to each other. A lieutenant colonel bent over to ask me something. I do not remember one thing he said, but I do know what I told him. I felt like in that situation what I said would not be held against me.

Very forcibly, I told the colonel the night sweep-and-destroy missions were dumb and whoever came up with the idea was stupid.

He listened, and then moved on to the next wounded warrior.

I later learned he was our battalion commander, Colonel Sweat.

Easing my pain with morphine, a medevac Huey flew me to a hospital in Qui Nhon, the 85th Evacuation Hospital.

One pellet had embedded itself in my lower right leg, another pellet passed through the palm of my left hand and a third cut a path across the right cheek of my buttocks.

Two doctors examined my leg and discussed the removal of the pellet.

Overhearing their conversation, I raised my head in an inquisitive manner.

One doctor looked at me and said, "If it's okay with you?"

"Fine by me, Doc" I said.

My hospital ward in Qui Nhon treated seriously wounded soldiers. Some never made it home alive.

The surgeon saved the pellet and gave it to me when I woke up. A cast stabilized my left forearm and hand.

After a few days in that coastal hospital, I flew on an Air Force medical evacuation plane bound for the 249th General Hospital, Camp Drake, Asaka, Japan via a one-night's layover at Clark Air Force Base hospital in Manila, Philippines.

The peroneal nerve in my leg had been injured, causing foot drop and required almost three months rehabilitation before I returned stateside to finish my enlistment.

FE TAYLOR

BORN ELEVEN MONTHS AFTER THE BOMBING of Pearl Harbor, FE Taylor spent the cold war years in Alabama and South Carolina. His move to South Carolina with his family exposed him to the nuclear age.

FE's father helped produce plutonium at the Savannah River Site. After receiving a degree in Forestry from Clemson, he married and began his career with a forest products company, managing forestland in southern Georgia. His career was interrupted in 1966 when he was drafted into the Army.

After discharge in 1968, he returned to his career and sequestered carbon until his retirement.

In retirement, FE is enjoying traveling, sailing, producing videos, photography, writing, hiking, tennis, golf, sketching, music, and grandchildren.

Ellen S. Thornton

26

By the Fire

By the fire, a flare of light

showed in your eyes

hidden wounds carried

alone, distant places

you would be going soon.

Outside the circling wind sends leaves

lifting and falling, scattering.

Somewhere, an eagle's cry.

That night you crossed the frozen river.

There could be no return

for your warrior's heart wanted only to go

where ashes were gathering soft as snow,

and shadows huddled,

waiting with dark wings.

By E.S. Thornton

February 2021

E.S. THORNTON

E.S. THORNTON'S POETRY HAS BEEN PUBLISHED in the *Concho River Review* and the *Connecticut River Review*. She was nominated for a Pushcart Prize for Poetry by the *Connecticut River Review*. Her work was recognized with an Honorable Mention in the *Writer's Digest* 72nd Annual writing competition. In fiction, her writing credits include a Bronze medal in historical fiction from the Military Writers Society of America for her debut YA novel, *The Girl Who Swam to Atlantis*.

She is a former newspaper reporter for the *Patriot Ledger*, *Honolulu Star Bulletin*, and *Wichita Eagle*, and a television reporter for *TVB* in Kowloon, Hong Kong. She has also worked as a technical writer and instructor in rhetoric and composition.

Ken Thurman

27

AMBUSHIN' IN THE RAIN

A N LOC IN CENTRAL SW VIETNAM was one of two provincial capitols the Viet Cong (VC) and North Vietnamese Army (NVA) were going all-out to capture and call their "People's Liberation Capitol". It was our mission to stop them—destroying as many as possible before they retreated back across the invisible line in the jungle called a border. Beyond which they were safe because we, play-fair Americans, couldn't cross. Sort of like killers' game of hide-n-seek.

Most of the NVA's invasion routes ran west-to-east, from the nearby Cambodian border to their favorite spots—used with deadly effect, multiple times, to ambush our convoys running supplies and necessities up Highway 13. Highway 13 was the vital supply line running south-to-north from the 2nd Brigade's base at Chu Lai to our company's 2nd Battalion firebase just outside An Loc.

After running into or being ambushed nearly every other day in practically every direction we moved, it was our turn to give the invaders a dose of their own tactics. As one of the few surviving squad leaders it was my turn to help plan, set up, and lead an ambush. Unfortunately, it was not an easy task since there were *so many* avenues of approach, *so many* trails, and *so many* thousands of bad guys around us. *Ah-h-h, the joys of leadership.*

During our daytime sweep, I rode on the platoon leader's Armored Personnel Carrier (APC/track) so we could work out with the company commander (CO) and he, in turn, with battalion operations (S3), the best places to catch the NVA on the move that night. We maneuvered along an irrigation ditch opposite the road, which defined the edge of a huge rubber plantation, seeing if we could draw fire or discover any bunker complexes nearby. After reconning a number of sites and not hearing any rounds or rocket propelled grenades (RPG) come our way or seeing new enemy diggings, the CO decided on a well-worn road paralleling a plantation drainage ditch.

"Okay, sir. Roger. Wilco."

I selected a good place to set up the ambush thinking, *Hm-m-m, we could a lot of damage if the bad guys try use this road tonight.*

The small road and drainage ditch ran straight for about three hundred meters coming from the west—the direction of their Cambodian you-can't-touch-us bases. It then took a near ninety-degree right bend where a footpath connected through rice paddies on the opposite side of the ditch and berm. After going a short distance of about ten meters, the path and stream turned back left and continued in the same westerly direction toward Highway 13.

It was fairly well protected from air sightings, but from the ground it had clear firing zones in both directions. Plus, the short dogleg would require any sizable unit to slow down and hinder a large charge toward us. And the best feature was (as we had learned in several bloody encounters with these clever Commies), we had the drainage ditch and the dirt (piled up by the French plantation irrigation builders) between us and them.

While continuing to roll so as to not arouse suspicion, we confirmed coordinates with the supporting artillery commanders and they, in turn, with air assets who would be available that night.

The afternoon downpour started, reminding us it was monsoon season. *Oh well, another free shower.* We needed it.

After arriving back at our base, it was my duty to round up/select a squad of eight to ten guys. Ambushes were not at the top of everyone's favorite to-do list and since I had a reputation for being a leader who would "blow the 'bush" if bad guys entered the killing zone, I was a little short on volunteers.

Some of the not-so-motivated draftees worried, "Yeah, but what if they're lead element of a whole platoon, or company, or worse?!"

My motivational rationale was along the lines of, "First, it's our duty and our orders. Besides, you want to let them go by so they can set up an ambush against us the next day?"

Despite the rain, a couple guys stepped up, knowing it might be an excellent opportunity to extract revenge for the guys we'd lost to earlier ambushes. Needing six more, I did the draw straws routine, as always. Reserving of course, final say on who we had to have.

Squad selected. Duties assigned. Then in my sternest nineteen-year-old command voice, I bark out, "Stop your bitching and get ready. We head out at dusk."

I rarely had griping. They were a good bunch of soldiers and they all knew Sgt Thurman would hump the M60 machine gun, so no whining allowed.

When doing an ambush you took only non-tracer rounds. Carried only what was necessary plus as many Claymore anti-personnel mines as possible, multiple trip flares, and lots of hand grenades. Knifes but no food—it wasn't a picnic. No mosquito repellent or scented letters from home. The gooks smelled you twenty meters away. No poncho, liners only—they heard the rain drops splash on anything unnatural ten meters away.

We checked each other out, including giving a good shake to make sure nothing banged together. Rubbed some extra dirt on exposed skin even though we were literally in a rain shower. No problem, there was plenty more... dirt and rain. We were ready.

Two APCs showed up. We loaded into and onto the first. The second provided covering fire if necessary or rapid pick-up if we got off in a really hot spot. Night started to fall, so we moved out. We maintained a pretty good pace, like we were on a dusk patrol sweep—stopping a couple of times to make 'em think we were checking things out.

The tracks slightly slowed as we neared the site. I gave the signal and the 'bushers rolled off the top and popped out the back, while the APCs kept moving. They slowly picked up speed and finished their dusk patrol back to base.

Well, here we are team. At least the rain has let up.

In the utter pitch darkness we did a touch count. All present and ready to move the final two hundred meters in a slow, zig-zag maneuver to the site. Everyone knew their position and was within two arms' length of each other (so with one roll they could be side-by-side if the shit really hit the fan).

The ammo carrier and I set up the machine gun on its bi-fold legs near the crest of the berm in the middle, just out of sight. The two end flankers slipped-n-slid over the berm and waded through waist-high water to set trip flares on the intersecting paddy path, and both directions of the dirt—now mud, road. The next two in and one from the middle crawled over and planted Claymores on the road-side of the dirt pile. Securing the fuse wires into the mines and around the legs so they couldn't budge, they crawled back over, stringing the wires to me. I knotted the wires together and plugged each into its detonator, safeties on.

Meanwhile, behind us in the center the radio man (RTO) set a couple of flares, covering our rear and for a worse-case scenario. He finished digging in and setting up the all-important connection to massive sources of air and artillery firepower.

I crawled to the first two guys on watch duty and set the bundle of detonators nearby, as they position themselves to see both ways down the road. Everyone else gave a thumbs up. We went heads-down behind the slippery red dirt for some rest.

Bush set. Now all we need is some good moonlight and sleep.

Alas, we would have neither.

What moonlight that had appeared was turned off by the next wave of monsoon clouds. *Ugh. Pucker factor raises. But at least it makes it harder for the bad guys, too. Oh well, sleep will be somewhat easier.*

Fat chance. The rain started again, harder. My bed—the ground—became thoroughly soaked, as did the poncho liner I was trying to hide under.

Damn. Okay, time to get everything to the same level of wetness so I can be evenly uncomfortable all over.

I threw back the quilted, rayon-stuffed poncho liner to let it and me get totally drenched. I threw the liner back over me and started generating heat with my shivering.

That's okay. The liner gets warmer faster and, like a good wetsuit, can actually keep one somewhat comfortable. Ah-h-h. Off to some much needed rest. But nature's little bloodsuckers soon got out of the pouring rain and under the protection of my personal tent, too.

Z-z-z. Z-Z-z-zt. Zz-Z-Z-ZT! Louder and closer they got to the only parts of me that could serve as their meal source—my head and ears.

You gotta be shittin' me! How can they navigate and fly through all that down-pouring rain, right to me? What do these little bitches do for food when some warm-bodied GI isn't lying around on the ground trying to hide?! No way could one swat them. They were way too agile and a killing slap would have given our position away. *Damn 'em! Okay, there's only one defense.*

I flipped back the poncho liner and let the sheets of rain wash them away. No cover at all. *But damn mosquitoes can't swim and I can maybe get some sleep.*

By then, the dirt wasn't just wet, it had turned into

muddy, slippery red clay. Rivulets of rain grew to two-inch-deep mini streams. Even doubling up my fists to use as pillows didn't keep my face out of the continuous flow of water.

Damn! The only thing that can keep my nose and mouth above water is my helmet. Ouch! Despite a camouflage cover "pillowcase" it was a *really* hard place to lay one's head. *At least I won't drown.*

Full-fledged waves of water—the monsoon monster rushed over, under, and seemingly through me. Pure exhaustion finally overcame nature and a semblance of sleep came over me.

About midnight, the second shift guard gently woke me.

"Here's the detonators. Nothing so far. Just rain, rain, and more fucking rain." Along with knotted Claymore wires, he handed me the Starlight night-vision scope. A nice advantage our military equipment industry invented for seeing in the dark. Outstandingly useful on guard duty back in base camps, where the bad guys already knew we were. On an ambush they had to be used judiciously. The soft green light coming back through the viewing end lit up the area around one's eye. Literally a dead giveaway when lying hidden in the pitch darkness of an ambush site.

Two hours of watching and hoping for targets to walk into our field of fire—nothing...except more torrents of rain. Spent more time and effort trying to stay on top of the berm than watching for the enemy, sliding back down the slippery slope time and again. *Ugh.* Then quietly as possible, crawling and clawing my way back up the four foot, red dirt, slip-n-slide. Only to ooze down again. Shouting in my mind, *This **really** sucks!* Then, the positive spin, *Well, at least I won't fall asleep or get bored to death.*

Finally, time came to pass the equipment and guard duties to next pair of fellow drenched-rat grunts. Whispering the orders, "Stay alert, if they come it'll be on your just-before-dawn shift. Oh, and don't drown."

Responsibilities complete, I curled up at the bottom "V" with the M60 resting on it's bi-pod legs directly up the slope from me and my steel pot pillow. Felt like the rain had subsided.

Ah-h-h, some well-earned sleep.

I was suddenly ripped out of my slumber by something heavy and hard smashing into the top of my head.

Holy fuck! I instantly thought, *The guard fell asleep or was dead and the bastards were on top of us!* I grabbed my bayonet and came up swinging.

Through the renewed sheets of monsoon, I slashed at anything and everything—my poor poncho liner caught the worst of it. Rolling away toward where the Claymore detonators should be, I clawed and groped for them, thinking, *I'll get some of these mutherfukers before they get all of us.* Found the detonators. But as I was feeling for the safety caps, I suddenly realized there were no follow-up hits and my slashing hadn't connected with anything solid. There were no gooks swarming us. Just silence and darkness... and the relentless water from the sky.

My mind whirred, *Huh? What the hell? What hit me?* Then, movement on my right. I tightened up. *Whew. It's the right-side guard.*

He slid over and grabbed me, scared shitless by my sudden thrashing and slashing.

"What the *hell* is the matter, Sarge?"

Pulling my wits together and my body back over to my sleeping spot, I felt the butt of my machine gun where my head had been. *Are you kidding?* The bipods had broken loose from the top of the berm, skiing down the torrent and made a direct hit on my bare, unprotected head.

"The M60 slid down and smacked my head. I thought the gooks were on us. I'm okay, just a cut." I heard and smelled the big sigh of relief from him as he rolled back over to his position.

With that, I pushed the M60 back up the slope and

shoved the legs into the mud as far as they would go, set the ammo can upright again, and wiped off the links as best I could (at least the rain helped with that).

Everything reset, including my nerves, I slid down to reposition myself thinking, *How bad is this? Ambushed and attacked by my own weapon. Can't even claim a Purple Heart despite the gash on my head!*

I was wounded by the *damn rain* instead of enemy action. Though ask any infantryman (grunt) who the real enemy was and he'll tell you, "The mud and the damn bugs!" *That's why the Army's most significant award is the well-deserved and hard-earned, Combat Infantryman's Badge. So much for thoughts of medals, I gotta get some sleep.*

I awoke to dawn and the radio crackling, "Situation? Over."

The RTO looked over to me, I gave the OK sign. He calls back, "Sit rep negative."

"Roger. Pick up will be in approximately forty minutes. Be there ready to load and go. Out."

RTO looked at me again, knowing the story of my M60's attack. He keyed the radio and added, "Correction. No gooks, but one wound. May need medic. Out."

With that, he and the guys within earshot ragged me—offering condolences and first aid, all the while laughing their asses off. I responded with grenades of sloppy red dirt. Which, being a bunch of young men who had just survived another night of ambushing, set off a mud fight.

As they disarmed the mines and flares, rolled up the wires, and repacked the ammo I, being NCOIC of the ambush, took advantage of "not having to do anything" by personally ambushing the laughers.

Scoops of stinking red mud flew through the air. They counterattacked. Soon we were even more covered in mud and rancid smells than what the night did to us. In the heat of our mud battle, we hadn't noticed the rain had stopped. Turned off, just like it turns on in monsoon season—instantly.

The radio screeched to life again, "We are entering the other side of the rubber. You ready for pickup?"

The RTO extended the handset to me, "Almost. We'll be there. Out." Then in my sternest command voice, I barked out, "Stop your laughing and get ready. We're outta here. NOW!"

We moved out to the morning pickup point in a beeline. Covered with mud and soaked to the bones, plus not having fired up or exploded any munitions, we all weighed about twenty percent more than when we deployed. Sloshing and sliding, we did our best double-time possible. What sights, sounds, and smells our band of brothers was.

In a frankly amazing accomplishment, we popped out of the undergrowth just as our company of 15 APCs started its U-turn for the day's sweep.

"Let's go. Load up!" was the platoon sergeant's morning greeting. On and up we clambered onto our respective vehicles. "Move out!"

And so started another day in the life of an infantryman.

"What's for breakfast?" someone asked, as if we didn't know.

Our new West Pointer platoon leader responded, "Whew. You guys look like hell. There're C-rations down there," pointing into the bowels of the APC. "We're expecting some heavy contact, so clean those filthy weapons first, especially that M60. Where the hell's it been, Sergeant?"

I curtly answered, "It's been in some serious contact, sir. By the way, where's our medic?"

My fellow 'bushers stifled their chuckles and smiles in their cans of breakfast C-rations. Our APCs lurched into motion along with the rest of the company.

We were off to find and kill some more mothers' sons for ... who?

KEN THURMAN

FROM FOUR-GENERATION GOLD DREDGING FAMILY IN California Gold Country. Grew up with children of rocket scientists & B52 crews at height of Cold War & space race. Amazing time and place! Joined Army at seventeen to get: GI Bill, reunited with first true love (AF Colonel's daughter), away from stepmother, and, oh yeah, save the world from communism. Chose Armor to accomplish goals. Almost worked out... except orders to Europe were switched RVN. *Damn!*

Deployed as tank commander with 1st Brigade of 5th Mechanized up to and in the DMZ. Transferred to mech squad leader in 1st Infantry on the Cambodian border. Lucky me... the intense hot spots of 1968-69. Silver, two Bronze, two Purples, and E-6 "blood stripe" later, survived to get out.

Started making love instead of war while using GI Bill to earn BBA & MBA from GaStUniv in Atlanta.

Work includes equal measure of:

Entrepreneurial; imports, contractor, auto repair shops, landlord.

Fortune 100 corporations; Certified Internal Auditor, Planning & Budgeting Director.

Professional; independent financial advisor, ChFC.

Community Service: Red Cross, credit unions' BofD, United Way, numerous veterans' organizations from Vietnam Rap Groups to MOPH Chapter Commander.

One very successful son, three sharp grandkids, and several extremely fine wives.

Jim Tritten

28

A Day in the Life of
a New Mexican

W HEN I READ THE *ALBUQUERQUE JOURNAL* on January 6, 2012, I was drawn to an article by the New Mexico History Museum Director. He suggested all New Mexicans sit down and write a bit about what happened the day New Mexico celebrated its statehood centennial. He asked us to send our stories to his offices, where they would be put into a time capsule and opened on January 6, 2112.

I wrote my thoughts, sent them off to be revealed in another hundred years, along with all the official pronouncements by government officials who likely wrote everything's coming up roses. I decided not to wait for the year 2112 for anyone to read my "Untold Story" of what life is like for an ordinary New Mexican veteran.

I was home alone on January 6, 2012, having put my wife on an airplane earlier that day. To not seem entirely so alone, I clicked on the television and looked at what choices I had for background noise while I crafted these words.

The first choice that looked interesting was *The Rocky Horror Picture Show*. I suspect few younger readers born in this century will have ever watched this cult classic comedy film. There is a generation of your elders who went to see this movie in theaters at the time. They brought water pistols, cigarette lighters, rubber gloves, toast, toilet paper, and other props to use when they mouthed the words to the entire production.

Yup, young people in the 20th Century had actually memorized the whole script of a screenplay—even if they could not identify most of the States in the Union or the world's nations. Funny movie, but no, my writing efforts on January 6, 2012 would not benefit from re-watching *The Rocky Horror Picture Show*.

I clicked some more through the selections and stopped briefly at *The Daily Show*—quite popular at the time with a significant segment of our population across the full spectrum of political affiliations.

Many of us enjoyed getting our "fake news" in the form of a comedy show with actors pretending to be news anchors. The show entertained and yet managed to inform without preaching or taking sides. No, not the right choice for that night either—I was just looking for background noise that would not interfere with some serious reflection.

I looked at our local public television station, KNME, and noticed it was going to broadcast a show about New Mexico. I started to watch, listened to a few seconds of acknowledgment that our state was celebrating its centennial—then it shifted to an analysis of Billy the Kid.

By the year 2112, when New Mexico celebrates its Bicentennial celebration and the time capsule is opened, I assume dragging out Billy the Kid will still be *in vogue*, and the controversies over his life and death will still be contentious—and good for tourism. Having read a bunch about the Kid already, I passed on the show and continued to search for something else to play in the background.

Next choice, a television series called *Monk* featuring a detective diagnosed with obsessive compulsive disorder. In that episode, Monk simultaneously tried to solve a murder and fend off his friend's efforts to celebrate his birthday.

Perfect. Just silly enough to provide some humor, interesting enough to continue to monitor while I typed, but not too absorbing to distract me from my mission. I left the show on as background.

So, how did I, a military retiree living in the semi-rural Village of Corrales, spend my day?

Well, you already know I took my wife to the airport. She was going to Denmark to visit her mother, other family, and friends. Next, off to Sweden to see her son and his family. My wife was, at the time, a citizen of Denmark but not the United States. She was required to carry what is commonly referred to as a *Green Card*—her proof of legal resident status while remaining a citizen of another country.

Resident aliens are afforded all the privileges of being citizens without being permitted to vote, serve on jury duty, or take many federal government jobs. She is an artist and an author, doesn't care about politics or working for the government, and quite frankly, being officially denied the ability to serve on a jury is a condition sought after by most citizens of our great nation.

[Currently, in 2021, there is still a lot of discussion about illegal aliens. Wait, the current President just instructed his immigration folks to stop using those words. Regardless, I lived with a *legal* resident alien in 2012. Later in 2017, my wife became a naturalized U.S. Citizen after legally entering the U.S. and carrying a *Green Card* for fifty-two years.]

After returning from the airport, I took glass bottles I had been saving to a recycling center in Albuquerque.

I have no idea why our village did not accept glass for recycling but about once a quarter, I still sneak across the county line and deposit my bottles in a disposal site run by the city of Albuquerque. I hope our meager efforts have made up for the utter devastation we bequeathed upon the Earth. Quite a contrast to how the Native Americans treated the land of New Mexico before the arrival of Europeans in search of gold, God, and glory.

I then went to a meeting with the head of our state's National Alliance on Mental Illness (NAMI) affiliate.

The organization is dedicated to assisting patients and family members of those patients dealing with mental illnesses. We strategized on ways to expand programs into the criminal justice system. Our governments and medical insurance conglomerates closed many inpatient and outpatient mental health treatment facilities and released the patients to fend for themselves. The result was many of those patients were then, and now, regular residents of our jails and prisons—many of them veterans.

The largest budgets these days for mental health treatment are contained within the criminal justice system. The Mayor and Chief of Police of Albuquerque had convened a summit meeting earlier in 2012 to start a dialogue about what could be done. My contribution was to lead an effort to initiate peer-run recovery support groups in jails and prisons. If those with a diagnosis did not come to programs, I urged NAMI to go where they were instead. Jails and prisons are a target-rich environment.

After this meeting, I went shopping, talked to a neighbor, came home, and took a nap. I checked my Facebook account to see what my grandchildren were doing and read the *Corrales Comment* to verify it contained an announcement about my upcoming course teaching chronic disease self-management. I briefly went back out to grab a bite to eat and then came back and set a trap for a feral cat.

In our small village, we are known today for not euthanizing feral animals. The price we still pay for adopting this moral high ground is folks from around the area drive into our village and dump their unwanted pets.

We noticed a white cat on our back porch three nights before eating the food we put out regularly to feed the occasional stray. We figured it had been recently deposited since it ate everything I had put out and did not run away when I went outside.

I picked up a trap from our local animal-friendly non-profit, but the cat did not come back over the next two nights. I set the trap again that night, hoping for a centennial surprise.

By the way, the *Corrales Comment* had no coverage of the state's centennial. Its front-page article was about expanding village access to the outside world. Only five roads connect us to the outside world. There also was coverage about whether a modest sewer system in the business area of the village would ever function.

A sewer line in the village had been built but not hooked up to discharge wastewater anywhere. So much for local New Mexican government.

I took a phone call from a friend who shares a passion for another of my volunteer activities. We both conducted oral histories of our nation's military veterans for the Library of Congress—the Veteran's History Project.

The effort was gratifying, and I am truly humbled by the acts of bravery many of my fellow veterans performed during World War II, Korea, Vietnam, and as part of the Global War on Terror.

What was life like in New Mexico on January 6, 2012, for an ordinary New Mexican like me? Let's take a world overview and drill down to our small village. The world that day, and still today, was somewhat insane.

A sizable portion of the world's population either advocates or acquiesces in radicalizing religion and the subordination of politics to religion. Didn't Europe try this centuries ago, which drove many of its residents to the eastern shores of the New World to escape? There are similar religious fanatics today who are equally irrational in their minds, and we are still at a loss how to deal with them.

The world has been insane before—witness Adolf Hitler and World War II. My generation had to deal with the world that existed after World War II and the start of this new era.

This Cold War period was also somewhat insane (threats of nuclear strikes) but a bit more rational. We lived through the Cold War and did not manage to destroy ourselves and the planet.

I am still unsure about the future and whether this new threat can be dealt with other than drastic physical means. The international future is not optimistic and very threatening. I hope there is someone still alive in the bicentennial year 2112 to read these words in English.

I noted that day our nation was sick and had strayed far from its founding principles and a proven track record of what made us once great. More people expect entitlements than those who view this magnificent land as a place of opportunity to make it independently.

In 2012 and today, a professional political establishment is out of touch with the average American and only out to feed at the public trough. I know each generation laments the passing of its values and questions how the youngsters will cope. I admit I have now joined that cohort.

I would expect by New Mexico's Bicentennial, the United States will have become a mediocre social democracy and transitioned from being the foremost world power. America will survive, but it will not be the United States that once served as the shining "city upon a hill" inspiring the world. I hope we will be as dignified in our decline as my wife's homeland of Denmark was in its decline from world power under the Vikings. Denmark is a wonderful place today—just a bit irrelevant.

New Mexico became part of the United States in 1850. It was denied statehood until 1912 because the folks in Washington viewed it as unstable and not civilized—remember Billy the Kid?

Today our state government remains dominated by a single group of power brokers who are an embarrassment to anyone with an ounce of education or ethics. Officials take government or educational jobs, do a poor job, then get bought out for outrageous sums.

Corporations beg us to contribute to *green* initiatives and then pay half-million-dollar bonuses to their executives—I refuse to subsidize such practices.

State officers are regularly sent to prison. A former governor could not even get a job with a new national administration. Newspapers publicize corruption, and the people accept the status quo.

If I were to hazard a guess about the state of New Mexico in the year 2112, the Land of Enchantment will still be viewed as provincial, corrupt, and still confused with the country of Mexico.

New Mexico Magazine even today runs a monthly column featuring stores about New Mexicans being told companies do not ship outside the U.S. or letters returned by the post office marked insufficient international postage.

Perhaps in our little community of just under 9,000 residents, in about 3,000 residences, and around 3,000 horses, we might find some normalcy.

Corrales, in 2012 was a semi-rural municipality without any municipal-supplied water or sewage. Many of us defend these lack of services since it is the only way to prevent development and growth in government at the local level.

Some newcomers to New Mexico want to turn an ideal rural paradise into an adjunct of either the big cities of Albuquerque or Rio Rancho. Transplanted Californians want municipal-supplied water, sewers, sidewalks, paved streets, and getting rid of the odor of outdoor animals.

Citizens have banded together in political action groups to oppose the heavy hand of Village Hall, attempting to do questionable things—things done in closed meetings without public scrutiny. My guess is the developers will eventually win this battle, and those who aid their cause will make lots of money and then move on to some other rural environment to do it again. At least I will not live to see it.

Regardless of development issues, the tiny Village of Corrales was a terrific place to live in 2012 and remains so today. The air is clear, and we still drink water right out of the aquifer. You can smell the *chile* roasting in the fall at the Wagner's Farms Store. The annual Harvest Festival is fun, and the Pet Parade is a kick.

Pet Parade instructions include lining up by the height of the pet with crickets to the front. I played Santa for many years in the annual Christmas de Caballos Parade. Our Fourth of July Parade lasts well over an hour. We have an extremely high per capita level of education and income. The second-lowest crime rate in the state. Not a great place for young people but well-suited for the retired set who want one-acre lots, the right to own large animals, and to live in peace. A place where cats can be dumped and perhaps survive a few nights before either being trapped or being hunted to death by packs of wild coyotes that still roam.

The sign upon entering Corrales used to say it is an animal-friendly place to live and that we coexist with coyotes. Someone took the sign down a few years ago. I see developers behind the removal.

New Mexico may have one of the most corrupt and embarrassing state governments in the nation, but it is also a great place to live. I can think of a hundred places that would be different, but I cannot think of any place better.

New Mexico has a different history than what I learned growing up on the East Coast. We are urged to support people of color and Native Americans. There are days where we celebrate both—separately.

If we investigate New Mexican history, we learn Buffalo Soldiers fought against Native Americans and committed atrocities. When I went to honorific ceremonies, I used to ask myself on whose side I was supposed to root.

It is beautiful in places and amazing in what can be discovered. The people are friendly, hardworking, and the food is addictive.

We had llamas until a few years ago, and many of our friends still keep large animals. We also coexist with four indoor cats—three rescued by the local animal humane society, and the fourth walked into our garage on his own.

New Mexico treats its veterans very well, and I am frequently thanked for my service to the nation by citizens I do not know. We held a Veterans Day parade in Corrales for a few years. I marched and carried a U.S. Navy flag. Nope, I might complain a little, but I have no intention of leaving the state, my village, nor my home in Corrales, except feet first in a pine box. New Mexico is the land of entrapment—not the land of enchantment.

I fly the U.S. flag daily—the flag presented to me when I retired from the U.S. Navy in 1989. It had been flown over the Capitol of the U.S. in Washington D.C. I used to be proud I had been presented with that particular flag. Still proud of the flag, just not of the politicians who blemish it.

I think it was more straightforward and less costly when politicians just outright bought votes with the coin of the realm (or beer) rather than invent all the bureaucracy to administer the harvesting of votes with tax dollars.

Sherlock Holmes said crime is often solved by what did _not_ happen. In the case of *Silver Blaze*, it was the "curious incident of the dog in the night-time" that broke the case—the dog did _not_ bark.

What did I _not_ do on January 6, 2012? I did _not_ attend the governor's centennial ceremonies in Santa Fe. I did _not_ read the centennial supplement to the *Albuquerque Journal*. I did _not_ purchase a New Mexican centennial stamp on its first day of issue. I also did _not_ exercise.

As I closed that night of January 6, 2012, I checked the trap. No cat. *The Rocky Horror Picture Show* had just started to play again. During two *Monk* episodes, the detective had to endure overcoming his obsessive compulsive disorder, was hoodwinked into attending a surprise birthday party, and solved two murders, including that of the inventor of the self-cleaning vacuum cleaner.

I hope this has given you readers a glimpse of what real life was like for an ordinary New Mexican veteran when we celebrated a significant day in our state's history.

My "Untold Story" will later be revealed by the New Mexico History Museum Director on January 6, 2112. You got an advanced view.

JIM TRITTEN

J IM RETIRED AFTER A FORTY-FOUR-YEAR CAREER with the Department of Defense, including duty as a carrier-based naval aviator. He holds advanced degrees from the University of Southern California and formerly served as a faculty member and National Security Affairs department chair at the Naval Postgraduate School.

Dr. Tritten's publications have won him forty-nine national and state-wide writing awards. He has published eight books and three hundred chapters, articles, and government technical reports.

Jim was a frequent speaker at many military and international conferences and has seen his work translated into Russian, French, Spanish, and Portuguese.

Marvin J. Wolf

29

SPORT OF THE INCA KINGS

(A TRUE STORY.)

GIVE CREDIT WHERE IT'S DUE: THIS was Barriga's idea. But Staff Sergeant Al Barriga was a cartoonist. He just didn't have the creative writing chops. Besides, even with over twenty years in uniform, there's no way he could have pulled it off on his own.

Like Dirty Harry said, a man's gotta know his limitations. So Barriga came to me, his boss.

* * *

I was back in South Korea, a new father, a very junior captain of infantry, and the Seventh Infantry Division Information Officer. And very, very bored. Barriga and the five other soldiers who worked for me were equally so.

Not that we had nothing to do. We put out *The Bayonet*, the division's weekly newspaper. Although this was widely ignored as Army propaganda—you can't fool the troops—we still tried to make it as interesting as possible.

We also pulled field duty, maintained our equipment, froze our butts off, and suffered the same lack of creature comfort as everyone else at Camp Casey. And like every other red-blooded American soldier, we endured a lack of off-duty attractions beyond those offered by the venereal disease distribution center outside our gates, better known as the village of Tongducheon.

Although working in a warm office was way better than dragging a rifle and combat gear up and down frozen mountains or through icky, sticky rice paddies—been there, done that—we were bored with putting out a newspaper that few read, filled with "news" that everybody either already knew or didn't care about.

The single exception was sports. Guys liked to read about intramural competition. There were bragging rights in sharing a Quonset hut with a member of a championship team, with being part of a unit that triumphed in sporting contests.

But it was late winter. Football season was long past. Basketball was finished. We had no hockey rink, and it would be months before baseball returned. Our sports page dwindled to almost nothing—troops got their only sports fix from *Stars & Stripes*, the semi-official Department of Defense daily, which, along with world and national news, carried pro and college scores and wire service features.

Then Barriga thought of a way to fill our sports page.

With assistance from the whole office, he invented a sport.

* * *

Barriga's parents were from Peru. His ancestors, he firmly believed, were Incas. So, we dubbed it *"grumaché"* and said it was the "Sport of Inca Kings."

We began by reporting the results of the first round of the [mythical] Mayta Cup, a [mythical] intramural grumaché tournament named for the Inca athlete king, Mayta Cápac. Because the winning team would be awarded a case of beer, the tournament was informally known as the Chicha Cup. In Quechua, *Chicha* [actually] means beer.

There really was a Mayta Cápac—750 years ago. Sportswise, nothing much has happened in southern Peru since 1533, when Pizarro sacked and looted Cuzco.

We began with the assumption none of our readers

spoke Quechua, the native language of the Central Andes. Not that Barriga did, either, but he knew a smattering of words and phrases.

To color our reports, we sprinkled game highlights with whatever he could recall. For example, we called the grumaché field *rit'i qewa*, which means snow-covered grass [maybe]. Other grumaché terms were mostly words used by Barriga's dad when he was drinking. Or by his mom, when his dad drank too much.

In reporting a baseball game, no contemporary sportswriter would bother to explain stuff like "strikeout," "infield fly rule" or "double play." So, while we used assorted grumaché terms, we rarely explained them. Nor did we describe the object of the game or the field it was played on, except in passing, or with Quechua words. And of course, we made up rules and changed them as we went along.

* * *

Think about what it would be like to read an account of a hockey game if you'd never seen one and didn't know the rules or even what equipment players used. That was the fun of it, knowing our readers would be scratching their heads and for the first time talking about something they read in our paper.

Not until our report of the third round of the semi-finals did we let slip that grumaché was played on a sunken hexagonal field about half the size of a basketball court. There was a *simi rumi* [stone mouth or goal hole] in each of the six sides, alternately defended by two opposing teams. The idea was to throw, kick or stuff a *rumi pupu* into an opponent's simi rumi. The rumi pupu could be thrown, kicked, or bounced but never carried or rolled—a rumi pupu, we eventually mentioned, was a fifteen-pound, leather-wrapped stone.

* * *

All these game details and others were slipped into stories, a few at a time, in no particular order. Eventually, discerning readers understood why, while fielding only seven men, a [mythical] squad needed thirty players. And why so many players suffered [mythical] bruises and serious [mythical] hand, head, leg, and foot injuries. Except we didn't say anything about them being mythical.

* * *

I should explain that, because I was very junior (a recently minted captain) every story we published, as well as every news release, was reviewed by my boss whom I will call Major Matero—the civil affairs officer. By 10:00 A.M. most mornings, however, Matero had sipped so much bourbon-laced coffee he would approve anything, including a test piece I submitted reporting that Amelia Earhart had been found working as a Tongducheon bar girl.

We had planned four stories, ending with final playoff results, which would get us almost within spittoon range of baseball spring training.

But then came a telex message from *Stars & Stripes* in Tokyo. I'd forgotten that they were on our distribution list. *Stripes'* editors browsed our pages looking for stories they could expand or report more widely. The sports editor asked me to send scores and highlights from our grumaché tournament.

Obviously, *Stripes* was just as desperate for sports news as we were.

So as grumaché disappeared from *The Bayonet*, weekly tournament roundups appeared every Saturday in *Stripes*. A million readers from Pearl Harbor to Hong Kong, from Sydney to New Delhi, scratched their heads over the mysteries of grumaché. Twice, editors telexed requests for an explanation of terms. I ignored these until an irate editor telephoned, then had Barriga create a skeletal grumaché lexicon in faux Quechua.

Desperate to end the hoax without giving ourselves away, we dreamed up a tournament grand finale: a prolonged, scoreless struggle between the 2072nd Radio Research Group and the 9th Ordnance Depot team. These were, of course, nonexistent units.

We did have a small Radio Research detachment, but its mission—mining North Korean Army radio traffic for useful intelligence—was classified. Anybody attempting to contact any unit called "radio research" was routed to a counterintelligence officer who scared them off. We also sort-of had an ordnance outfit, but its men and equipment had mostly deployed to Vietnam, leaving behind a skeleton force. They rarely answered their phone. I suspected they all hung out in the PX cafeteria drinking coffee until it was time for dinner.

To tie things up in a bow, we created an exciting finish we hoped would forestall all further requests for grumaché news. Through four scoreless periods, the Radio Research guys would hold off several clever *asnu* [donkey] *sonqo-suwa* [heart-stealer] feints by the Ordnance team. With only minutes before sunset—grumaché play was suspended until daybreak so that *qolqe* [money] could be *erk'eta munay* [given affection]—the 2072nd's *qoyllor* [star] *songollay* [sweetheart] fractured his knee while attempting the difficult *munay usa* [love louse] maneuver.

With both sides out of ambulatory replacements, the *kura* [priest] ran onto the field yelling "*Soq'oita q'owai,*" ["Give me something to drink!"] to halt play. He then declared *am urubamba* [a plain of snakes, e.g., a draw], whereupon both enraged benches limped onto the *rit'i qewa* and pelted each other with *ukuku wiqsa kuna* [bear heads, e.g. worn-out rumi pupu]. After MPs restored order, it was decreed that grumaché would no longer be played in the Seventh Infantry Division.

Just as we were ready to ship this masterpiece to Tokyo, Major Matero's liver failed and he was evacuated stateside for treatment. Until a replacement arrived, Master Sergeant Miller (not his real name), the chief of staff's sharp-eyed proofreader would review our press releases for style and punctuation. The chief of staff himself would spot-check content.

There was no way we could sneak even a single rumi pupu past that master sergeant, and the chief of staff would have kittens the first time he encountered a phrase like "*Soq'oita q'owai.*"

I decided to cancel the last piece.

* * *

Then the *Stripes* editor called from Tokyo: He'd planned to run our final piece as the lead story in Sunday's sports roundup. When I made excuses, he asked for my boss' phone number. I faked static interference as an excuse to hang up, but it was plain he'd call back.

We were screwed.

Barriga was scheduled to rotate stateside and then retire from the Army. I arranged for him to leave Korea immediately. Cleaning out his desk, I found a letter he'd written in which he accepted all responsibility for the hoax. I might have been tempted to keep it, except it was so full of misspelled words and make-you-cringe grammar no one would believe that particular cartoonist could have written anything published in *Stripes*.

In any case, as senior officer I alone was responsible. I made an appointment to see the chief of staff—a humorless, no-nonsense full colonel, and confess all. If by some twist of fate, I was spared a court-martial I could expect immediate reassignment to infantry duty on the DMZ.

I began packing.

And then the weather turned unseasonably warm. A forecast blizzard became an intense, slow-moving rainstorm

that washed out roads and bridges from South Korea's
Yellow Sea coast to the Straits of Tsushima.

A miracle.

I telexed the sports editor in Tokyo that, due to severe
weather, our tournament was canceled.

* * *

I heard no more about grumaché until a few weeks later
while attending a Public Affairs conference in Tokyo. The
last day's events included a tour of *Stars & Stripes*. As I
traversed a top-floor corridor en route to a briefing, a flinty
Marine colonel hailed me through his open office door.

The new commanding officer of *Stars & Stripes*.

"Seventh Division?" he said, eying my shoulder patch.

"Yes, sir," I said.

"Then you'd be the public information officer?"

"Yes, sir."

"Grumaché—that was pure, unadulterated, bullshit,
right?"

"Sir?"

"Tell me that it wasn't a hoax."

"No, sir, I can't tell you that."

He threw back his head and laughed. "Captain, you just
made me a hundred dollars richer," he said. "A bet with
my predecessor."

"Glad to be of service, sir," I said, carefully choosing
my words.

He turned my blood to ice with a withering glance.

"Pull something like that on my watch, and I'll see you
in Leavenworth," he growled.

"Yes, sir," I said. "I mean, no, sir."

"At the Naval Academy, I took four years of Spanish,"
he said, studying me. "So, when I graduated in 1939 and
chose to serve in the Corps, my first duty station was the
embassy Marine detachment in Lima, Peru."

I was beginning to understand.

"Spanish is useful in Peru," he continued. "But back before the war, the locals mostly spoke Quechua. There isn't a helluva lot for a young man to do at night in Lima, so the first Quechua every embassy Marine learns is '*Chicha*'—beer.

"And the first phrase we learned was 'get me a drink'— '*Soq'oita q'owai.*' You can't shit the troops, Captain."

My heart went down faster than the Titanic.

"Grumaché!" he said, barely able to contain his mirth. "The Sport of Inca kings! Really—the very idea!"

Still laughing, he waved me away.

MARVIN J. WOLF

ARVIN J. WOLF SERVED THIRTEEN YEARS on active duty with the US Army, including eight years as a commissioned officer. Enlisting in February 1959, he served as an infantryman in the Fourth and the Seventh Infantry Divisions. As a sergeant, he served as an Infantry School instructor and as a drill instructor at Ft. Jackson, SC. In March 1965, he re-enlisted as a private. Wolf served as a combat correspondent in the First Cavalry Division (Airmobile) in Vietnam and was appointed a second lieutenant, infantry in November 1966 at An Khe, RVN.

Wolf left active duty in 1974 and, after a few years in corporate communications, turned freelance. He is the author, co-author—or ghost author of twenty books and one produced screenplay. One of his photos appeared in the Ken Burns documentary, *Vietnam.*

His military books include *Buddha's Child, the memoir of VNAF General and RVN Prime Minister Nguyen Cao Ky*; *Abandoned In Hell, The Fight for Fire Base Kate*, and *They Were Soldiers, the sacrifices and contributions of our Vietnam Veterans.*

His six novels include the *Rabbi Ben Mysteries* and the *Chelmin and Spaulding CID Mysteries.*

He lives in Asheville, NC, with his adult daughter.

Dr. Bob Worthington

30

FEEDING THE GREEN MACHINE:

TRAINING THE SOLDIERS TO SERVE IN VIETNAM

T HE BEST ASSIGNMENT FOR AN INFANTRY captain is commander of a company.

In the mid-1960s, the war in Vietnam was not going well. General Westmoreland, senior commander in Vietnam kept asking for more troops. Politicians were divided between the hawks and the doves while young people protested the war, the draft, and the government in general. Times were bad for everyone.

The Army needed more soldiers for Vietnam and procuring them became more difficult. It took the Army eight weeks to convert civilians into soldiers. Then they would be trained in their chosen (or selected for them) military occupation. Their introduction into the Army began with Basic Combat Training (BCT).

As commander of a BCT company, this is my story of the challenges and difficulties I faced preparing young recruits for Vietnam.

Twenty-five percent of the recruits were draftees, conscripted men—most very unhappy because their education, careers, and lives were drastically interrupted for two years. Additionally, the demand to push more soldiers through the pipeline for Vietnam reduced the enlistment standards.

Many recruits were physically or psychologically unable to succeed as soldiers.

My first official day as a company commander for a year began on Monday 28 August 1967 in the Army Training Center at Fort Benning, Georgia.

Each company started with about 210 recruits, but by the end of the eight-week BCT cycle only about 190 graduated. The ten percent loss was due to a host of reasons: medical, psychological, discipline, or unsuitability to become a soldier. Turning civilians into soldiers in eight weeks was not an easy task.

The company operated in ten-week cycles—eight weeks of BCT and then two weeks of cadre training, preparing for the next cycle, personal leave, and maintenance of buildings, equipment, or grounds. Those two weeks were never a relaxing "down time" but a busy period of arduous work.

Busses and trains delivered over 1200 civilians to Fort Benning's Army Training Center Reception Station each week. Orientations explained the process. Hair was lopped off (they became bald), uniforms fitted and issued, more physical exams conducted, and additional aptitude testing done. Classification interviews confirmed what Army assignments were appropriate for each recruit, and continued training was established. Two dog tags were made and handed to each recruit. All information was entered the recruit's permanent Army personnel file. That takes a few days and, when enough recruits to fill a battalion for basic training were processed, they mounted up in trucks and were driven to their new home at a Basic Combat Training company.

Each company had the CO, two or three training officers (lieutenants), a first sergeant, a supply sergeant, a mess sergeant (and some cooks), a senior drill sergeant, five drill sergeants, and two spec fours (armorer and company clerk). Our real estate consisted of several WW II, two-story wooden barracks, and single-story buildings for the mess hall, supply, and administration.

Arriving recruits were grouped, lectured by our drill sergeants, explained what they would be doing for the following couple of months, and then assigned barracks. The drill sergeants demonstrated how beds were made, how footlockers and wall lockers were set up, and how to keep their barracks clean. Fire guard duty was clarified, in that the recruits stood four-hour night shifts to roam the barracks while everyone else slept, ensuring everything was safe—mainly keeping alert for fires and providing heat during winter months by maintaining the coal furnace.

Recruits were also introduced to KP (kitchen police) or mess duty. During the eight weeks, each recruit served KP several times, but only one day at a time.

Training began with drill and ceremony, marching and saluting, as well as PT (physical training). Guard duty and general orders were covered. Saturday morning inspections were held in the barracks and outside in ranks.

All formal training was conducted by officers and NCOs of the Training Center Committee Group. While committee instructors introduced all formal training, it was the drill sergeants' responsibility to supervise the hours of practice necessary to develop a degree of proficiency in basic military arts. Therefore, the company officers and NCOs, themselves, had to be competent in everything the Committee Group taught.

Outdoor training included hand-to-hand combat and bayonet instruction, followed by a bayonet obstacle course and training with the infamous pugil stick (a heavy stick, about five feet long, ends covered with thick padding). Recruits were dressed in a football helmet with a face guard, heavy gloves, and diapers (which were thick groin protectors).

Armed with a pugil stick, recruits practiced encountering an enemy, armed only with bayonets (on rifles). Some perfectly followed through with their bayonet fighting training. Others flailed about, knocking their opponent to the ground, using the pugil stick more like an axe, sword, or mace.

Indoor classes were interspersed with outdoor instruction. Recruits were issued an M-14 rifle (a select-fire automatic .308 caliber shoulder weapon, which used a twenty-round magazine). While a specific rifle was assigned to every recruit, it physically remained locked in the company arms' room until issued to the recruit for use. [The M-14 replaced the WW II .30-06 caliber, semi-automatic, eight shot, clip-fed, M-I Garand in 1961.]

By the middle of the cycle, recruits shot on the 25-meter range to develop familiarity with firing their rifle and learn how to zero their weapon. Zeroing meant to adjust the rear sight, so the rifle hit the target at a desired spot at a specific range. The next step was the field firing range, where they shot at pop-up targets anywhere from seventy to 300 meters away. Electrically controlled, when hit the targets fell. The culmination of rifle training was firing for qualification—testifying to one's skill as a rifleman.

Schooling continued with CBN (chemical, biological, and nuclear) classes and a trip to the tear gas building. Inside a room full of tear gas, wearing a protective mask, the recruit must remove it and recite name, rank, and service number before being allowed to exit.

Throwing hand grenades was scary for many recruits—afraid of pulling the pin and then accidentally dropping the grenade in the small-walled throwing pit. [I never saw or heard of this happening.]

Other sessions involved advanced combat training in the infiltration course where recruits crawled under 100 yards of barbed wire (and other barriers), while real machine gun bullets pierced the air above their squirming bodies, and positioned explosive charges detonated around them.

Toward the end of the cycle, one big event was the week-long bivouac. A march of several miles with rifle and full combat gear initiated the exercise. In the field,

each man carried half of a military pup tent (called a shel-
ter-half) two men joined to create a two-man tent. Many
of the combat skills learned were put into practice, living
outdoors as soldiers.

The eight weeks terminated with a plethora of testing. The Physical Combat Proficiency Test encompassed
five different events to measure a man's physical ability
to possess the strength, agility, and stamina needed to
function as a combat infantryman. It included a one-mile
run; forty-yard low crawl; run, dodge, and jump; grenade
throw; and horizontal ladder. While we had run the recruits
through the test many times, it was done the final time for
score. The last big evaluation was the G-3 Proficiency Test.
Many of the subjects taught in academic classes, outdoor
military training, and drill and ceremony were examined
by a special team of NCOs. Individual scores in each area
were tallied to arrive at a recruit's overall final score. The
cycle terminated with a battalion parade and the presentation of individual awards (to both recruits and cadre),
and company awards for the best company in a variety of
areas—from best mess hall to highest company scores in
the PCPT, rifle qualification, and G-3 Tests.

McNamara's Folly

A major problem we contended with was a special
program developed by Secretary of the Defense, Robert
McNamara, titled Project 100,000. When John Kennedy
assumed the office of U.S. President in 1961, he asked
McNamara to serve in his cabinet. McNamara chose the
Department of Defense (DoD).

Being a numbers-cruncher, McNamara preferred a system's analysis approach to problem solving and decision
making. One problem he faced was finding enough men to
support the war in Vietnam. His solution was a simple one
for number-crunchers—lower the eligibility requirements

for being inducted into the Army. The available supply of eligible men immediately increased. The problem was, we got recruits who were not capable of becoming successful soldiers. The program was a fool's response to solving a manpower problem.

The total number of men accepted and processed is questioned but was probably between 320,000 and 354,000 men. Project 100,000 began in October 1966 and ended in December 1971. Fifty-four percent of the group was recruited, forty-six percent drafted.

Here was who McNamara sent me: many Puerto Rican males who could not speak English—not when they joined my company, not when they left; men who were grossly out of shape—so overweight or so underweight they were physically weak and had no stamina; men so emotionally or intellectually deficient to the point they were unable to pass BCT—they could not handle the pressure of the training regime. Essentially ten percent of my company caused ninety percent of my problems.

Some recruits did very well in BCT. They were allowed the opportunity to serve in the Army and they were motivated to do just that. Some were just able to get through.

One of their biggest downfalls was discipline. The rigid environment of the military became unacceptable for many of the recruits. They rebelled by acting out, challenging authority, or going AWOL (absence without leave).

Later research on Project 100,000 revealed the men (as a group) were not successful as soldiers, were killed more often in Vietnam, and (after service) were not as successful in their vocational or personal lives as their non-veteran peers.

Another time-consuming problem were RBIs—Reply by Indorsement. This military term referred to a letter passing through the military chain of command to a soldier, typically addressing a nasty problem the recipient had. It requested the recipient specify, in writing, how he planned to resolve the problem. The formal correspondence dictated to the recipient: For appropriate action and return.

Essentially, the letter originated from the Army's highest levels of command. Every commander who passed it down added his own comments, until it finally arrived at the lowest level in the chain of command, me—the BCT company commander.

As a BCT commander, I received several RBIs each training cycle. Here's why: One quarter of the recruits were not there voluntarily, having been drafted. Many had just begun life when they were drafted—yanked out college or the start of a lucrative career. They were not happy being an Army private.

Others voluntarily joined the Army to escape, attempting to find a better life, willing to risk their lives as a commitment to their country. But in every cycle, there were those (draftees and volunteers) who disliked the training so much they exaggerated the truth and wrote fabrications home about what they experienced. A very few wanted to convince the home folks they were rough, tough, and mean and their training was making them even more so. Both types penned letters, lying about their training.

Little Johnnie wrote home explaining how tough the training was. He described sleeping less than four hours each night, losing twenty pounds, and forced to run twenty to thirty miles every day on only one meal.

There were recruits who hated BCT, hated their drill sergeants, hated the Army, and blamed everyone for their miserable existence. They wrote Mama depicting the horror and inhumanity of what was being done to them and the other recruits. Their letters described the depraved personalities of the cadre, from the company commander down.

Believing the letters to be truthful, Mom and Dad contacted their senator or congressional member. A staff member then spoke with the parents and made a few copies of the letter. Then, a letter (signed by the senator or representative) arrived at the Pentagon. At that point, the letter was required to be read and sent to the appropriate general in command of the Army Training Centers. The letter eventually landed on the desk of the Commanding General of the U.S. Army Training Center at Fort Benning and turned over to his deputy commander or the chief of staff (both full colonels), requesting appropriate action by me.

Everyone in that chain from Congress (through the generals, colonels, to captain), most likely knew what little Johnnie described was totally false. But they all had to play the game, go through the motions, and at the end get little Johnnie to admit, in writing, what he said was a lie.

My indorsement (with Johnnie's statement attached) was then returned through the chain of command. The senator or representative's staff member related what they had accomplished, and that little Johnnie tended to stretch the truth a bit, but he was okay and doing very well. Sometimes the parents accepted that, knowing their little Johnnie. Others were convinced everyone in the federal government was promoting a major cover-up and hid the truth. Each RBI took a lot of time to resolve. Receiving one, despite the outcome, negatively impacted a company commander's Officer's Efficiency Report.

My workday usually began around 5:00 AM. I got up, shaved, showered, and dressed. Sometimes I grabbed something to eat, but often I breakfasted at my mess hall. I checked with the CQ (Charge of Quarters—a company NCO who took charge of the entire company and essentially represented the commander during the night) and inquired how the night went.

Sometimes I went home for supper but returned to the company area to do paperwork or handle with recruits' problems (like little Johnnie's letters to Mama). Oftentimes, I would not get home until eight or nine at night. I arrived home in fatigues and combat boots, so tired I stretched out on the living room carpet to just relax for a few minutes, only to be woken a couple hours later by my wife telling me to go to bed. We repeated that nearly six-and-a-half days a week.

A BRIGHT SPOT IN TRAINING

During the summer, we encountered a very unusual job. Instead of the typical eight-week cycle of recruits, my company was tasked with participating in an incredibly special Army ROTC program. The program was being offered to college graduate students who wanted to join ROTC. We would train them to be soldiers (in a special BCT program designed just for them) and when back in grad school they would complete the senior ROTC classwork. Upon graduating, they'd be commissioned. We provided a special six-week BCT cycle, which counted as the first two years in a regular four-year ROTC program. All our students came from schools in Utah. Most were Mormons.

First off, the students were there because they wanted to be. Secondly, they were older, more mature, educated, and very bright. Training them was a piece of cake. They quickly recognized what had to be done in both their military training and maintaining their barracks. There was one slight problem during inspections relative to the footlocker display—what was to be done with their Temple Garments.

Adult members of the Church of Jesus Christ of Latter-day Saints participated in an Endowment Ceremony, in which they promised to be faithful to their religious beliefs and teachings. Upon completion of the ceremony, both males and females are required to wear a Temple Garment, as underwear, day and night. The garment (in 1968) was a white, single piece which sort of resembled what a T-shirt and pair of shorts (with the legs reaching almost to the knees) would look like if they were one piece instead of two separate pieces. Since our cadets were adults, most had garments rather than regular underwear. The garments held a deep religious significance so we had to decide what should be done.

It seemed each floor of the cadets had a spokesperson who reflected the wishes of their group. I meet with the spokespersons, and we arrived at a uniform way to display their garments that would not disgrace the religious importance of their garments.

The six weeks with that group were the most relaxed we ever encountered.

My tour as a BCT company commander was the most stressful of my twenty-five-year military career. Even more so than combat. Why? In addition to the many challenges described and the long hours, our battalion commander insisted on perfection. The following cycle had to be better than the previous. He demanded higher scores, more company awards, fewer dropouts, and less RBIs.

Being a company commander was supposed to be the best assignment for an infantry captain. For me, it was the worse job I ever had.

Dr. Bob Worthington

D R. BOB WORTHINGTON ENLISTED IN THE U.S. Marine Corps in 1957 as a college dropout, serving two years then returned to college and Army ROTC. Commissioned in 1961, he served on active duty until late 1969 when he left to attend graduate school, remaining in the active reserves. As a Psychology PhD student, he was returned to active duty in 1971, retiring in 1981.

During his first fifteen years in the military, he spent most of his time in infantry and unconventional warfare assignments. The last decade, he was a senior Army clinical psychologist. During his military career he served three combat tours, being awarded the Combat Infantryman Badge, seven decorations for valor, the Purple Heart, an Air Medal, and the USMC Combat Action Ribbon. After Army retirement, Worthington was a university professor, retiring in 1997. Between tours he served as a BCT company commander.

As a professional writer he has over 2500 publications. His latest book (about his first tour in Vietnam as a combat advisor), *Under Fire with ARVN Infantry*, received a MWSA Gold Award in 2020. His next book (about his second tour as a combat advisor in Vietnam) will be published in mid-2021.

Jerry L. Burton

31

COPING WITH FEAR

NONE OF US ARE WITHOUT FEAR. My father manned a 20mm anti-aircraft gun aboard a cruiser, the USS *Columbia*, in the Pacific during World War II. Below is a picture of him when a Japanese kamikaze struck the fantail of the *Columbia*. You can't really see him because of the flames. But he's in there, still at his assigned duty station.

I remember asking him if he was afraid when he saw the Japanese plane bearing down on the ship.

His answer was, "I'm sure I was, but I was too busy doing my job to let it distract me."

USS Columbia, Lingayen Gulf, Luzon, Philippines, 5 Jan 1945; ©2007 MFA Productions LLC Image in the Public Domain; Naval Historical Center; Unknown; Public Domain; Photographed: 5 January 1945; Accessed 10 November 2020

Dad kept firing at the kamikaze until just before impact. Then he squatted down in his "tub" and the flames and debris passed over him.

After telling me the story, Dad pointed his finger at me and said, "I would expect you to always do the same—do your job."

As flyers, we carry a lot of responsibility. We all have had scary experiences—some in battle, some in weather, some because we did something stupid, and some just 'cause. Fear is a normal reaction and to offset it, we develop personalized coping mechanisms. Dad's coping mechanism was focusing on carrying out his duties.

I thought for a long time people who became test pilots and astronauts were fearless—a special breed of human being who laughed at fear. It was comforting to me to hear the following story of my friend's fear and how he coped. He was an F-104 test pilot, Ken Luedeke.

This incredible man was kind enough to give me permission to paraphrase his stories. They are written below in the first person—as Ken telling his story. So, without further ado, I give you Kenneth Luedeke, Major, USAF (Retired)!

* * *

KENNETH D. LUEDEKE

I JOINED THE UNITED STATES AIR Force after one year of college. I had 350 flight hours and anticipated being welcomed into a flying slot and receiving a commission. It didn't work out that way.

The Air Force had set their standard at two years of college. So, I began a career as a clerk typist. After graduating from typing school near the top of my class, I had my choice of assignments. I was given several locations. I quickly scanned them.

No, no, no, not that one, either. St. Louis...not real exciting. Washington, D.C., maybe. Colorado Springs, could be. Fairbanks, wait a minute. Typing—boring. Fairbanks— Arctic Circle, high mountains, rough terrain, northern lights...that sounds pretty good. All those things might off-set the boredom of all the typing.

So, Fairbanks it was!

It didn't occur to me that when I reported in January of 1952 there would be very short, very cold days. When I left Alabama, it was sunny with temperatures in the 70s. When I arrived at Eielson AFB, it was dark and stayed that way. The temperature was minus forty degrees Fahrenheit.

My first assignment at Eielson was to the Form 5 section. I maintained the pilots' flight logs—Form 5s. It was very boring. I soon got transferred to the Aircraft Dispatcher section. There, I was able to utilize my former pilot training and experience.

One of the pilots who knew I had a private pilot's license and was gung-ho about flying, told me Eielson had an Aero Club—a flying club for military personnel. I checked out in a four-place Stinson Voyager. I built flight time by taking guys in the barracks on short flights and sharing costs.

The Air Force was flying WB-29s out of Eielson, gathering data for weather research and forecasting. I thumbed a ride on some of those missions. On one of the missions, the pilot, Captain Jack Davis told me he owned his own plane—a Seabee Amphibian.

Sometime later, Jack flew some people down to southern Alaska to do some hunting. He landed on the Kalahaga River, near Yakataga. The tide at the time was extremely low and the airplane got stuck on a sandbar. The plane and the people were stranded, spent the night in the airplane, and were rescued the next morning by an Air Sea Rescue team from Elmendorf AFB. The personnel were returned to Eielson, but the aircraft was left where it was.

Jack immediately planned the recovery of his aircraft. He knew I was checked out at the Eielson Aero Club and that my work schedule was fifteen days on and five days off. He asked me to rent an Aero Club aircraft and fly him down to Yakataga so he could get his aircraft. He would pay all expenses.

His plan was to fly down to Yakataga together in a two-place Aeronca. We would spend the night in Yakataga. The next day, we would fly up the coast to the mouth of the Kalahaga River and land on the beach.

From there, we would hike up the river to the sandbar where his plane was stuck. He would change the spark plugs, run up the engine, and check the airplane out. Then, if all were well, Jack would fly his airplane to Yakataga.

I would hike back to the mouth of the river, take off from the beach in the Aeronca, and fly to Yakataga where I would meet up with Jack. We would spend the night there and fly out in the morning, Jack in his Seabee and me in the Aeronca. Piece of cake.

I was apprehensive about my ability to do that kind of flying. The idea of flying through high mountains with wilderness below was unsettling. Of course, Jack would be with me on the way down, but I would be by myself on the way back. I reminded myself I would be experienced at it on the way back.

I didn't know proper techniques for a beach landing. I had never done it before. But, again, Jack would be with me on the landing, and taking off shouldn't be too bad with only me in the airplane. The whole plan sounded scary to me, but at the same time was alluring. I told Jack I was in.

When the day came to make the trip, I went to the Aero Club and checked out an Aeronca Champion. It was a light, two-passenger aircraft with a 75-horsepower engine. Survival gear consisted of a 32-caliber rifle—just enough punch to make a grizzly bear terribly angry—and a one-man raft—of limited use in the mountains or against an angry grizzly who has just been popped with a 32-caliber projectile!

The aircraft was equipped with a magnetic compass. It had no flight instruments, no radios, no lights, and no navigational aids. The magnetic compass was of marginal use. Every heading was off by about twenty-five degrees, due to magnetic variation in that part of the world.

I had drawn a course line on my sectional chart. Along the course there would be no roads, power lines, railroad tracks, or towns to help with navigation. My en-route checkpoints would be limited to rivers and mountain peaks.

Aircraft performance was another critical factor to consider. The pass we were flying through to get into Copper River Canyon was about 10,500 feet above sea level. The service ceiling on the Champ was about 10,500 feet. Service ceiling is that altitude at which the airplane can climb at no more than a certain rate. For the Aeronca Champion, that rate of climb was a painfully slow 100 feet per minute. The other factor was there would be two people and tools in the airplane, not just one person and an otherwise empty airplane.

The good news was Jack would be with me. I could rely on his experience and judgment.

On the flight down, we climbed awhile to get through the incredibly narrow pass. Aside from that, the remainder of the flight to Yakataga went very well.

We refueled at Yakataga and flew to the mouth of the Kalahaga River, then up the river to confirm Jack's Sea-bee was still there. It was. We circled and returned to the beach, landed, and hiked back to the Seabee.

The recovery effort was not as easy as we had hoped, but Jack got his airplane into the air and back to Yakataga. I hiked back to the beach and successfully took off, but not without scaring myself.

I flew over the area where Jack's airplane had been just to make sure he had not crashed. Then I flew to Yakataga.

Jack was there, adjusting his airplane's magnetos. We spent the night there, as planned.

The next morning we were greeted by heavy fog and light drizzle. Fog was forecast for the entire day along the coast. I was relieved because I was sure we wouldn't fly in those conditions. I was certified only as a VFR Private Pilot.

Jack's Seabee was equipped for instrument flight, so he took off first. Our first destination was up the coast at Cordova. If the weather was good enough for me to fly, he would radio back and let me know.

About twenty minutes after takeoff, Jack reported to Yakataga Radio the fog was breaking up and the visibility was improving. I should take off and fly to Cordova.

I took off with one-mile visibility and a 300-foot ceiling. Immediately after takeoff, I turned toward the gulf. I wanted to be sure I avoided the mountains that rose abruptly from the shore.

I was watching the ground below me as I passed over the shoreline. As I looked up, I became immersed in a fog bank. I carefully descended out of the fog bank and flew along just barely above the water. With no flight instruments, I had to keep visual contact with the water to determine how high I was. Forward visibility was roughly fifty yards. Visibility to either side was about the same. I set a compass heading I felt would keep me offshore, therefore clear of mountains.

Based on Jack's report, I expected to break out of the fog at any moment. For ten minutes I flew my heading, expecting to break into the clear. I did not. I felt claustrophobic. I forced myself to concentrate on flying the aircraft to fight off panic.

I decided to turn around and try to find my way back to Yakataga. After all, they had a fairly good ceiling and visibility when I left. Of course, I had no navigational equipment to help me but I reversed course, anyway.

I had no idea what course to hold. I was really lost by that time. All I could see was fifty yards of water all around me. I held a constant magnetic heading for about ten minutes.

Then, panic really set in. I started talking to myself, saying, "Calm down. Think. Think clearly. You can get out of this situation."

I retraced my actions. Jack had said the weather got better down the coast to the west. I should be able to head west from there until I found a break in the overcast and fog. I turned again, that time to magnetic west. I needed to define a starting location. I assumed I was just off the coast opposite Yakataga.

Then, I remembered there was a twenty-five-degree east magnetic variation I had to apply to my heading to fly a true course of west. I took a quick look at my map and estimated a true course of 285 degrees to the mouth of the Copper River. Of course, a magnetic heading of 285 degrees would not get me where I wanted to go. I would have to adjust the 285 degrees by adding or subtracting 25 degrees.

Which is it? Add to or subtract from? If I made the wrong correction, it would result in an error of fifty degrees.

What was the little saying I learned when I first started flying at Lake View Airport near Celina, Ohio?

"East is least, and west is best."

I decided I had to subtract the twenty-five degrees from 285. I turned to a magnetic heading of 260 degrees. Then, I questioned myself over and over in my mind. I finally decided I must have done it right.

In Ohio, I had subtracted the magnetic variation, and in Ohio it had been somewhere around five degrees east.

I now focused on maintaining wings level and a 260-degree heading. Judging from the minimum wind effect on the water's surface, I assumed I didn't need to make a crosswind correction.

Again, I looked at my chart, estimated the distance to the mouth of the Copper River, and figured I would arrive there in about one hour. All I had to do was hold a good course and be patient. I expected to fly out of the fog and be able to fly on the Cordova. It wouldn't be long. If I could just settle down and remain calm, soon it would be over.

The struggle with panic subsided.

The engine RPM suddenly surged up and down. I had been so pre-occupied and focused on the heading and maintaining positive control of the aircraft, I had allowed ice to build up in the throat of the carburetor. The ice cut off the flow of air to the engine. I was facing a possible ditching in the Gulf of Alaska.

I quickly pulled the carburetor control to full heat. The RPM dropped even lower. I was only fifty feet above water, and I lacked the power necessary to maintain level flight. The aircraft slowly descended toward the icy water below.

I increased pitch a little in order maintain altitude, but when the airspeed approached stall, I had to trade altitude for airspeed and allow a slow descent. Panic was like another person trying to take over my brain. The aircraft flew lower and lower.

I maintained the airspeed at just above stall as the icy water appeared to rise toward me. I was out of ideas. My heart raced and panic pounded on my door. There was nothing I could do. I was doomed.

The engine coughed. But instead of dying, it suddenly came to life. The carburetor heat had melted the ice in the throat of the carburetor and the RPM surged several times. The engine steadied out at full power. I gained some airspeed and then climbed back to fifty feet above the waves.

As the adrenaline subsided, I felt very weak—but not so much I couldn't keep my grip on the carburetor heat control.

After a very tense hour of straight and level on the 260-degree magnetic heading, I saw an island emerge from the fog. I had to climb a little to clear the island's taller trees.

What a wonderful sight. My hope soared. I thought about ditching in the water close to the island and swimming ashore. I was so relieved to see land again that I didn't want to leave it. But I decided ditching the plane was not really a good idea. I continued in hopes of finding clear air up ahead.

I located the island on my chart. It was just off the coast from the mouth of the Copper River. I quickly altered my course to the right and took up a more northerly heading. About fifteen minutes later, the fog darkened. I feared I was flying toward a mountain. I prepared myself to turn at the last minute, if necessary. Then several islands came into view. They were followed by the beach with the mountainside just beyond. The fog was lifting and so were my spirits. What a beautiful sight!

I turned toward the west and followed the coastline. I soon saw some abandoned railroad tracks that ran up toward the Cordova airfield. I was no longer lost.

When I landed at Cordova, Jack came running out to greet me. He had alerted Air Sea Rescue and reported me as missing. He also told me he had run into worse weather shortly after his first call. He called Yakataga a second time to tell me not to take off, but I had already left.

I went into the airfield office and laid down on the couch with my face toward the wall. I felt very weak. Jack gave me a few minutes, then asked me if I was ready to fly back to Eielson since the weather had improved. I told Jack I was never going to fly again. I would catch a bus back to Eielson and the Aero Club could send someone down to get the airplane.

After a while the weather improved, and my courage returned. We both flew back to Eielson. My aircraft was lighter without Jack and his tools, so I had no problem flying back through the high pass.

I grew up a lot that day. My courage and confidence soared. I had fought off panic and developed a coping mechanism for fear.

It would serve me well as an Air Force test pilot.

* * *

The Rogue Drone

K ENNETH D. LUEDEKE HAS BEEN A friend for at least
a decade. We met through Civil Air Patrol. I didn't
have the pleasure of flying any missions with him,
but he's been a regular at the Civil Air Patrol breakfast
we have once a month.

Ken is a retired USAF major. He flew F-100s in combat in Viet Nam. He was also an F-104 test pilot. I admire
his record of service and his character. Ken is a very
humble, intelligent man with many interests. He also has
many interesting stories, some of which he has given me
permission to share in my writing.

Ken and I share several things in common. He grew
up around Dayton, Ohio. I lived in a suburb of Cincinnati
during my high school years. We both attended Miami
University, Ohio but at different times. We both have farm
country in our backgrounds. We both had Air Force careers
which included F-100 time. But the thing I like most about
what Ken and I have in common is that he and I both had
to fight a medical battle to have our careers.

Ken's Air Force flying career far surpasses my own.
Having been a test pilot in the F-104 Starfighter was an
incredible achievement. He was instrumental in the development of the QF-104 drone program. Ken achieved Mach
2 flight multiple times—it was a part of the standard test
flight profile on F-104s that entered the drone program.
Pushing the Starfighter past Mach 1 and 2 was his favorite
part of the program.

Ken also worked with other, less glamorous aircraft.
One of his tales involved a drone training flight at White
Sands, New Mexico in March of 1955. He flew a DT-33

from the back seat. The instructor pilot, Glenn Kaufman was in the front. Glenn was an experienced pilot with Korean War combat time in a B-26.

Their mission was a typical training profile. It involved flying formation with a QF-80 drone. The unmanned drone was a modified F-80 Shooting Star—a jet fighter-interceptor. Ken flew the DT-33 and Glenn flew the QF-80 by sending remote signals from the front seat of the DT-33 to the autopilot of the QF-80. His duty position was referred to as the Beeper because every signal he sent to the drone resulted in a beep in his headset.

Ken and Glenn took off and climbed through 1000 feet AGL (Above Ground Level) when the drone began to fly erratically.

Flying close formation with manned aircraft required a lot of focus, especially if you're the lead aircraft. Timely communication between aircraft was important. If you were flying radio silent, focus became more important because you communicated through hand signals. Trying to fly close formation with an unmanned drone that has decided to make its own decisions raised the pucker factor way high.

Glenn's problems increased as he signaled the drone. His sending unit or the drone's receiving unit may have been experiencing low power. If that were the case, Ken needed to fly as close to the drone as possible. Of course, if the drone made a sudden, unexpected maneuver, Ken needed to be able to quickly respond to avoid a mid-air collision.

"Something suddenly didn't feel right. The drone moved ahead of us. I moved the throttle forward to obtain more thrust. Still the rogue drone increased its separation. Kaufman was urging me to, 'Keep up! Keep up!' Something had gone seriously wrong," Ken said.

The drone had outdistanced them enough, it was safe for Ken to break focus and perform a quick scan of his instruments. The problem then became apparent. Ken's engine had flamed out.

They were at 1000 feet above the desert floor, heading north about two miles from the airfield. Ken quickly turned east toward the field. The DT-33 wasn't going to be able to glide that far.

Ken quickly scanned the desert below. Then he made another turn toward the south and aligned his flight path with a desert arroyo—a deeply eroded trench formed by wind erosion in the sand.

His aircraft was only 200 feet above the ground. There were no decisions to be made. With the engine-out and too low to turn, a straight ahead, off-field landing was inevitable.

Ken extended the speed brakes, lowered the flaps. He kept the landing gear up, flared, and settled onto the only flat area of the desert for miles around. The aircraft slid to a smooth stop.

They opened the canopy, shut off all switches, and stepped out onto the wings and congratulated each other on a successful dead stick landing.

The aircraft was recovered.

It was a sad sight as it returned to Holloman on the back of a flat-bed truck. The maintenance crew replaced the engine, the flaps, the speed brakes, and the tip tanks. Minor repairs were made to the fuselage. The aircraft was flying again within a week.

The cause of the flame-out was determined to be fuel starvation. That puzzled the pilots because they had almost a full load of fuel when the flame-out occurred. Then, as they talked through the flight, they realized Glenn was so focused on the erratic drone he'd forgotten to gang-load the fuel switches. The gang-load switches were located in the front cockpit. Gang loading all on allowed various tanks to cross-feed. With the fuel selection not ganged, the engine was only being fueled by the 95-gallon fuselage tank.

Both Ken and Glenn were so focused on the rogue drone neither of them noticed the fuel level in the main tank rapidly drop to zero.

The unscheduled off-field landing was categorized as an incident and considered part of the hazards of operating in a test environment. Test environments were more prone to unknown and unforeseen conditions than more predictable and more regulated environments.

Jerry L. Burton

J ERRY L. BURTON IS AN ORDAINED minister with a PhD
in Church Administration. In the secular world, he has
held top executive positions in several international
corporations and is a retired US Air Force Lt. Colonel. His
extensive background includes science, religion, business,
and education. He has advanced degrees and practical
experience in all those areas.

Jerry's deep belief in the worth of every person drives
his passion for sharing his knowledge and experiences.
He has published articles and training manuals in science,
business, and education and is now venturing into books in
the areas of military memoirs/history, religion, and humor.

His passion for sharing God's word in an understandable
way has led Jerry to write a three-volume study guide to
the Bible. *Volume One, Get-A-Grip on the Bible: Genesis
through Ruth*, was published in November of 2020 by
WestBow Press, a division of Thomas Nelson and Zonder-
van. Volumes Two and Three will be completed by the end
of 2021.

A military memoir/biography, *Clouds of War, Past,
Present, and on the Horizon* was published in September
of 2020 by Xlibris.

Mari K. Eder

32

AN OFFICER AND A CODEBREAKER:

THE GIRL WHO STEPPED OUT OF LINE

"I 'VE BEEN LOOKING FORWARD TO MEETING you. You come so highly recommended. We've all been waiting for you to arrive." The young petty officer gushed with excitement. Ensign Betty Bigelow had just arrived at the U.S. Navy's Communications Annex on Nebraska Avenue, in Northwest Washington, D.C. It was a typical, steamy and sticky July day in the steam bath the nation's capital knew as summer. Betty felt like she was breathing under water.

"Really?" Betty was flattered. She had come straight from the train at Union Station. Her puppy-dog sponsor escorted her on their way to the Post Chapel for what Betty understood would be a welcome session.

Betty had already dropped her duffel at the reception center and once her picture was taken had been issued a staff badge. Now this and she would be introduced to her shipmates at her new duty location. Afterward she'd be able to unpack in the temporary officer billets and have time to familiarize herself with the Annex campus.

Betty looked around and wiped the sweat from her upper lip. It was 1944 and Washington, D.C. was sweltering. Having grown up in the northeast, Betty found the swampy heat and humidity of the capitol city to be oppressive. But

Betty was a woman of few words, just perfect for her new life as a Naval officer in the big city.

So far though, she wasn't enamored with her surroundings. Betty said later, the whole complex, "appeared to be a huge encampment of ugly temporary buildings surrounded by a high fence and secured by Marine guards.[i]" It definitely wasn't Vassar

Her escort noticed Betty's frown. "We call it the USS *Mount Vernon*," she confided. It was supposed to be a joke.

Betty snorted. Her officer training school had had a similar ship-like name, the USS *Northampton*. It didn't look any more like a ship than these drab old buildings. But she didn't say a word and listened carefully to her escort talk about how the Annex worked. She still had a lot to learn.

* * *

There were women in uniform everywhere on the campus, Betty noticed. More than 4,000 of them, she would later discover. The Navy's cryptanalysis center was eighty percent female.[ii] Women outnumbered men in every working unit at the center. In the Pacific decryption unit where Betty was assigned, there were 254 male sailors and 1,252 WAVES (Women Accepted for Voluntary Emergency Service), plus thirty-three civilians.[iii]

Betty had been in the Navy at that time for three months. She was only twenty years old.

* * *

Elizabeth (Betty) Bigelow was born in 1923 in Newark, NJ. She grew up with two brothers and attended boarding school. She chose Vassar, one of the prestigious Seven Sisters women's colleges in the Northeastern U.S. She majored at art history but decided she wanted to be an architect. That meant math and Betty took a lot of math classes.

In her junior year she signed up for a class in mechanical drawing. The professor was Dr. Grace Hopper, who quietly worked on her own entry into the Navy as an officer. Betty thought Professor Hopper was brilliant. She stood in front of the class and wrote on the blackboard in German—with her left hand.

"When her hand arrived directly in front of her nose she would switch the chalk to her right hand—she was ambidextrous—and continue writing in French." Betty shook her head in amazement. Professor Hopper also incorporated animation and rocket design into her lessons.[iv]

Hopper's mechanical drawing classes were designed to draw students in and challenge young minds. One day she said to Betty, "The Navy is looking for women like you. But we can't tell you any more about it. Are you interested?"

Betty nodded, intrigued. But nothing else happened. A month later, an official-looking letter arrived, inviting Betty to an interview. She came to a plain office in one of the campus administration buildings and spoke with a male Navy officer.

"I see you're an art history major. Why are you taking all of these math classes?" He asked. Her grades sat in front of him. They were impressive.

"I want to become an architect," Betty said. "I need mechanical drawing and some of the math classes for that." She waited. Betty never talked more than was necessary.

He finally said, "Go on."

"Math is reliable. You perform the same calculation a hundred times and you get the same result. A hundred times." What more was there to say?

"I see," he said with a small smile. The interviewer scratched a short note in her file.

Next came the follow-on interview. The letter announcing her acceptance into the WAVES officer candidate program arrived after that. But because she was only twenty, Betty needed her parent's permission.

They agreed, understanding that it was personal for their daughter to want to make her own contributions. Her two brothers were already serving in the Pacific.

In the fall of 1943, Betty returned to Vassar for her final year of college and found a new course listed on her schedule. All it said was math, but as Betty quickly learned, it was actually a class in cryptanalysis. There were seven other women in her class. They were cautioned to not talk about the course with each other or outside of the classroom at all. Betty was fine with that.

* * *

The WAVES were established on July 21, 1942. While Congress and the President were reluctant to open the service to women, they recognized the need. Women in the Naval reserve were to be assigned to shore duty, freeing up men to go to sea. The more than 86,000 WAVES were assigned to 900 stations in the U.S. While it was a mostly white organization, eventually seventy-two African American women served[v].

It felt like a huge compliment to be personally recruited by the Navy. It was and it wasn't.

"It was generally believed that women were good at doing tedious work—and as I had discovered early on, the initial stages of cryptanalysis were very tedious, indeed," recalled Ann Caracristi, a well-known codebreaker who went on after the war to serve with the National Security Agency for forty years, retiring as Deputy Director[vi].

By 1944 when Betty was recruited, the Navy had the process down.[vii] The war meant Betty's last semester of college was curtailed and soon after commencement in May of 1944, she was off to WAVE training.

New male officers were called "90-day wonders" because their initial officer training lasted only three months.

* * *

Betty's training was only sixty days long, but it covered all the basics. WAVE officer training was held at the Northampton Midshipmen's School at Smith College in Massachusetts. In Officer Candidate School (OCS) she learned to march, how to take orders, and then how to give orders[viii]. Marching was easy enough and Betty learned how make her bed 'shipshape.'

Later she recalled she'd had a tough time making the daily mandatory formations.

"I wasn't very good at being on time," she said wryly.[ix]

* * *

Betty didn't know her former professor, Grace Hopper had gone through the same training the summer before. Betty made it through with little trouble other than the demerits for being chronically late. She could recognize types of aircraft and ships, write reports and correspondence Navy style, recognize ranks and observe protocol. She could talk the lingo, too. She learned to say deck instead of floor, overhead instead of ceiling, and bulkhead instead of wall. The language was the easiest part of the Navy culture to absorb.

When cautioned about her tardiness, Betty replied, "Aye, aye, sir." She managed to not roll her eyes.

The candidates didn't have much access to news from the outside world. Betty was late because she'd been reading a note one of the cadre had posted on the company bulletin board. That's how Betty learned of the D-Day invasion—through a simple note posted on the bulletin board in her barracks. Not long afterward, Betty graduated from OCS, took the oath, and was commissioned an ensign.

That first day's welcome ceremony in Washington was nothing more than a lecture, and it wasn't like any of the typical Navy lectures Betty had grown used to. It was a fire and brimstone-filled speech, a sermon on security that went beyond the typical mantra of "Loose lips sink ships." Betty and the other newly arrived WAVES were duly impressed by the warning they would be shot if they ever revealed what they did inside the gates of the compound.[x]

* * *

Betty made friends during her time in the Navy, and some she corresponded with for years. During her two years in Washington, Betty had the opportunity to get to know the city. She lived in apartments in various neighborhoods from Chevy Chase to Georgetown.

"Washington was lovely," she recalled, "But we didn't get to see much of it."

She had the opportunity to go out with colleagues from work, but since everything they did was compartmented, no one talked about their jobs.[xi]

It was no different for other codebreaking operations, whether that of the U.S. Army at Arlington Hall Station or at Bletchley Park in the U.K. At Bletchley, incoming staff were required to sign the Official Secrets Act. Most never spoke about their wartime service after the war at all. It was more than fifty years later when stories about Enigma, Bombe machines, and the role of codebreaking leaked out.

Betty found the work at once tedious and stressful. There was a 'zero defects mentality' to codebreaking and it meant she had to give every message her best effort.

It was hot in the building where she worked, often over 90°F by 8:00 A.M. All through the first long summer, Betty and her colleagues felt their uniforms stick to their backs. Sweat ran down their legs. It was relief to simply get up and walk over to pick up the incoming message that arrived from pneumatic tube from the building where the codebreaking machines did the initial work.

The codebreaking machines, Bombes, were built in Dayton, Ohio and shipped into Washington. The machines were seven feet high, ten feet long and weighed 5,000 lbs.

A run on a Bombe took twenty minutes. Once the results were verified by a supervisor, they were sent to Building 2 where the analysts waited.[xii]

BOMBE

* * *

"I was assigned to work on Japanese Navy codes, in 'Keys,' or codebreaking," Betty recalled. "When the messages arrived, they were coded at the beginning and the end with a date/time group set of numbers. There was one type of message—at the diplomatic level, and the other dealt with convoys, or weather stations. The second type accounted for the heaviest traffic and was highly classified."

Betty worked on the famous "Purple Cipher," a complex set of Japanese codes. She recalled there were many accomplished academics at the Navy Communications Annex. Her boss was a man, a former professor at the University of Minnesota.

"Was it difficult to break these codes?" an interviewer asked her years later for the Veterans History Project. Betty explained she didn't have to know Japanese—it was all numbers.

"The military mind always structures things in the same way," she said, in her understated way. To her, that meant it was easy to break the codes for weather report messages, then move on to more difficult topics like Japanese fleet locations and convoy operations.

"One day, a message came in and they wanted it deciphered as quickly as possible. I did decipher it and a Japanese convoy was sunk as the result. I remember being terribly pleased about that."[xiii]

* * *

When the war with Japan ended in August 1945, Betty and selected other WAVES stayed on until the remaining messages were completely finished and the files organized and cleaned up. Betty remained at the Annex until August 1946. By that time, she had been promoted to Lieutenant JG.

When she was discharged from active duty, she had to sign another non-disclosure agreement, stating she would never reveal what she had done during the war. To anyone. The secrecy oath was binding—for life.[xiv]

That fall, Congress lauded the work of the codebreakers. Speaking on the floor of the House of Representatives in October 1945, Rep. Clarence Hancock said, "I believe our cryptographers...in the war with Japan did as much to bring that war to a successful and early conclusion as any other group of men."[xv]

The women were never mentioned. Or publicly thanked.

* * *

Betty experienced the limitations of her secrecy oath first-hand as she tried to use her GI Bill to go back to school and resume her pursuit of a degree in architecture.

"Sorry," she was told. "All billets are being held for men coming home from fighting."

It didn't matter she was a veteran, too. And even if she had said she'd worked at the Navy Communications Annex in Washington, people would have assumed she worked as a clerk. That was their cover story, after all.

Betty ended up at Princeton, working as an assistant for an architect. There she met her future husband, Keith Stewart, a graduate student in English Literature. They married following his graduation and moved to Charlottesville, Virginia where he taught for three years. Later he accepted an offer with the University of Cincinnati. They relocated to Cincinnati where Betty worked with the University's budding computer sciences program.

Betty's work in Navy communications was the perfect foundation for her new-found career in computer science. As a codebreaker, she had been on the cutting edge of "Where the machine era of cryptology began, the era of brute force, women operating machines the size of rooms, American Bombes and some of the first IBM punch-card computers."[xvi] At the University, she helped students de-bug their programs and build their research projects. [xvii]

Betty remained in the Naval Reserve until she and Keith started their family. They had a son and two daughters and, as he continued his academic career, they enjoyed two sabbaticals in the U.K. Later, upon returning to Cincinnati, Betty became president of the local Vassar Alumni club and was active with the University library.

While Betty moved away from Navy life and found her new path, the work she and others did at the Navy Communications Annex (with the Army at Arlington Hall Station, and at Bletchley Park in the U.K.) continued to have a major impact on the development of future signals intelligence operations. The FBI expanded. The OSS fathered the CIA. And the work the cryptographers did became the foundation for the National Security Agency (NSA).

The NSA was created by President Truman in 1952, just as Betty and her husband were on the road, moving to Cincinnati. The new agency was to be separate from the Defense Department and other intelligence agencies because of the unique nature of its mission. Once it activated at Fort Meade, MD, many elements of wartime cryptography that had existed at the Naval Security Station in Washington relocated there. Intelligence operations continued to migrate to Fort Meade until 1995.

No one broke their oath of silence. Like Betty, most of the 10,000 women codebreakers in World War II kept their secrets from friends and family. They typically didn't participate in veterans' groups or organizations, either. Betty didn't give speeches or talk with school groups. The women codebreakers were quietly forgotten.

It wasn't until March 22, 2019—seventy years after the end of World War II—that the codebreakers held their first reunion. Five of the veterans, all in their mid-nineties, were honored by the Veterans History Project at the Library of Congress.[xviii]

Unfortunately, Betty Stewart, like many of her contemporaries, wasn't among them. She passed away on May 21, 2015.

[i] Mundy, Liza. Code Girls: The Untold Story of the American Women Code Breakers of World War II. New York: Hachette Books, 2017. P. 178.

[ii] https://blogs.loc.gov/folklife/2018/03/breaking-codes-and-glass-ceilings-in-wartime-washington/

[iii] Mundy, Liza. Code Girls: The Untold Story of the American Women Code Breakers of World War II. New York: Hachette Books, 2017. P. 190.

[iv] Williams, Kathleen Broome. Grace Hopper: Admiral of the Cyber Sea. Annapolis, MD: Naval Institute Press, 2012. P. 12.

[v] https://en.wikipedia.org/wiki/WAVES

[vi] Mundy, Liza. Code Girls: The Untold Story of the American Women Code Breakers of World War II. New York: Hachette Books, 2017. P. 21.

[vii] https://stories.vassar.edu/2019/190308-cracking-the-codes.html

[viii] Williams, Kathleen Broome. Grace Hopper: Admiral of the Cyber Sea. Annapolis, MD: Naval Institute Press, 2012. P. 22.

[ix] https://www.google.com/search?q=veterans+history+project+betty+bigelow+stewart&oq=veter&aqs=-chrome.1.69i57j69i59j35i39j0l2j69i61l3.20338j1j7&sourceid=chrome&ie=UTF-8

[x] Budiansky, Stephen. Battle of Wits: The Complete Story of Codebreaking in World War II. New York: Simon & Schuster, 2000. P. 263.

[xi] https://memory.loc.gov/diglib/vhp/story/loc.natlib.afc2001001.68970/?loclr=blogflt

[xii] https://www.dhs.gov/history-nac

[xiii] https://memory.loc.gov/diglib/vhp/story/loc.natlib.afc2001001.68970/?loclr=blogflt

[xiv] Fagone, Jason. The Woman Who Smashed Codes: A True Story of Love, Spies, and the Unlikely Heroine who Outwitted America's Enemies. New York: Harper Collins, 2017. P. 319.

xv Mundy, Liza. Code Girls: The Untold Story of the American Women Code Breakers of World War II. New York: Hachette Books, 2017. P. 31.

xvi Fagone, Jason. The Woman Who Smashed Codes: A True Story of Love, Spies, and the Unlikely Heroine who Outwitted America's Enemies. New York: Harper Collins, 2017. P. 252.

xvii https://www.legacy.com/obituaries/cincinnati/obituary.aspx?n=elizabeth-stewart-betty&pid=174958006&f-hid=5472

xviii https://connectingvets.radio.com/articles/womens-history-month-female-wwii-veterans-have-their-first-re-union-over-70-years?fbclid=IwAR1LxKAXqKQgxMBwvJ97p5TNFJQ_T08CIDxnGGqis3YbM9hhd73IHN5ufdl

Mari K. Eder

ARI K. EDER, RETIRED U.S. ARMY Major General, is a renowned speaker and author, and a thought leader on strategic communication and leadership. General Eder has served as Director of Public Affairs at the George C. Marshall European Center for Security Studies and as an adjunct professor and lecturer in communications and public diplomacy at the NATO School and Sweden's International Training Command. She served in several senior positions in the Pentagon, on the Army Staff, as Deputy Chief of Public Affairs and Deputy Chief of the Army Reserve, and with DoD's Reserve Forces Policy Board.

General Eder is the author of *Leading the Narrative: The Case for Strategic Communication*, published by the Naval Institute Press. Her latest communications book, *American Cyberscape*, was released in November 2020. An inspirational book, *The Girls Who Stepped Out of Line: Untold Stories of the Women Who Changed the Course of WWII* will be published in August of 2021. When not writing, lecturing, or traveling, she works with rescue groups and fosters rescue dogs.

MWSA Authors

M.T. Falgoust

33

The Cicada's Coda

T HE CRUNCH FELT FINAL.

"What'd you go and do that for?" The reedy pipe of my eleven-year old morality demanded. "He didn't do you nothing."

"*Anything*, Bug." Zach underlined his correction with a beefy, All-State shove into my thin white shoulder. "You're so stupid."

He gave the dead creature a thirty-yard field goal kick. "Like this dumb cicada. It's not even supposed to be out yet."

My molars nearly rattled out of my jaw as I smacked, bony-ass first, into the chunky, crushed slate of St. Mary's driveway under the elm tree.

The path home from the bus stop always brought us past the old church. Maybe that's what inspired Zach to play God as he crushed the cicada underfoot.

Didn't make it right.

A sharp, searing pain shot from my hand up through my arm as the jagged rock bit into the fleshy part of my palm. I leveled a blistering stare at my older brother.

The stare wasn't the only thing that blistered. An early summer stuck to my back, plastering the cotton of my pink shirt to damp skin. It was only early May, but the mercury was already boiling into the low nineties.

"Global warming," Mrs. Nowak had explained in science class.

Global warming, I thought. *Maybe that's why the poor, confused insect had crawled its way from its grounded nest and out into the harsh glare of a burning sun a month early.*

Zach might have been a dumb jock, but he wasn't wrong. The seventeen-year cicadas weren't due to emerge for at least another few weeks. Mrs. Nowak had told us all about them. The insects lived most of their lives underground, emerging for a brief four- to six-week period to mate and continue the life cycle, and then they died.

Unless some jerk football player decided to stomp on them first.

"Shithead," I lobbed my progressive new vocabulary word at Zach. Half for the dead bug.

Half for me.

No sooner had the epithet dropped from the puckered Cupid's bow of my mouth than the bell in the campanile tower tolled a sonorous reprimand. It echoed out over Main Street, down past Rentschler's Ice Cream Parlor, and on to our house where I was certain Babci could hear it, clear as crystal, from her rocking chair post on our front porch.

I ducked a repentant, progressive head. My grandmother didn't care much for progress. You could hear it in the sandpaper scratch of her Lucky Strike-tempered voice.

Like later that night when I got all decked out for the middle school dance.

* * *

The greying tufts over her piercing ice blue eyes arched high. "Where are you going dressed like that, Robaczku?"

Little Bug.

Maybe I had been a little heavy-handed with my mother's *Maybelline.* I had just wanted to be more...progressive. I blinked the two huge black spiders that had taken up residence on the edges of my eyelids.

"I have a dance, Babci. At school," I explained. "And I'm late."

Babci blew a skeptical puff of air through wrinkled lips. "Late?" Babci licked a wrinkled, nicotine-stained thumb and rubbed at the mascara. I tried ducking. No dice.

"Late?" Babci repeated. "Robaczku, if anything, you rush too early. All things in time."

All things in time, I thought. Yeah. Their own sweet time. I was the only girl in my grade who hadn't gotten her period yet. Georgette Dubicki had had hers since fourth grade. Now she had boobs that made guys Zach's age drool.

I wondered for a half a minute if Babci had found the box of tampons I kept in my room. Or worse. What if she'd found the ones I'd soaked in red *Kool-Aid*, just to see how much liquid they could actually absorb?

I shuddered.

If she had found the tell-tale feminine products, Babci didn't say a word. She just sat, like she always did, rocking on the porch, sucking on her contraband candy.

"Babci! Your diabetes. Doc Langley says no candy!" I snagged the chocolate-covered marshmallow fluff from her hand and air-balled it into the ashcan. I growled. No period *and* no game.

"Pah! What does he know?" Babci tugged at her chusta.

I pulled the trapped edges of her shawl loose and draped them around her thin shoulders. The red, press-on tips of my stubby little fingers reached for the afghan that had slipped from her legs. It lay in a crumpled heap on the wood planks of the porch Dziadziu had built all those years ago. She nodded and waved her hand.

"Go. In the chest. By my bed," she rasped. "Bring me your grandfather's collection."

"Dziadziu's bugs?" I sighed. "I really don't have time, Babci. I gotta go. They're supposed to be playing some really great music and I don't want to miss anything."

"Then you make time. Go," she said. "Bring me what I ask."

Disagreeing with a Polish grandmother was like trying

to convince Trump to eat Taco Bell. I blew a stray hair off my forehead and headed inside.

The pungent smell of caramelizing onions hung thick through the house. I followed my nose to the kitchen where my mother was absorbed in the latest "reality" show while actual reality burned behind her. I whisked the blackened pierogis off the stove and tossed the smoking pan into the sink. I doused the whole stinking mess in cold water, sending up a steaming cloud scented with overcooked root vegetables, a pungent mix of potato and onion. *Great! I smelled like the bleenie boys at the St. Mary's Annual Block Party. The guys were going to be lining up to dance with me tonight.*

Mother didn't even turn her face from the television screen. "You finishing dinner for me, Mads? Thanks so much. It was a helluva day at the factory."

"Yeah. Sure, Mom."

"Thanks, babe."

Zach thundered down the stairs and into the kitchen. He pulled up short and wrinkled his nose. "Whoa. Way to jack up dinner, Maddie. Think I'm gonna eat out tonight. Mom, I'm going over to Raz's house. He just got the new X-Box One X and it is supposed to be killer. I might stay over."

"Sure, hon. Text me, or whatever." She waved a dismissive hand. I huffed.

"Hey, Mom. I'm thinking about getting a nipple ring," I muttered as I headed for Babci's room.

"That sounds great. Take pictures."

I opened the door to my grandmother's room. Going into Babci's space was always like stepping through a wormhole. The old brass bed sat, neatly made, under a framed painting of an anonymous farmhouse. I'm pretty sure Babci's mother hand-stitched the quilt that covered the mattress. An array of glass perfume bottles and atomizers cluttered together on a mirrored tray on the dresser.

I grabbed her old, silver-plated hairbrush. Some of the

plating had worn through over the years. I held it up, a makeshift microphone, and sang a few bars. A howl erupted from the neighbor's dog.

Everybody's a critic.

I replaced the brush on the vanity tray. I wondered for half a minute if Babci ever sang into a brush microphone with some of her old music on the Victrola. I picked up one of the vinyl records she had neatly stacked next to the old clunker. I squinted through remnants of clumped mascara. *Who the heçk was Glenn Miller?* Guy sounded like a mailman. I plopped the paper-sleeved disc back on the pile. Who needed this old stuff anyway? I wanted music, I just pushed a button on my phone and shoved my headphones in my ears. I could drown out the world.

It was awesome.

My eyes roved over the framed photos in the room. Babci and Dziadziu on their wedding day. Dziadziu in his Army uniform from World War II. Dziadziu in front of the old St. Nicholas coal breaker near Mahanoy City. Not sure why, but Babci had kept Dziadziu's boots he had worn while working at the breaker. They were still, to this day, covered in a fine film of fossilized plant life. Black and grimy. *Gross.*

Then there was Dziadziu's chest.

I pushed open the heavy lid that groaned under the weight of its history. Thick photo albums were stacked inside. Newspapers in tall stacks. Some yellowed. Some less so. I looked at some of the headlines.

August 6, 1945—First Atomic Bomb Dropped On Japan; Missile Is Equal To 20,000 Tons Of Tnt; Truman Warns Foe Of A 'Rain Of Ruin'

October 23, 1962—We Blockade Cuba Arms; JFK: Blast Reds If Castro Attacks

November 5, 1979—U.S. EMBASSY SEIZED, HOSTAGES
HELD IN IRAN

July 7, 1996—PARK EXPLOSION; 2 REPORTED KILLED
AS BLAST RIPS THROUGH CROWD.

I shuddered. Why would my grandfather keep these
particular papers? I started having second thoughts about
the dance.

About a lot of things.

I shook off the heebeejeebies and moved an old year-
book on top of the frightening words. I finally found what
I was looking for. Dziadziu's bugs.

The box wasn't big. Only about a foot wide and
maybe about three inches deep. The sides held a deep,
reddish-brown stain and a thin pane of glass fit neatly
into two channeled grooves on either side. It wasn't the
box itself that was particularly interesting, however. It
was the disconcerting collection of pinned bugs inside. I
shuddered again before closing the chest lid and making
my way back out to Babci.

"You found what you are looking for?" Her voice
creaked as I stepped back out onto the front porch, bugs
tucked neatly under my arm.

"I found a bunch of dead bugs, Babci," I mumbled and
handed her the insect coffin. "Why did you want me to get
these weird old things?"

"Come," she smiled. She patted the empty chair next
to her. "I want to tell you a story."

I rolled my eyes. "But, Babci, I really have to go.
Everything will be over if I don't go soon."

"And I tell you everything will be over if you do." The
sudden rebar in her voice made her seem taller than her
hunched frame would allow. I sat.

The steel in the blue-gray of her eyes softened. She
patted my stockinged leg. "Your grandfather? He proposed

to me when the cicadas sang. I will never forget it. You have not been alive long enough to hear their music, but soon you may."

"I know about the cicadas, Babci. We talked about it at school."

"Ah, but what you don't know is our family's history with the cicada."

"We have a history?"

"Yes, my little bug. Your grandfather was born with the singing of the cicada. This cicada," she tapped the glass. "This cicada sang when your grandfather came into this world. His mother saved this as a reminder of their magic song. And this one? When this one sang to his mate, your grandfather, he sang to me. Quite badly," she laughed. "But, still beautifully. He took me as his wife after that day."

She smiled a memory.

She tapped the glass with a thick, cracked nail. "This one? This one marks the year your mother came to us. We tried for many years to have a child, but began to think we could not, but still she came. Each of the creatures you see hear marks another beautiful moment in our lives. We waited for each one. Sometimes the years between were long and hard. But, we waited, patiently, for the cicadas to come back."

Her words lingered as her blue eyes drifted away on a memory. I thought certain she was having another spell when she snapped alert and her gaze pierced mine.

"Nothing good comes quickly. Your grandfather believed the cicada's song marked us as blessed. As long as the cicada's returned, our family would thrive."

"It's kind of superstitious, though, isn't it, Babci? I mean. They're just bugs." I judged the fat black bodies with their bulging red eyes.

Babci clucked her tongue. "Oh, they are so much more than that. There are some who believed the cicadas were once men. Men who fell under the influence of the Muses and were so moved by their beauty they sang and sang. They sang without any thought for food or drink and died."

"Died?" I yelped. "Babci, that's horrible!"

"No, no, no, little bug. The Muses brought these men back to life. They live on as cicadas whose only job is to sing on and watch for the ones who honor the Muses."

I peered in at the ugly bugs, searching for signs of magical inspiration.

"Why are you telling me this story, Babci? What does it have to do with me?"

"The cicadas don't rush. When the larvae hatch, they fall to the ground and they burrow deep. Waiting. Watching. Growing slowly. And when they emerge, their song fills the air and the Muses bless mankind. Do not rush, Little Bug. Grow slowly. Wait for your blessings."

She strained as she reached into her pocket. She pressed two worn dollars into my hand. "Now, you be a good girl. Go to Rentschler's. You buy me Ptasie Mleczko, yes?"

Babci's voice faded on her close. Her chin dropped slowly to her chest. Her grip loosened on the box. I slipped the box from her hands and set it gently on the porch. Her breathing was ragged, but steady. I took one more look at the creepy little bug bodies and slipped off the porch to catch my ride to the dance. I pocketed the bills. I'd stop by the store...after the dance. Babci and her bugs would still be there when I got back. I patted the tube of mascara in my pocket.

* * *

Babci passed away that night, just two weeks before the cicadas were due to officially emerge. Farmers and gardeners across the northeast had been lamenting the arrival of the parasitic scourge. You would have thought it was the coming of the eighth plague the way they moaned and groaned. Strangely, however, the cicadas never came. The skies remained silent. The music never came.

M.T. Falgoust

M.T. Falgoust is an internationally award-winning author, illustrator, and veteran of the United States Navy. Since her time in the service, her writing has appeared in *Reader's Digest*, *Alfred Hitchcock Mystery Magazine*, *Writers' Journal* and with *Harlequin Books*.

Other titles have garnered awards and accolades from the NY Book Festival, the Oshima Picture Book Museum Int'l Picture Book Competition, and the Green Book Festival.

Her action-thriller, *The Eye of the Storm*, was recognized as a finalist in the Clive Cussler Adventure Writer's Competition.

CPSIA information can be obtained
at www.ICGtesting.com
Printed in the USA
BVHW052003021021
617893BV00006B/136